The Boy in the Woods
A J WILLS

Cherry Tree Publishing

The Boy in the Woods

Copyright © A J Wills 2024

All rights reserved. No part of this publication may be reproduced, stored in a retrieval system, or transmitted, in any form or by any other means, without the prior written permission of the author, nor be otherwise circulated in any form of binding or cover other than that in which it is published and without a similar condition being imposed on the purchaser.

This book is a work of fiction. Any resemblance to actual persons, living or dead is purely coincidental.

Prologue

She tilted her head back and stretched out her arms, bathing in the moon's silvery glow.

'Are you scared?'

He was terrified but couldn't admit it.

Just one slight trip, one misplaced step... It made his stomach lurch just thinking about it. There was no way you'd catch him up there, at least not without a dozen safety ropes.

But she was completely lost in herself, oblivious to the danger, with a smile of ecstasy curling on her plump lips.

'We should get back.' He reached a hand up to her.

'Don't be such a bore. Aren't you having a good time?'

'Of course,' he lied. He'd wanted this more than anything. Well, not *this* exactly, but to be with her. Alone.

She looked incredible with her honey-blonde hair tied back in a ponytail and a tight-fitting dress that skimmed the swell of her breasts and hips. She'd never looked twice at him at school, preoccupied by the dazzling attentions of the older, sportier boys and their confident chat. But now, here they were. Together. It should have been the best moment of his life, but his guts were churning.

Why wouldn't she just come down?

After the party, she'd kicked off her Converse and run through the trees, guided by the light of a full moon slipping in and out behind wispy grey clouds, towards the bridge with its high stone walls where during the day you could watch peregrines soaring from their nests in the pines.

He'd run after her, laughing, his legs powerful, feeling like he could run a marathon without breaking into a sweat.

She'd hitched up her skirt and clambered effortlessly onto the parapet, bare feet scrambling up the stone, calves straining.

'What are you doing?' he panted as he ran to her, alarm growing.

She stood like a tightrope walker, steadying her balance. She took a step, pointing her toes, her nails painted the colour of ripe cherries.

'Hey, come on, be careful.' His heart looped in his chest.

'I feel like I could fly. Do you feel it too?' She looked sylphlike in the glimmering light.

It wasn't how he'd imagined the evening would turn out when she'd allowed him to pop that tiny square of blotting paper on her tongue, his fingers grazing her wet lips.

'Please, I'm begging you.'

She skipped and stumbled, almost falling, then caught her balance, giggling. Tottered on the edge. 'I'm on top of the world,' she shouted, her words echoing down the valley.

'Please, don't.'

'It's fun.'

'It's dangerous.'

'Is it?' She glanced over her shoulder into the dizzying depths of the gully, as if unaware the world disappeared into the dark below. She craned her neck, her body swaying.

She wobbled and rocked, placed a foot down, but only half on the wall. Her arms flailed, wheeling through air, terror painting itself across her face.

And then she was falling. Tumbling over the edge like something out of a nightmare.

He lunged for her, clawing for her hand but grasping only thin air.

In the blink of an eye, she was gone.

Her petrified scream lasted less than a second before her body hit the ground with a dull thud.

Then there was only silence and the rush of blood in his ears.

He stood for a moment, his brain frozen.

He didn't know what to do. What to think.

So he turned, and he ran.

Chapter 1

Tyson pulls up to a sudden halt, planting his paws firmly on the ground. He cocks his head with his ears pricked. I urge him on, yanking at his lead, but he's rooted to the spot, resolutely refusing to move. I don't know what he's heard, but he won't budge. Probably a pheasant in the bushes or a rabbit scurrying back to its hole.

'Tyson, it's going to be dark in a minute.' He glances at me with big brown eyes and whimpers. 'Come on, don't be so pathetic.'

I rub his head behind his ears, stroking his velvety, chocolate-coloured coat, but he's not moving. It's so typical of him. He's totally neurotic. I'm not sure if all boxers are like this, but at two years old, he couldn't be any less like his famous namesake.

Hank, a somewhat less nervous black labrador, tugs my arm violently in the opposite direction as he dives under the low-hanging branches of a beech tree, desperate to follow his nose and a new smell he's picked up, while Biscuit runs rings around my legs, wrapping her lead around my ankles, as if she's determined to trip me up.

It's like this every time. Walks in the woods always descend into total chaos. I never claimed to have any qualifications when I set up the dog-minding business, but I'm sure my clients would wonder what kind of amateur I really am as their beloved pets run rings around me yet again.

I'm paid to look after five dogs during the week. As well as Tyson and Hank, and our own ditsy cockapoo, Biscuit, who we bought for the boys when they were younger with the misplaced idea it would teach them about responsibility, there's Bertie, a docile Hungarian vizsla with the most beautiful, silky russet-gold coat and Rosie, an adorable brown and white springer spaniel with soft, floppy ears whose back end wiggles like she's twerking whenever she wags her tail.

The only way to free myself is to momentarily drop Biscuit's lead. I uncoil it from around my muddy boots and step out of the tangle, but before I can retrieve it, Biscuit bolts off, barking ferociously at something through the trees. And in an instant she's gone.

'Biscuit!' I yell, fumbling in the pouch around my waist for one of the chicken-flavoured treats she loves.

She'll usually do anything for a treat, but as her bark fades into the distance, it's clear that whatever's caught her attention is a more powerful lure.

As I sigh, wondering what I'm supposed to do now, Bertie sneaks under my arm and snatches the treat from my fingers.

I'm going to have to go after her. I can't risk her snagging her lead on a branch and doing herself a serious injury. Plus, in half an hour, it's going to be dark and I need to get the other dogs back to their owners.

'Come on, you lot. We need to find her.'

Reluctantly, they follow as I jog inelegantly in my Wellington boots along the trail, following the sound of Biscuit's incessant barking.

Sweat soon dampens my T-shirt under my jumper and coat as my breathing becomes laboured. I'm not used to running anywhere and the effort has my thighs burning and sharp stabs of pain shooting up my shins as my feet slop around inside my ill-fitting boots.

'Biscuit!'

I slow down to a fast walk as Biscuit's barking ceases suddenly, but what I hear instead sends a sliver of dread through my body. A yelp of pain that pierces through the mist, hanging low and needling through the trees like gun smoke.

She's injured herself. Oh god, that's just what I don't need right now. I dive off the footpath into the scrub where brambles and creepers snatch dangerously at my feet.

'Biscuit! Where are you?'

I home in on her whimpers, brushing branches out of my face as I run.

Eventually, I find her sitting in a small clearing, fussing with her front paw. She stares at me with sad eyes as I approach.

'What have you done, you silly girl?' I kneel at her side and run a comforting hand over her head.

Gently, I take her paw and immediately spot a huge thorn embedded in one of the soft pads. At least it doesn't look serious, which is just as well as I could do without a vet bill to worry about this month. With our recent move, and the extension to our mortgage, money's tight.

I tie the other dogs to a nearby tree and take a closer look. Although the light's not great, I'm able to grab the splinter between my thumb and forefinger and tug it out with little effort.

Biscuit jumps up as if nothing's wrong and turns to stare at something in the distance. She throws her head back and barks. I follow her gaze, but the gloom really has set in now. Low, grey clouds fill the sky and the mist is getting thicker.

With a wince, I pull myself to my feet, clinging tightly to Biscuit's lead, which is soaking wet and covered in mud.

In between Biscuit's barks, snatches of raised voices carry on the still air. I haven't seen anyone since I left the car park, but I can definitely hear two people. And although I can't make out what they're saying, it's obvious from the aggressive tone that they're arguing. Shouting and yelling. A man and a woman, I think. His voice is deep and gravelly. Hers a shrill scream. I've always shied away from confrontation. Rory and I never yell at each other like some couples, and in the calm sanctity of the woods, I find the aggression deeply unsettling.

The mist billows and clears for a second, and I finally spot the source of the shouting in the distance. A young couple, standing close to the trunk of an old oak tree. Teenagers, possibly?

He's taller than her, his head hidden under a hoodie, and they're not just arguing, they're physically fighting. Grappling. He's holding her wrists above her head, his naked aggression setting my heart racing.

Every muscle in my body contracts. I don't want to get involved, but I can't walk away. Is she being attacked? What if she needs help? But instead of acting, all I can do is stand and watch helplessly. I'm in shock. Too horrified to move.

Biscuit barks again, then growls.

The boy turns his head, glancing over his shoulder towards us, and my heart almost jumps out of my mouth.

I can't distinguish his face clearly at this distance, but there's something familiar about the way he's standing, with the weight slightly favouring his right foot. His build. His manner.

No, it can't be. It's my imagination projecting my worst fears.

But the girl looks familiar too, with her long blonde hair and petite frame.

He's seen me now. Noticed I'm watching. We hold each other's gaze for a moment or two.

'Leo?' I gasp under my breath.

Please tell me it's not. We've been through enough trouble with that boy to last a lifetime. I couldn't stand to go through it all again. It would be the death of me.

I squint, but it doesn't help. It might be Leo. It might not. I'm too far away to be sure.

While he's distracted, staring at me, the girl pulls free of his grip and runs, threading through the trees and disappearing into the gathering darkness. His head snaps back around and watches her go.

He casts one more quick glance my way and then chases after her, vanishing in the same direction.

In an instant, they've both gone and I'm left wondering what I've just seen. Whether my eyes have deceived me. Whether I've just watched my son attacking a girl in the woods. Physically assaulting her.

And I stood there and did nothing.

Chapter 2

It's hardly a surprise that I'm suspicious after everything Leo's put us through this year. We've had to move house, send the boys to a new school, uproot our lives and abandon our friends. Our names and reputations have been dragged through the mud, I've been forced to give up my job at the school and Rory's commute into London is now even longer. All because of Leo. It's been a high price to pay to keep my family together.

My legs are trembling, my mouth's dry and the pulse threading through my veins is like a jackhammer. Of course, I could have been mistaken. I couldn't see clearly. Just because the boy was of a similar height and build to Leo, with a skinny frame and shoulders beginning to broaden with youthful muscle, it doesn't mean it was him. And lots of kids wear dark-coloured hoodies and jeans. Guilt balloons in my chest. I shouldn't have been so quick to jump to conclusions. Even if it was him, there's probably an innocent explanation.

Just like there was an innocent explanation with Heather Malone?

I shudder.

The encounter has left me shaken, like that time I was in a pub when I was a student and a fight broke out between two men right next to me. It was horrible, watching them throw punches at each other. So animalistic. So brutal. I didn't go out for six weeks after that. I couldn't. I felt too vulnerable. So sickened. Why do men always have to behave like Neanderthals?

And the girl? For a moment, I thought she was Olivia, our neighbour from across the road, but why would Leo be fighting with her? She certainly looked a little like Olivia, the girl who walks to school with Leo most days. She's much smaller than him, with long, blonde hair and pretty features, so it could have been her, I suppose. But I thought they were friends. Maybe even something more than that.

I don't know Olivia that well. She's been around to the house a few times to hang out with Leo, although I've not really had the chance to speak to her. Leo's ushered her in and out before I've had the opportunity, like he's embarrassed of what I might say. I suppose they could have fallen out about something, but that still wouldn't excuse Leo's behaviour, the way he was grappling with her hands, pinning her against the tree.

Biscuit finally stops barking, distracted by something she can smell in a clump of brown, dead ferns. I really need to get the dogs back to the van before the last of the light. I don't have a torch and I don't want to be stumbling around the woods in the dark. But I'm drawn to the big oak where I thought I spotted Leo and Olivia, because there's something else I'm sure I saw.

I'm almost certain they dropped something in the struggle.

I untie the dogs, loop their leads around my hand and tentatively guide them across the uneven ground towards the tree, its branches like an old man's gnarled and arthritic fingers.

The only indication that anything untoward has taken place is the ground, which has been trampled flat. Brown, decaying bracken has been crushed down and footprints have churned up the peaty mud. It doesn't tell me anything. But then, what was I hoping to find?

Disappointed, but not surprised, I take a deep breath and cast my eye around to locate the footpath. It must be close by. I'm sure we didn't wander that far from the trail, but in every direction, all I can see are trees and scrub. I should have paid more attention when I went chasing after Biscuit. Not that it's her fault. It's mine for not keeping a tighter grip on her lead.

I turn through a full circle, trying to establish my bearings. My boots squelch in the soft mud and catch against something hard in the ground. Instinctively, I glance down, expecting to find a jagged rock protruding from the earth, but discover something far more disconcerting.

A knife, half hidden under a pile of yellowing, fallen leaves, with a blade about four or five inches long and a shiny black handle. Like something you'd use to chop fruit or vegetables. A kitchen knife.

My breath catches in my throat.

A coincidence? It seems unlikely, especially as when I kneel to take a closer look, I spot a smear of red across the tarnished blade. It looks like blood. Fresh blood. Bright red and sticky.

Biscuit shoves her head under mine, sniffing curiously at my discovery. I push her away forcibly. She's done herself enough harm today without cutting her paw open.

'Go away, Biscuit,' I hiss in her ear. She whines and turns her back on me.

An awful thought barrels into my head. But the idea is too heinous. Too unbelievable. Whatever Leo's done in the past, that's not my son. He's not violent and he wouldn't deliberately do anything to hurt anyone. He was brought up better than that. He's not a monster, despite what some of those foul-mouthed, out-of-control online trolls had to say.

And yet, what other explanation is there?

You read about kids in inner cities arming themselves with knives, don't you? It has become almost endemic if you believe the news. But surely not here. Surely not my son.

I glance around, the cold chilling my bones. What am I supposed to do with it now I've found it? It's dangerous. If I leave it here, a child could stumble across it. Or an animal. It would be irresponsible of me.

I zip up my coat to my chin as I stand.

There's no real choice. I pick the knife up carefully with the tips of my fingers and use a tissue from my pocket to wipe it clean of mud and blood, then slip it into the pouch around my waist with the dog treats.

The dogs are getting restless. We ought to get back. Away to my right, I finally pick out a trail, one I'm fairly sure I recognise and that leads directly back to the car park.

'Let's get you all home, shall we?'

The car park is deserted and the last light is fading fast. One by one, the dogs jump into their cages in the back and settle down on the beds I've made for them from old towels.

I clamber in behind the wheel, unzip my coat and check my phone. The mobile phone signal in Clover Wood is sketchy at the best of times, although you can sometimes pick up a signal in the car park. Today, I have an impressive two bars. It should be enough to make a call.

It's one I don't really want to make, but I know I have to. I need to speak to Leo and put my mind at rest. I need to know if he's been anywhere near the woods this afternoon.

Chapter 3

The darting shadows of two playful bats swoop and plunge past the windscreen as I find Leo's number and make the call. He'll go mad if he thinks I'm accusing him of something, especially if I'm mistaken, but I need to ask the question.

Of course, there's every chance he'll lie to me, but all I can hope for is that if there is something going on, some issue with Olivia, he feels able to be honest with me. He agreed after Heather's death that if he ever found himself in trouble like that again, he'd tell us and not try to deal with it on his own. We're not ogres after all.

Typically, he doesn't answer. His phone goes to voicemail and an emotionless, automated female voice informs me the person I've called is unavailable and invites me to leave a message.

I consider it for a split second, as Leo will see I've tried calling, but I'm not sure what to say. He's so curt with me lately, so angry all the time, I don't want him to think I'm making accusations. Our relationship is fragile enough as it is. The slightest thing seems to set him off these days and I'm constantly walking on eggshells to avoid upsetting him. I only have to ask how his day's been at school or whether he has any homework, and I'm accused of prying. Or asking too many questions about things that have nothing to do with me. It's utterly exhausting.

Instead, I hang up, clip my phone into the holder on the dashboard and plug in a power cable. It's better if I speak to him face to face, anyway. I'll catch him at home after I've dropped off the dogs.

I'm sure he was nowhere near the woods and that I was mistaken. It's more likely he was hanging out with a friend playing video games or making a nuisance of himself outside the corner shop, although since we moved to the new house and transferred the boys from their old school, Leo has been struggling to make friends. There's Olivia, of course, but I've not heard him mention anyone else by name.

I think that's partly why he's become so uncommunicative and moody lately. He never used to be like this. He was always such a charming, happy-go-lucky boy. But then it was awful for all of us when Heather died. I know he resents me for moving the family away, but one day he'll come to appreciate that I did the right thing.

It's only a two-minute drive back to the estate. I slow to a crawl as I pass our house, checking to see if there are any lights on. Downstairs is ablaze and I catch a shadow flit past the kitchen window. It looks like it could be Casper. He's usually home first. Leo's probably in his bedroom, where he seems to spend most of his time when he's home.

My first stop is at Anthony and Zac's house to return Tyson. I pull up outside and walk him to the front door, sorting through the keys on my ever-expanding bunch. Most of my clients have given me keys to their houses to let myself in as I please.

Tyson scratches at the door with one paw as I open the deadlock and release the latch. I let him off his lead and he races inside, his feet scratching on the hard wooden floors, excited to be home.

The house is immaculate. Of all my clients, Anthony and Zac have by far the best taste. I adore their beautiful slate-grey kitchen with its fancy coffee machine, chrome fruit squeezer and tastefully arranged bottles and jars dotted around on shelves. They have expensive sofas in the lounge, matching wooden furniture throughout, and all kinds of amazing modern art on the walls. It's the sort of house I could imagine being featured in a magazine.

Sometimes I picture myself living here, but it wouldn't be practical for us, not with all the dogs and two teenage boys who are unbelievably hard on all the fixtures and fittings. For a start, where would we store all their sweaty trainers in a house as minimalist as this?

I scoop up a pile of post from the mat, sifting through it on my way to the kitchen. Not that there's anything of interest. A brown envelope that looks suspiciously like a tax demand, junk mail from some local retailers, and what looks like a greetings card addressed to Anthony in looping handwriting. I drop the mail on the side and fill Tyson's bowl with a scoop of dried food from a container in one of the cupboards.

We've made some good friends on the estate since we moved here a few months ago. Everyone's been warm and welcoming, but I really like Anthony and Zac. They make me laugh, the way they constantly rib each other. Neither of them takes themselves too seriously, which is a refreshing change. Anthony's a personal trainer at a gym in town. Generously, he's offered me a free session whenever I fancy, although I've been putting it off. I'm not sure the world's quite ready to see me in Lycra yet. His husband, Zac, is a flight attendant working short haul into Europe. They're both busy people, which means we don't see them as much as I'd like.

Happy that Tyson is settled, I head back to the van, locking up after me. Next, I return Bertie to Fergal and Hanna, who live five doors down from us. They're friendly enough, especially Hanna, who's Swedish and runs an online clothing company from home. She has the most adorable accent and the kindest nature. She'd do anything for anyone, although I think she's lonely working from home. She's always trying to grab me for a chat at the most inopportune moments.

Her husband, Fergal, isn't around much. He's tall and muscular and completely bald, but it suits him. He also runs his own business. Some sort of consultancy, I think he told me once.

I knock before letting myself in. 'It's only me. Sabine,' I call out as I push open the door.

Bertie pads nonchalantly along the hall and settles in his bed under the stairs with a yawn as Hanna appears at the top of the stairs, her eyes sparkling and her lustrous blonde hair falling over her shoulders in springy curls.

She always makes me feel under dressed, especially as my clothes are invariably covered in mud and dog hairs, my nails bitten down to the fingertips, and my hair a ragged, greasy mess with the roots needing a touch up.

'How was he today?' she asks.

'As good as gold.'

'Will you stay for a cup of tea?' Hanna asks, wafting down the stairs like she's floating. She never misses the chance to chat, but I want to get home. I need to speak to Leo.

'I can't really—'

'Did you see they've put planning in for another hundred houses behind St Peter's Church?'

'No, I—'

'As if the town really needs any more houses. Are they going to build more schools to cope? A new doctor's surgery? You can't get an appointment as it is,' she says.

I agree, but it seems hypocritical to complain about new houses being built when we've both moved onto an estate that was only completed in the last year on a greenfield site. The second tranche of the project is currently being built, with another twenty homes going up behind ours. Although there's a narrow strip of woodland between the back of us and the construction site, we've been plagued by noise and dust since the day we moved in. I'll be glad when they've finished.

'I'm sorry, Hanna. I've got to get going.' I edge towards the door.

'I'm thinking of starting a petition. You'll sign it, won't you?'

'Sure. I'll see you in the morning.'

She's still talking as I pull the door closed behind me and take a deep breath. I like Hanna, but she leaves me exhausted. She's totally draining.

Opposite their house is Kwame and Zahara's place. He's some big shot in the music industry, if you believe the gossip. Zahara's in events management, but has the looks of a supermodel. She's also the most serene, unflappable woman I've ever met. She's kind and generous and never has a bad word to say about anyone. Her job, which takes her all over Europe, sounds high-powered, but I imagine she's brilliant at it. She's the kind of woman who'd make a success of anything she turned her hand to.

Neither of them is home this afternoon. I pop some food in a bowl for Rosie, their brown and white spaniel, and while she eats, I wander into the lounge where there's an enormous TV hanging from the wall and a sound system linked up to four big speakers on stands. On one of the walls hang framed platinum discs of albums even I've heard of, each with a plaque crediting Kwame for his contribution. I'm impressed, and even more so when I spot a series of photos of Kwame with a variety of semi-famous recording artists.

Rosie bounds into the room, looking for me, licking her lips.

'Have you finished, girl?' When I scratch her ears, she rolls over and offers me her tummy to rub.

'I'd better get going. I'll see you in the morning.'

She comes with me to the door and whines when I leave.

My final call is to Jerome and Faith's house with Hank, the boisterous black labrador. They live opposite us, with their daughter, Olivia.

As I head up their drive with Hank in tow, a vision pops into my head of the two teenagers I'd seen in Clover Wood. Leo wrestling with Olivia? Gripping her wrists, a knife in hand?

I close my eyes and shake my head. I didn't even see a knife at the time, which just goes to show the tricks your mind can play on you. Even so, my arm feels like a dead weight as I lift it to knock at the door.

Maybe Olivia will answer and I can ask her directly whether she was with Leo earlier in the woods and settle my doubts. It would certainly save me from having to quiz Leo and face the sting of his irritation.

Olivia's a bright girl, from what I've heard. She's probably been at home studying since school finished. She wouldn't lie to me, I'm sure.

But to my disappointment, Olivia doesn't answer the door. It's her father, Jerome. He's still in his work clothes, heavy-duty trousers with patches on the knees and an olive-green fleece jacket with the name of the electrical company he owns embroidered on the breast.

'Sabine!' he says with a delighted grin, like he's not seen me in years and I'm the most exciting thing that's happened to him all day.

I glance at the ground and bite my lip. Jerome's friendly enough, but I find him a little odd. A little too forward. Too flirty. He has a mischievous glint in his eye which puts me on edge, and he always finds a reason to touch my arm, my shoulder, my leg. I wouldn't say he gives me the creeps exactly, but I wouldn't want to be left alone with him for too long.

'How's my boy been today?' he asks, stooping to make a fuss of Hank.

'Trouble, as usual.'

Jerome grabs Hank's head and holds it steady to look into his eyes. 'Have you been giving Sabine the runaround?' he asks in a sing-song baby voice like he's talking to a toddler.

'Doesn't he always?' Jerome stands and when he lets Hank go, the dog dives inside the house and disappears. 'Bye then, Hank. See you tomorrow,' I call after him.

Jerome shrugs. 'So rude. Sorry.'

I wave a hand dismissively. 'Don't worry. I won't take it personally,' I chuckle. 'He's probably gone to find Olivia.'

'He'll be lucky. She's not home yet.'

My stomach somersaults. 'Oh?' I say.

'I expect she'll be back when she gets hungry.'

'Right, okay. Talking of which, I'd better get home and think about what I'm going to cook my lot for dinner.'

'Thanks, Sabine.' Jerome rests a hand on my upper arm and I have to fight the urge to flinch. 'Hank really loves spending time with you, the lucky sod.'

'It's my pleasure.' I force a smile. 'I'll see you in the morning.'

'I'm looking forward to it already.'

Yuck.

I pull away and hurry down the drive without a backwards glance, conscious of Jerome watching me. Checking me out. I pity poor Faith for having to put up with a man like that, although whenever I've seen them together, they've been behaving like a pair of lovesick teenagers.

Biscuit's grateful to finally be freed from the van and trots happily at my heel towards our front door. As I slot the key in the lock, I glance over my shoulder. Jerome's still watching me from across the street. He raises a hand and waves. I nod and slip inside, glad to be out of his view.

But I don't have time to worry about Jerome Hunter. I have more important things on my mind, like speaking to my son.

'Leo?' I yell, heeling off my boots. 'Are you home? I need to have a word.'

Chapter 4

When there's no reply, I wander into the lounge, following the sound of a video game being played at full volume.

Casper is sprawled out on the sofa with a controller in his hands and his tongue wedged between his teeth as he concentrates on the TV screen. When he notices me at the door, he sits up but can't drag his eyes away from his game as the character he's playing launches a violent assault on a comically muscular warrior carrying armfuls of weapons and ammunition.

'Casper, can you turn the volume down a bit?' I yell as the sound of gunfire and explosions reverberates around the room. It's so loud, the TV speakers are distorting.

'Hang on, Mum,' he says. 'Just got to kill this guy.'

A few seconds later, he tosses the controller onto the couch with a cry of despair.

'Did you get killed?' I ask, not sure what's going on in the game.

'There was a guy hiding in the bushes. I didn't see him.' He finally mutes the volume.

'I'm sorry.'

'It's okay. How was your day?' he asks.

'Not bad. I didn't lose any of the dogs, so that's a bonus.'

I'm grateful that he laughs at my joke. He's the only one in this family who finds my amusing quips funny.

'Well done,' Casper says.

'Although Biscuit got a thorn stuck in her paw.'

'Oh.' He frowns. 'Is she okay?'

'She'll live. Have you seen your brother?'

'No,' he says, collecting his controller and switching off the TV.

'Is he home yet?'

'Don't think so. What's for tea?'

I've not thought about dinner and right now it's the last thing on my mind. 'I don't know yet. I'll have to see what's in the freezer. Let me get in the house first,' I snap, peeling off my coat.

'Want some help?'

'It's okay,' I sigh. 'I can manage.'

Casper's always been the thoughtful one of the two. The one who offers to carry in the shopping from the car. The one who'll clear up the plates after dinner without asking and who always asks after my day, even though I don't suppose he cares in the slightest. He's so different from his brother, I sometimes wonder if one of them might have been switched at birth, although you only have to look at them together to tell they're related. They're like two leaves from the same branch. They share the same eyes. The same shaped nose. The same quirky way they have of holding their heads slightly to one side when they're concentrating.

I guess my chat with Leo is going to have to wait.

The freezer is predictably empty and doesn't throw up much inspiration, unless we want to eat ice cream or those blackberries we picked and froze last year and brought from the old house.

Fortunately, I find a couple of breaded chicken fillets and two old pieces of cod buried at the bottom of one of the drawers. Plus some oven chips and frozen sweetcorn. It'll have to do. It's all a bit yellow, but it's better than starving and I'm not ordering takeaway on a Monday night.

'Want me to lay the table?' Casper asks cheerily, appearing in the kitchen with his games console tucked under his arm.

'Thanks, love. That would be great.'

He returns a few minutes later and hops up onto a stool at the breakfast bar to watch me laying out our frozen meal on two baking trays. It's not exactly cordon bleu cooking.

'How was school?' I ask.

'Yeah, it was okay. We had biology today, which was okay, and maths, which wasn't. Doug reckons he's been scouted by a football coach to play for United, but he's so full of crap. He's always making stuff up like that.'

'Uh-huh,' I say, not really listening. I'm glad he's made friends. Unlike Leo, Casper's taken the move to a new town and the transfer to a new school in his stride.

He's even joined a few after-school sports groups. I genuinely think he's happy here, which only serves to highlight how miserable his brother is.

Leo blames me for the upheaval, but that girl's death wasn't anything to do with me. If we'd stayed where we were, we'd never have been allowed to forget it. I'm sure in time, Leo will appreciate there was no other option, and that it's been difficult for all of us, but we had to get our lives back. Leo might be on the cusp of adulthood, but he still has a lot of growing up to do. Then maybe he'll realise the sacrifices we've all made because of what he did.

As I slide the trays into the oven, turn up the heat and set the timer, the front door crashes open. I hear a bag being thrown onto the floor and heavy footsteps tramping up the stairs. The familiar sounds of my eldest son returning home.

'Leo? Wait! I need to talk to you.'

I race after him, but he's already reached his room when I make it to the landing, wiping my hands on a tea towel. He slams his door shut, rocking the foundations of the house.

'Leo?' I put my ear to the door and knock gently.

'What?' he snaps.

'Can I come in?'

'What do you want?'

Charming. If I'd spoken to my parents the way he speaks to me, I'd have had the biggest hiding of my life. I ease open the door, smiling, determined not to start off on the wrong foot.

'How was school?' I ask.

He's sitting on the edge of his bed, scrolling through his phone. He huffs and rolls his eyes. 'What do you think? Shit, if you must know.'

He's wearing his black hoodie and skinny-fit jeans. As he crosses his leg, I notice splatters of mud around his ankle.

'It can't have been that bad.'

He lifts his eyes momentarily from his phone and stares at me contemptuously, with eyebrows raised.

'Come on, Leo. I know you didn't want to move or change schools, but we couldn't stay. You know that. You only have to give it a year and you'll be off to university wherever you like,' I say. We've been through this so many times.

'If I get the grades.'

'Don't you think you will?'

He shrugs. 'Is this just a social call or did you want something?'

I grit my teeth. There's no point rising to it or we'll end up in a screaming match again. 'I was with the dogs in Clover Wood earlier,' I say, observing his expression. He doesn't react. 'I thought I saw you with Olivia.'

'Nope.'

'Oh. Are you sure? It looked like you.'

'Why would I be in Clover Wood with Olivia?'

'I don't know. I was hoping you could tell me.'

'I just told you, I wasn't there.'

A sigh slips from my lips. 'Are you absolutely sure? I thought I saw the two of you arguing.'

'Arguing?' He finally lowers his phone and meets my eye.

'Arguing, Leo. You know what arguing is, don't you? You do enough of it with me.'

'There's no need to be sarky.'

'I'm not. I'm asking you to be honest with me.'

'So you don't believe me?'

I hate these games he plays, twisting my words and making it sound like something it's not. 'It's not that, but if you're in any kind of trouble -'

'I'm not.'

'You'd talk to me, wouldn't you? Or Dad?'

'Yes,' he snaps.

'It's just that I saw someone and it looked remarkably like you.'

'Well, it wasn't.'

'So where were you, then? Where have you been for the last two hours? School finished at half-three.'

'Seriously?' he asks with incredulity. 'You're checking up on me now?'

'I worry about you, Leo. I'm your mother. And you can hardly blame me, can you?'

'I was with a friend.'

'What friend?'

'You don't know them.'

'Give me a name, then.' I fold my arms across my chest. It would be easier extracting teeth.

'You don't believe me, do you?' he screams, jumping up. He's a few inches taller than me these days and he can be quite intimidating when he wants to be. 'Why do you always think the worst of me? I can't do anything right, can I?'

He's blowing this completely out of proportion. Trust needs to be earned.

'I just don't want you getting into any more trouble. It's an important year and you could do without the distraction. I thought you would have learnt by now that if something's happened, you can talk to me,' I say.

'Again? I didn't kill Heather,' he yells in my face.

'That's not what I meant.'

'But you still think it was my fault, don't you?'

We've been through this a million times. He might not have forced Heather to take those drugs, but he knew she was only fifteen, he knew she was vulnerable, and he gave them to her anyway.

I was as surprised as anyone that the police didn't charge him with the supply of a Class A substance, if nothing else. He was lucky. It could have ruined his chances of getting a place at university or a decent job. Not that Heather's parents saw it as lucky. Understandably, they blamed Leo for their daughter's death and were all for lynching him, as were half of the community and every keyboard warrior on social media when his name came out publicly.

'I just want the truth, Leo. You promised, no more lies.'

'I'm not lying.'

I study his face, trying to read him. 'You'd better not be.'

'Christ, Mum, when are you going to let it go?'

Maybe he is telling me the truth this time. Maybe it was all in my imagination, but how can I be sure?

'I found something.'

'What?' he grumbles.

'Wait here.'

I run back down the stairs and into the utility room where I've hung my waist pouch. I snatch it off the hook and carry it back to Leo's room. He throws me a puzzled look when I hold it up.

'Recognise this?' I pant, sliding open the zip.

'Your pouch?'

'No, this.' I carefully pull out the kitchen knife. 'It was in the woods. It had fresh blood on it.'

'Blood?' Leo blanches.

'Yes, Leo. Blood.'

His Adam's apple bobs up and down and he sucks in his bottom lip like a sulky child. 'Well,' he says, 'it's got nothing to do with me.'

Chapter 5

'Sorry I'm late.' Rory comes up behind me and plants a kiss on my cheek, the whiskers of his ridiculous grey beard tickling my skin.

'Again,' I point out. It's becoming a bad habit.

The boys and I have already eaten and I'm in the kitchen wiping down the work surfaces and contemplating whether I could justify a glass of wine on a Monday night. After the day I've had, I could really use one.

'I couldn't get away. Alison's meeting overran and I missed my train.'

I know we've moved further away from London and the nearest train station, but there have been far too many excuses lately for not making it home on time. Tonight of all nights, I could have done with Rory's support.

Some adult company over dinner would have been appreciated too. Leo was predictably sullen as we sat at the dining table in silence, and even Casper was distracted by his phone. It wasn't exactly an enjoyable meal.

'Mine in the oven?' Rory pulls out a baking tray of shrivelled-up battered cod and overcooked chips, and pulls a face.

'If you'd have been home on time, it wouldn't be ruined.' I don't mean to snap but Leo's been trying my patience, and I'm worried about him. He couldn't disguise the look on his face when I showed him the knife. What was it? Horror? Guilt?

'I didn't say anything. It looks lovely,' Rory protests.

'No, it doesn't, but I didn't have anything else in the house. I've not had the chance to go shopping.'

'It's fine.'

'No, it's not.'

Rory lifts the tray to his face and sniffs. 'Mmmm, delicious.'

'Perhaps you'd like to do it yourself next time.'

'Hey, what's wrong? You look tired.' Rory sets the tray on the side and puts a hand on my shoulder.

'Take a guess.'

'Leo?' he says, arching his eyebrows. 'What now?'

He serves what's left of his poor excuse for a dinner onto a plate and hitches himself up onto a stool at the breakfast bar to eat, popping overcooked, crunchy chips into his mouth with his fingers.

'I thought I saw him in Clover Wood this afternoon with Olivia,' I say, folding a tea towel over my shoulder.

'Jerome and Faith's daughter? So?'

'They were fighting.'

'Right.'

'I mean physically fighting. He had her by the wrists and pinned against a tree. It was awful.'

'You're sure it was Leo?'

I hesitate a beat. 'Yes. No, not really. It was getting dark.'

'Have you talked to him?'

'I've tried, but you know what he's like. You can't have a civil conversation with him.'

Rory ponders as he chews. 'What did he say?'

'That I don't trust him.'

'Do you?' Rory asks.

'I don't know. Sometimes.' I clear my throat. 'Do you think he's...'

'Back on the drugs?'

'He promised he wouldn't touch them again.'

'You want to get him tested? We could order some kits online if it would make you feel better.'

I run a hand over my brow. 'No,' I sigh. I can imagine how that would go down in Leo's current mood. 'There's something else. I found a knife with blood on it.'

Rory's face creases with surprise. 'What? Where?'

'In the same spot I saw them arguing. And now I don't know what to think.'

'But knowing you, you thought the worst.'

'Well, what would you think?' I step into the utility and fetch the knife from my treat pouch. I lay it on the counter in front of Rory.

'This it?' he asks.

I nod.

'I thought you said it was covered in blood.'

'Not covered in blood, but there was blood on it. I wiped it off.'

'Why?'

I shrug. 'I don't know.' Why *did* I clean it? Was I subconsciously trying to protect Leo? 'Leo says he's never seen it before.'

'But you don't believe him?'

'I don't know what to believe. I want to believe him, but—'

'You don't trust him.'

I let out a long sigh. Does it make me a bad mother?

'Why don't you give the boy the benefit of the doubt for a change?' Rory suggests. 'Don't you think you're overreacting?'

'Overreacting?' I scoff. I grab the knife and wave it under Rory's nose. His eyes open wide with alarm. 'What if he took this knife to the woods to meet Olivia and was going to use it on her?'

'Don't be ridiculous. Why would he do that?'

'I don't know. That's what I've been trying to find out. Oh god, I really thought the move was going to be the restart we all needed, but it's happening all over again,' I cry. 'I feel like I don't know my son at all these days. He won't talk to me and even when he does, it's to tell me how much he hates me. He hates his school, and he hates living here, and he thinks it's all my fault.'

'That's not true.' Rory unbuttons his waistcoat and pushes the remnants of his meal to one side of the plate before licking his fingers clean, one by one.

'Isn't it?'

What's happening to us? We used to be such a tight team, me, Rory, Casper, and Leo. The Sugars against the world. We did everything together, and we used to have fun. We laughed all the time. United against the world. But those days all seem so long ago. I can't talk to Leo without him biting my head off, and why do I constantly feel as though I'm fighting with Rory's office for his attention? Since Heather's death, we've been drifting further and further apart. Becoming a family of four individuals doing their own thing. We hardly ever even sit down together to eat.

I knew it would happen eventually, that the boys would grow up, leave home and have lives of their own, but I never imagined it would happen so soon. Or so suddenly. It's all slipping between my fingers like the finest grains of sand.

'So I was thinking,' I say, drawing a circle on the counter with my finger.

Rory groans. 'What now?'

'Maybe you could have a word with him. Talk to him man to man.'

'Me?'

'You're his father. He might be more open to talking to you.'

Rory looks horrified. He's a good dad. He always has been. When the boys were small, he loved fighting and wrestling with them, building dens under the table with their duvets, helping them construct elaborate Lego buildings, and playing football with them in the garden. But he's never been good at talking to them about things that matter. That's always been my domain.

Like when Casper was being bullied by a Year 4 pupil, it was me he confided in, and me who sorted it out. When Leo was struggling with the pressure of his schoolwork, when Rory's father was diagnosed with terminal cancer and given only a few months to live, when Casper was cast as Joseph in the school nativity and was worried about performing in front of all the parents, it was me they came to. Not Rory. He's a typical man. He's never been any good at the emotional side of parenting.

'I don't know, Sabine.'

'Oh, for god's sake, Rory, I'm only asking you talk to him.'

He hangs his head. I don't know why it should be down to me all the time.

'Is everything okay? I heard voices.'

I jump at Casper's sudden appearance. How much of that did he hear?

'Sorry, love,' I say, wiping tears of frustration from my eyes. 'We didn't mean to shout.'

'What were you arguing about?' Casper asks innocently, knocking a pair of headphones off his ears.

'Nothing for you to be concerned about,' I tell him. 'Nothing at all.'

I glare at Rory, but he refuses to meet my eye.

Chapter 6

After he's finished eating, Rory takes himself off to his study to work, leaving me to unload the dishwasher. A waft of steam hits my face as I open the door. I start by putting away the pans and the plates, then remove the basket of cutlery.

Among the knives and forks, teaspoons and dessert spoons, is the kitchen knife I found in the woods. It's come up beautifully, the blade so shiny I can see the scratches where it's been sharpened. It probably wasn't hygienic to put it in with all the other dishes, but I didn't know what else to do with it.

'Mum, can I have a glass of milk?'

Bloody hell. I wish Casper would stop creeping up on me like that and scaring the living daylights out of me. I spin around guiltily, hiding the knife behind my back.

'Yeah, sure. Help yourself.'

When he turns away to dive into the fridge, I shove the knife into the back of a cupboard above the kettle, slipping it inside a plastic sports bottle no one ever uses.

I don't know why I feel the need to hide it, but I don't want it left around. Maybe I'll drop it into the recycling bin later. Are you allowed to put knives in with the recycling? I don't know. I wouldn't want someone cutting themselves.

'I might go to bed,' Casper says as he pours a generous helping of milk into a glass.

'Okay, but don't let me catch you up there playing video games at midnight.'

'Mum,' he moans. 'I'm not ten.'

'I know.' I pull him towards me and kiss the top of his head. He attempts to wriggle out of my grasp, squirming in disgust, but I'm not ready to give up on cuddling my youngest son quite yet. 'Love you.'

'Love you too.'

An hour later, there's still no sign of Rory. I've tried watching TV to unwind, but I can't find anything to hold my attention and have been flicking mindlessly from one channel to the next, until finally I give up. I lift Biscuit's head off my lap and she peels open a sleepy eye. Thankfully, her paw doesn't seem to have given her any further problems, so I'm hopeful that unless it becomes infected, we can avoid the vets.

I leave her dozing on the couch and head off to find my husband. He's still at his desk in front of his computer, working on a design. I wish he wouldn't bring his work home. We don't see much of him as it is, especially as he's spending increasingly long hours at the office. Does he really need to work in the evenings as well? Or is it an excuse not to spend time with me?

'Did you speak to Leo yet?' I ask, putting my head around the door.

'Not yet.'

'Are you going to?'

'Yes,' he snaps. 'I just need to find the right time.'

'How about now?' I suggest.

'I'm in the middle of something. I'll do it later.'

We both know he's making excuses and that he has no intention of speaking to Leo tonight. Honestly, he can be so emotionally stunted sometimes.

'You know what? If it's too much trouble, don't bother.' I pull his door shut aggressively. Why is he so incapable of doing this one simple thing for me? I don't ask much of him.

Fine. Well, if he won't speak to Leo, I'll do it myself. This needs resolving. If Leo is in some kind of trouble again, I'm going to get to the bottom of it.

Upstairs, a glimmer of light glows under Leo's door. I knock and let myself in without waiting for an invitation.

Leo's lying on the bed but jumps up when I walk in, hiding something under the duvet, his face flushing.

'What are you doing?' I ask.

'Nothing.'

'Look, I'm sorry. I didn't mean to shout earlier,' I say, hoping if I strike the right chord, and don't make it sound like I'm accusing him of something, Leo might open up to me.

'Okay.'

'But I'm worried about you.'

'I'm fine,' he says, shoulders hunched, a dark scowl of suspicion on his face.

He's growing up so fast. He'll legally be an adult next year, but he's at that awkward stage where he looks like a man, but still has the maturity and emotional intelligence of a child.

I miss my little boy who used to look up to me, who needed me. Who'd hold my hand to cross the road and didn't care who saw, and who would roll into our bed in the middle of the night and snuggle up on my pillow with his warm, sweet breath on my face.

I knew it was coming, but I could never have imagined he'd morph into this sullen, moody, distant creature who couldn't stand to be in the same room, let alone talk to me. When I speak to him now, it's as though we're talking in different languages and every word I utter, every sound I make, seems to drive him to distraction.

'You would tell me if there was something wrong, wouldn't you?' I ask, folding my arms and then lowering them again, conscious not to appear defensive.

'Yeah.'

I cross the room and sit on the bed next to him. 'I worry about you, that's all. I'm your mother. I can't help it.'

'I said I'm fine.'

'I want you to be happy.'

'If you wanted me to be happy, you wouldn't have made us move here.' He glances at me with narrowed eyes.

It's as if he thinks what I did was a betrayal when all I was doing was trying to protect my family.

'You know we couldn't stay.'

He shrugs. 'Why not? Because you were worried about what people were saying about you?'

The barb cuts like a razor. 'That's not fair. You know we couldn't stay.'

At first, we tried to ignore the nasty comments, threats and abuse, made largely on social media by people in the town who should have known better. We had all sorts of ignorant vitriol thrown at us. Then, even our friends and neighbours started keeping their distance after Heather's death, as if Leo had murdered her and got away with it.

What they don't seem to realise is that no one forced her to take that LSD she got from Leo. No one encouraged her to climb onto that bridge when she was off her head. And nobody pushed her. She fell. It was a tragic accident, but Leo will have to live with the consequences for the rest of his life. He didn't mean her any harm. The only thing he's guilty of is stupidity. He should never have been experimenting with drugs and he should never have been pressured into giving them to a fifteen-year-old girl.

If anyone's to blame, it's Heather's parents. They were the ones who let her attend a party that was supposed to be for sixth-formers only. They should have kept a closer eye on her, but I never once saw any criticism flung their way.

'Are you taking drugs again?' I ask.

'What? No, course not.'

I look him in the eye and hold his gaze. 'I want you to be honest with me.'

'Mum!'

'Alright, I had to ask.'

'I'm not stupid, you know.'

He was stupid enough to supply an underage girl he hardly knew with drugs once before, but I don't challenge him. I can only hope he has learnt his lesson.

'And how are things with Olivia?'

'She's not my girlfriend, if that's what you think.'

I raise an eyebrow. 'You could do worse. She's a pretty girl.'

'She's just a friend.'

'Okay. And everything's alright between you, is it?'

'Yes,' he huffs.

'You've not fallen out?'

'I don't know what you think you saw today, but it wasn't me, okay?' He raises his voice as he picks at his fingernails.

'I'm only asking. There's no need to shout.'

'I wasn't in the woods and I wasn't with Olivia. Whoever you saw, it must have been someone else.'

'Okay, fine. I believe you.'

Leo snorts. 'Really?'

'Yes. You've looked me in the eye and told me it wasn't you fighting with Olivia in Clover Wood earlier, or threatening her with a knife, so I believe you. I trust you not to lie to me.'

'Right.' He swallows and looks down at his hands. 'Is that it?'

'I just wanted to check in with you. You're still my baby.'

'Mum! You don't need to worry about me,' he says.

But I do. I can't help it, especially as I don't believe a word he's just told me.

Chapter 7

The first thing I notice when I step out of the house the next morning is the police car parked outside Jerome and Faith's house. I hope the Hunters haven't been burgled during the night. This is supposed to be a safe part of town. Not the sort of estate that's prone to break-ins. Or at least I thought not.

Despite the injury to her paw she picked up yesterday, Biscuit jumps effortlessly into her cage in the back of the van and settles down on her bed. I'm due to collect Hank next, but I'm not sure if I might be interrupting something. The police don't turn up at your house first thing in the morning unless it's important, do they? But Jerome and Faith will be expecting me and maybe glad for me to take Hank off their hands if they have more important matters to worry about.

I lock the van and tentatively cross the road, scanning the house for signs there's been an intruder. A broken window. A ladder that shouldn't be there. But everything looks exactly as it did when I dropped Hank off last night.

I knock at the door and take a step back.

Hank barks, and I hear his claws scrabbling across the floor.

When the door opens, he comes bounding out with his tongue lolling. His ears fall back and his tail drops when he sees it's me. He fusses around me like I'm a long-lost relative, almost bowling me over with his exuberance.

I wrap my arms around his neck and ruffle his fur as he springs up and down, trying to lick my face.

Faith appears at the door wrapped up in a thick towelling dressing gown, looking like a ghost. She's normally so well turned out, I don't think I've ever seen her without make-up before. She's deathly pale, her hair flattened and her eyes rimmed red like she's been crying. My first thought is that someone's died.

'Faith? Is everything okay? I saw the police car outside—'

She stares at me blankly, as if I'm a complete stranger.

'Faith?'

'Sorry, Sabine,' she says, snapping out of her trance. 'I'll fetch Hank's lead.'

She shuffles back into the house and returns with it a few moments later. As she hands it to me, she bursts into tears, her body crumpling.

'Faith? What is it?' I grab her elbow and help her stand as she sniffs and wipes her eyes.

I'm at a complete loss what to say or do. Something's happened, obviously. 'What is it? Is it Jerome?'

'I'm sorry, Sabine. It's been a rough night,' Faith says. 'It's Olivia. She's missing.'

'Olivia?'

Faith nods, searching in her pocket for a scrunched-up tissue that she uses to wipe her nose. 'She didn't come home last night and we're going crazy with worry. It's just not like her.'

It's no wonder she looks so awful. I doubt she's slept a wink.

'I'm so sorry.' I don't know what else to say.

'We've called around all her friends, but nobody's seen her. It's not like her to go off without letting us know.'

'What about her phone?' I ask, stupidly. As if they've not tried calling her mobile. I can't imagine the suffering Faith's going through. If it had been Leo or Casper who'd vanished, I'd be completely out of my mind.

'It's switched off. We can't get through. I don't know what to do.'

Inside the house, I hear the low rumble of voices. Jerome's familiar, deep tones, strained with emotion, and two others I don't recognise. Police officers, I guess.

'I'm sure there's a logical explanation and she'll turn up soon.' The words trip lightly off my tongue, but they're empty platitudes. I've no more idea than Faith whether Olivia's likely to be found soon or not.

My mind goes into overdrive imagining all the awful things that could have happened. I'm sure the same fears have been running through Faith's mind all night and if she's anything like me, like any concerned mother, she'll have come up with a dozen catastrophic scenarios.

'I just can't shake the feeling that something awful has happened to her,' Faith wails, dabbing her eyes with the tissue. 'The police have been so good. They came straight out last night and have people out looking for her, but they haven't found anything yet.'

'Well, it's reassuring they're taking it seriously, isn't it?' Although I'm not surprised. As far as I'm aware, Olivia has never run away before, and a pretty, young girl from a decent home vanishing without trace must have set all the alarm bells ringing.

'I just want to know she's safe.' Faith bursts into a renewed fit of tears, which leaves me feeling even more helpless.

'Is there anything I can do?' I ask.

Faith shakes her head. 'We've been trying to trace her last movements,' she says. 'We know she left school at around three-thirty, but after that, nobody saw her.'

The ground feels as if it's falling away from my feet. My stomach tightens and my throat narrows.

Leo assured me he wasn't in Clover Wood with Olivia yesterday afternoon. I want to believe him, now more than ever. I want to believe it was my imagination merely projecting my deepest fears. That he was never there. That he has nothing to do with Olivia's disappearance. But the niggle of doubt chews at my insides.

'The police are going to see if there's any CCTV footage which might have picked her up on the way home,' Faith says hopefully.

Thank god there are no security cameras in Clover Wood.

'Fingers crossed.'

'You'll keep an eye out for her, won't you?' Faith says. 'And let me know if you hear anything.'

'Of course. It's the least I can do.'

I know I should tell her what I thought I saw in the woods yesterday, that maybe Leo was the last person to see Olivia before she vanished, but I can't bring myself to do it, because then I'd have to tell her everything. About how I thought I saw Leo fighting with her daughter, grappling with her, and then what's she going to think? She'll have to tell the police, and if they start digging into Leo's past and discover his connection to Heather Malone's death, they're bound to jump to the wrong conclusions. They'll think he has something to do with Olivia's disappearance. And maybe they'll stop looking for her. I know my son. I know he's not involved. But if I tell Faith what I may or may not have seen, it's only going to complicate things and interfere with the search.

No, it's better if I keep my mouth shut for now. At least until I've had another chance to speak to Leo.

'Do you still want me to take Hank?'

'If you could, that would be a big help.' She sounds so grateful.

While we've been talking, Hank's wandered into the garden and is sniffing around the base of a leafy bush in a world of his own. I call him to heel, but he ignores me, trotting off with his nose pressed into the lawn.

'I'll bring him back at the usual time,' I assure Faith with a stoic smile.

I'm about to walk away when Jerome calls out from inside the house. 'Faith? Who is it?'

'Just Sabine, here to pick up Hank.'

Suddenly, he's in the doorway with his hand protectively on Faith's shoulder. He looks drawn with worry, his face dark and unshaven.

'I'm so sorry to hear about Olivia,' I mumble. 'I was saying to Faith, if there's anything I can—'

'Will you speak to your son, Leo?' he says, running a thick, calloused hand over his chin. 'Find out if he's seen her. They've become friendly in recent weeks, I think. He might know something.'

'No, I don't think so,' I blurt out without thinking. 'I mean, of course I'll speak to him, but I doubt if he knows anything.'

Jerome's brow furrows. 'I appreciate it, Sabine. Thank you.'

'I'd better be going. Will you keep me posted if there's any news?'

'Of course.' Jerome's smile is thin-lipped.

How awful for them both. It's bad enough worrying about two teenage boys. I don't know how I'd cope with having a daughter.

'Hank,' I call. I pluck a treat from my pouch, recalling with horror it's where I put the knife I found in the mud. My heart races a little quicker as my brain connects the dots.

It's just a coincidence. There's nothing at all to suggest that Olivia's disappearance has anything to do with Leo, but if he has lied to me about where he was yesterday afternoon, he might have been the last person to see her. I need to talk to him again. I can't let this spiral out of control,

Hank comes bounding over and snatches the treat from my fingers. I'm conscious that Jerome and Faith are still standing on the doorstep, watching me.

'Okay, I guess I'll see you later,' I call over my shoulder as I attach Hank's lead to his collar and guide him across the road to my van.

He hops in the back with Biscuit, still crunching his treat, and folds himself into his bed.

I hang up his lead, secure the doors and lock the vehicle, before rushing back indoors, hoping to catch Leo before he leaves for school.

Casper's sitting on the bottom stair pulling on his shoes, his tie hanging loose and the top button of his shirt undone. Normally, I'd give him a lecture about taking more pride in his appearance, but I don't have time for that this morning.

'Where's your brother?' I ask.

'Dunno. I think he left already.'

I glance at my watch. That's not like him to be so punctual. 'For school?'

'I guess. Why? What's wrong?'

'Olivia from across the road is missing.'

'Really?' Casper says with surprise.

'She didn't make it home last night. I thought Leo usually walked to school with her?'

'Dunno. Sometimes, I guess,' Casper says with a shrug.

'Great, that's really helpful. Thanks.'

'You're welcome,' he says, grinning as he stands and grabs his rucksack. He throws it over his shoulder and heads out of the house with a cheery, 'See you later,' as if he doesn't have a care in the world.

Didn't he hear what I said about Olivia? What is it with teenagers? Maybe it's just teenage boys who seem to live in a world of their own.

I pluck my phone from my back pocket and try Leo's number. Predictably, it goes straight to voicemail. I shouldn't be surprised. He never picks up my calls.

'Leo? It's Mum. Can you call me? It's urgent.' That should get his attention, but to be sure, I add, 'It's about Olivia. She's gone missing. The police are over with her parents and they were asking if you'd seen her. Anyway, just call me, okay?'

In case he doesn't bother to listen to it, I send him a text with a similar message. If he knows anything about what happened to Olivia, he needs to tell me. Otherwise, I can't help him.

I'm late now to pick up the other dogs, but I make one more call while I'm still in the house. This time to Rory. I'm still angry that he didn't speak to Leo for me last night, but I can't keep this to myself.

'Sabine?' he says, sounding slightly out of breath as he answers my call. I guess he's walking to the office from the station. 'What's wrong?'

It's rare that I call him at this time of the day and I can hear the concern in his voice.

'Olivia's missing. The police are with Jerome and Faith.' I pause to let my words sink in and the ramifications of what I'm saying percolate through his brain. 'Apparently, she didn't make it home last night. They're worried something's happened to her.'

'Shit, really? I saw there was a police car outside when I left, but didn't think anything of it,' he says.

'I'm worried.'

His voice is momentarily drowned out by the sound of a passing vehicle. 'You don't really think...?' he says.

'I don't know. Maybe. Leo might be the last person to have seen her before she disappeared.'

'Have you spoken to him this morning?'

'No, he left early and he's not picking up his phone.'

'I wouldn't jump to conclusions.' The noise of the traffic dies away as I guess Rory steps inside his office. His voice echoes, like he's in a large tiled hallway.

'I'm not jumping to conclusions but - I don't know. I don't know what to think.' I run a hand through my hair, letting my fingers graze my scalp.

'I'm sure there's an innocent explanation.'

'How can you be sure? Especially after...'

'This is totally different.'

'A girl died.'

'It wasn't Leo's fault,' Rory says. 'You know that.'

I take a deep breath, trying to bring my racing pulse under control. 'I got the impression he was hiding something. He definitely wasn't telling me the truth.'

'Okay,' Rory says. 'Well, why don't we speak to him tonight? Together?'

'You promise?'

'Of course.'

'Thank you.'

'But look, don't fret. I doubt Leo has anything to do with it.'

I wish I shared his confidence, but I have a niggling bad feeling about it. 'You're right. I'm probably worrying unnecessarily.'

'I've got to go. I'm late for a meeting. I'll speak to you later.'

Chapter 8

Rory hangs up with a sigh and shoves the phone into his coat pocket. Why's Sabine getting herself so worked up? What does she think Leo's done to Olivia? Abducted her? Killed her? He's their son. He wouldn't harm anyone. It's not in his nature. But that's Sabine for you. She thrives on a crisis. And if there isn't one, she'll do her damnedest to create one. Life was supposed to be better when they moved to a new town. How is this better?

Leo made one mistake, admittedly a big mistake, but Sabine seems to be obsessed with making him pay for it. She's on his back all the time, but that's not going to help him move on and grow. She doesn't give him any space. She needs to chill out a bit. Let Leo be himself or she'll push him away forever if she's not careful. She thinks she's doing the right thing, that she's protecting him, but he's almost an adult now. She can't keep mothering him. He has to learn to make his own mistakes and stand on his own two feet.

Rory doesn't know much about Olivia's parents, Jerome and Faith. They're certainly not friends. They're the kind of people you'd stop for a quick chat with if you saw them in the street. Nothing more. He has absolutely nothing in common with Jerome, other than they live in the same street on the same estate, and he's never particularly warmed to him, although he wouldn't wish having a child go missing on any parent. It must be awful for them both.

Jerome's an electrician. A one-man self-made success who's probably spent his working life avoiding the taxman with no-questions-asked cash-in-hand jobs. It's no wonder he can afford such a big house. Life would be easier for everyone if they didn't have to hand over half their hard-earned cash to the Inland Revenue.

It's not as if Faith's florist shop in the town can be that profitable either. Business rates, even for a small premises like hers, are astronomical. You'd have to be selling a lot of roses to clear a profit, although Rory's seen the price she charges for a bouquet and it's enough to bring a grown man to tears.

Clutching a takeaway flat white he picked up at the station, Rory swipes his pass over the electronic reader and lets himself through the automated barriers into the building the charity shares with a dozen other organisations. He avoids the lift, opting to take the seven flights of stairs on foot. With a job that means sitting at a desk for eight hours a day, it at least means he gets some exercise.

The charity occupies the entire sixth floor. It's one of those modern, open-plan workspaces that looks more like a warehouse than an office, with rows and rows of desks alongside each other, where nobody has any privacy or quiet, unless they book one of the fancy space-age meeting pods placed strategically around the perimeter by the windows. Management thinks it helps foster creativity and that by taking away the walls between them, they're brainstorming and sharing ideas all the time, when in reality they spend most of their time chatting and gossiping about almost everything apart from work.

At least the design department has its own corner, with views over the London skyline and the impressive dome of St Paul's Cathedral. It's called the design department but is just half a dozen workstations at a rectangular collection of desks.

As he approaches, he notices someone has gone to some trouble decorating Marney's workstation with a colourful display of balloons and bunting. There's a scattering of glitter across her desk, a pile of greetings cards and a banner stretching across her computer screen announcing it's her twenty-first birthday.

A part of Rory dies inside. He's happy that someone's gone to so much effort for one of his colleagues, but he can't even remember how he celebrated his twenty-first. At forty-seven, he's not exactly ready to be put out to pasture, but he's conscious of time slipping away, his hopes and ambitions fading with it. In the blink of an eye, he's gone from fresh-faced university graduate to a tired and faded father of two teenage boys, tied to a job he no longer loves but can't afford to give up. He has a wife who's convinced their eldest son is out of control, and he lives in a soulless new build in the suburbs he neither wanted nor likes. It's not what he thought life would be like when he was young and ready to put the world to rights.

Age is already against him, and any career ambitions he once had have long been abandoned. He's become part of the furniture at the charity these days. His role's too cosy, his salary too cushy, to embolden him to push for more, or, god forbid, find a new job.

'Looks good, doesn't it?' Toni slips into her seat at the computer opposite with a mug of tea.

'Did you do it?'

'God no,' she says with a grimace. 'Not my style.'

'I can't even remember turning twenty-one.'

When she laughs, her eyes crease, and it's like sunlight breaking through grey clouds. He enjoys making her laugh. It makes him feel young again.

'You're not that old, granddad.'

'Hey, less of the old,' he smirks.

She leans back and stretches, yawning. 'Sorry,' she says. 'A bit of a late one last night.'

He catches the faint hint of ethanol on her breath.

'Were you out?'

She nods, using the back of her hand to stifle a second yawn. 'Just to the pub.'

'On a school night?'

'It what the young people do.' She laughs again, the tight ringlets of her hair bobbing up and down over her shoulders. She has a rash of freckles across the top of her nose and her skin is glowing. What else was she doing last night that's left her so tired, but in such a good mood, he wonders.

When Marney arrives, she screams in delight and presses a hand theatrically to her chest.

'Oh my god, who's done this?' she squeals.

Rory watches with detached amusement. It's only some balloons and a bit of glitter. No need for her to be so effusive. One member of the fundraising team looks up from her laptop and stares.

'Happy birthday, Marney.' Toni claps her hands with glee.

Marney unwraps a long, knitted scarf from around her neck and picks up the pile of greetings cards on her desk, ripping them open like a child tackling a pile of presents on Christmas morning.

'Oh god, you guys. This is too much. Thank you so much.'

'Happy birthday,' Rory says. He feels bad that he's not bought her a card, but nobody mentioned it was her birthday. Or if they did, he totally forgot.

The rest of the team gather around Marney, offering hugs and air kisses. There are tears in her eyes. Just wait until she's nearly fifty. Rory bets she won't be so keen on everyone making a fuss then.

'I hope you're all coming to the Wellington tonight to help me celebrate,' Marney says as everyone finally returns to their desks.

'What time?' Toni asks.

'Straight after work? I've booked a table from five-thirty.'

'Count me in.'

'What about you, Rory? Will you come?' Marney asks.

'Me?' He's surprised to be included. They treat him like the ageing uncle of the group and he's rarely asked to join them at the pub, even for their regular Friday lunchtime drinks. He's turned them down too many times. 'I'm not sure. I told my wife I'd be back early tonight.'

Marney pouts. 'That's a shame.'

'Come on, Rory. You can come for just the one, can't you? You don't need to stay long.' Toni kicks him under the desk.

'I'm not sure,' he mumbles, tempted but uncertain. He promised Sabine he'd be back to talk to Leo.

'Please,' she whines, cocking her head and making puppy dog eyes at him. 'I'll buy you a drink.'

How can he resist? Of the two options, going out to the pub for a swift pint with his team is by far a more appealing prospect than dealing with a stroppy teenager at home. He can still be back by eight. Nine at the latest. That's plenty of time for him and Sabine to have that chat.

'Go on, then,' he says with a smile. 'But I can only stay for the one, okay?'

Chapter 9

I've been watching Jerome and Faith's house from the kitchen window for the best part of the day, praying one of the many police cars that have come and gone would turn up with Olivia in the back, safe and well. But I've not seen or heard anything, so I assume she's not been found.

Meanwhile, Leo hasn't responded to any of my messages, even though I can see he's read my texts, which makes me even more anxious and suspicious. I know Rory thinks I'm overreacting, but I've been replaying the events in Clover Wood yesterday in my mind, and I've convinced myself it must have been Leo I saw with Olivia. I don't want to think the worst of him, but it's suspicious that she's disappeared and now I can't reach him.

Maybe a year ago, I wouldn't have thought anything of it. I wouldn't have drawn the dots. But a year ago, I would never have imagined Leo would experiment with drugs or be implicated in the death of a girl and picking up a police caution. Perhaps we weren't such good parents as I thought. Maybe we were too soft on Leo when he was growing up.

Biscuit rushes into the kitchen and barks, with Rosie close behind. Those two are never far apart.

I glance at the clock on the oven. It's gone four. I should have taken the dogs out for their afternoon walk by now, but I've not been able to tear myself away from my vigil.

'Alright, I'm coming.' I crouch to scratch Biscuit's ears.

Hank lollops in and nudges my hand with his head, encouraging me to give him some attention too.

I decide against going back to Clover Wood. It was crawling with police search teams this morning and half of the trails were cordoned off. Instead, I take them to the recreation ground on the other side of town. It's further away and there are more young children and dogs around, but I keep mine on a short lead and soon have them back in the van, tired out, hungry and ready to go home.

When I drop off Rosie, I run into Zahara pulling up at the house in her sporty Mercedes, home early. She's wearing a pair of leggings and a tight-fitting crop top. Her hair is tied back and slightly damp. She looks as though she's come from a magazine photo shoot rather than the gym. I can only fantasise about looking that good after a workout.

'Any idea what's going on?' She nods towards the police cars parked outside Jerome and Faith's.

'It's Olivia. She's missing.'

Zahara raises four beautifully manicured fingers to her mouth, her eyes widening in shock. 'Oh my gosh, really?'

'She didn't come home last night.'

Rosie shuffles towards Zahara, her tail wagging like a whip. Zahara scoops her up in her arms and buries her face in her fur. 'How awful. Poor Jerome and Faith. Have you seen them?'

'They're not doing too well.'

'I'm not surprised. Such a sweet girl. I'd hate to think anything has happened to her. We've grown quite fond of her lately. I wonder if there's anything we can do.' Rosie starts wriggling and Zahara puts her down.

'I don't really know her,' I say, intrigued. 'I hear she's very bright.'

'Totally. She was hoping for a place at Oxford. And she's majorly into her music, of course. She's always popping around to hang out.' Zahara leans towards me conspiratorially, touching my arm. 'To be honest, I think she's a little starstruck by Kwame, and of course, he can't help himself, bragging about all the artists he's worked with.'

'Oh,' I say, a little surprised. I'm sure Olivia's relationship with Kwame is entirely innocent, but I wonder if the police are aware. If Jerome and Faith know.

'Not that we've seen her for a while,' Zahara continues. 'Between you and me, I don't think she's very happy at home,' she whispers.

'Really?' Jerome and Faith have always struck me as good parents, but then I think about my relationship with my son. 'Mine's the same. Leo's going through a difficult stage at the moment. We seem to clash all the time. I think it's their age. They get fed up with their parents and are desperate to move on. Not that I'd fancy Leo's chances of looking after himself. He'd probably end up living on takeaways and bringing his washing home to me at weekends.' I laugh and Zahara gives me a tight-lipped smile. She doesn't have kids, so I can't even warn her she has all this ahead of her.

'Do you think I should pop around and see if they need anything?' Zahara asks, goose pimples mottling her stick-thin, bare arms.

'I'm sure they'd appreciate that.'

She nods. 'Probably better to have a shower first.' She points her keys towards her door and I take the hint.

'I'll pick Rosie up tomorrow morning at the usual time,' I say, heading back to my van.

'Thanks, Sabine. Let me know if you hear any more about Olivia.'

My last drop off of the day is the one I've been dreading. I park outside our house and walk Hank across the road with trepidation. It was bad enough facing Jerome and Faith this morning. If Olivia's still missing, I hate to think what kind of state they're in by now. Should I be offering words of comfort or bringing them a lasagne so they don't need to worry about cooking? What is the right thing to do? I have no idea. At least I've looked after Hank for them for the day, I suppose.

I'm surprised when a police officer in uniform answers the door. He looks me up and down and I'm suddenly conscious of how scruffy I must appear with my muddy Wellington boots and coat covered in dog hair. But there's no point making an effort with my appearance when I have five energetic dogs to look after.

He looks at least ten years younger than me, but he still makes me nervous. It must be the uniform.

'I - I was looking for Faith. Is she in?' I ask with a guilty-sounding tremor in my voice. What the hell's wrong with me? I haven't done anything wrong.

'And you are?'

'Sabine,' I announce. 'Sabine Sugar. I live across the road.' I point to our house. 'I look after Jerome and Faith's dog.'

He glances at Hank, who's sitting obediently by my feet, and back up at me, his eyes narrowing.

A trickle of sweat runs down my spine.

'Just a minute,' the officer says, pushing the door closed in my face. Charming.

When it opens again, it's Jerome looking grey and defeated.

'I brought Hank back.' I offer him the lead.

Jerome blinks twice and glances at Hank, who whimpers and then barks. 'Right, thanks.'

'No news?'

Jerome shakes his head and sighs. He's normally so exuberant. The life and soul, but he looks broken and small. 'No, nothing yet.'

'I'm so sorry. If there's anything we can—'

'Did you speak to your son?'

'Well, I - I've tried, but he's not returning my calls and he's not home from school yet. I will do, though.'

Jerome nods. 'They're friendly, aren't they, he and Olivia?'

'Ummm, I think so. He'll certainly be upset to hear Olivia's missing.'

'One of Olivia's friends said she saw her going off with Leo yesterday afternoon, heading towards the woods.'

It's like a wrecking ball hitting me square in the sternum, knocking the breath from my lungs. 'Oh?'

'Which means he might have been the last person to have seen her before she... she vanished.' When his body folds and he cries, it's so unexpected, I don't know where to look or what to do.

Jerome is a giant of a man with the physique of a rugby player. He's over six feet tall and broad with it. A man's man with a broken nose and a barrel chest. Not someone I ever expected to see crying or showing any kind of emotion.

'I miss her so much,' he cries.

'I know.'

'But anyway,' he says, composing himself and wiping his cuff across his squashed nose, 'I thought I should let you know. I've mentioned it to the police, so I expect they'll want to have a word with him. Can you let him know?'

A lump swells in my throat.

'Sure,' I croak. 'I'll warn him.'

Chapter 10

It's like someone has poured concrete into my boots as I trudge back towards our house. The last time we had to deal with the police, I had no idea what to expect. Now, I'm all too aware and I dread it. Strangers intruding into our lives again, asking awkward questions and poking their noses into our business.

It was a Saturday morning when they turned up the last time, a week after Heather Malone had been found dead. We'd heard that she'd died, of course. It's all the parents at school were talking about, and of course, it was all over the local news and social media. There had been wild speculation that she'd been at a party and was either drunk or high or both and had fallen to her death, intoxicated. We had no idea Leo had any involvement, or even knew her, until the police knocked at the door one morning in July.

They made me wake Leo and drag him out of bed. At first, they were friendly enough. We all sat around the dining room table with mugs of tea while they asked Leo about the party he'd been to the previous weekend. They asked him if he'd met Heather, if they'd known each other before, and whether he knew how she'd come to have traces of LSD in her bloodstream.

I'll never forget the look Leo gave me before hanging his head in shame and admitting that yes, he'd seen her at the party, that he didn't really know her, although they were at the same school, and that he'd supplied her with a small quantity of drugs.

It was like walking in front of a juggernaut. I no longer recognised my own son. I'd never had the vaguest suspicion he was taking drugs, letting alone supplying them to other kids, because he'd always been so vehemently against them when he was younger. But here he was, not only admitting to possessing LSD, but to supplying a fifteen-year-old girl he barely knew and who'd died as a result.

The carefully constructed walls of my world fell away and I was left listening, numb with shock, as Leo explained how the evening had unfolded. How Heather had sought him out and begged for a tab of acid, how he'd accompanied her into the woods when she started acting strangely, and how he'd tried and failed to talk her down from the parapet of the old railway bridge. He admitted he'd been with her when she fell and made an anonymous, panicked call for an ambulance, which is how the police, who'd traced the number, ended up at our door.

Even though Leo had called as soon as Heather had fallen, it was too late to save her. A post-mortem examination revealed Heather died instantly on impact with the ground and there was nothing paramedics could do to save her.

After going through his story, the attitude of the two detectives who questioned him changed. Their sympathetic tone hardened and their friendliness evaporated. They snapped handcuffs on Leo's wrists and treated him like he was a common criminal. They marched him to a car outside, read him his rights, and whisked him off to the local station. I'll never forget that look of sheer terror and confusion on his face.

As any mother would, I imagined the worst. I thought they'd throw the book at him and charge him in connection with Heather's death. So when he walked away with only a police caution for the possession of a Class A substance, we couldn't believe our luck. After all, it wasn't his fault Heather had died. He hadn't encouraged or coerced her into taking the drugs, and he'd actually tried to do the right thing, talking her down from the bridge and raising the alarm when she fell.

But if we thought that was the end of it, we were being naïve.

Heather's death was the talk of the town for weeks, and although Leo's name never appeared in any news articles, it was eventually leaked online and spread like a virulent virus. He might have been cleared of any wrongdoing by the police, but Heather's family, friends and seemingly anyone with an opinion still blamed him for her death and thought he'd got away with murder.

They made our lives hell. As well as the online abuse, which was bad enough as it was so relentless, there was the damage to our car. The paint thrown at the house. People walking across the road to avoid us. Friends we'd known for years shunning us. All of them judging us and blaming us when they didn't understand the facts.

I can't even imagine what it must have been like for Leo being at the centre of it all, but there's no doubt it changed him. He used to be such a cheery boy, but after Heather's death, he became withdrawn and difficult. Casper didn't come off lightly either, verbally abused and ostracised by kids in his year group because of what his brother was perceived to have done. It was destroying us all. It couldn't go on, and because we couldn't fight it, we ran. We sold our beautiful Victorian home at a bargain knockdown price and used the proceeds to buy new in a new town. I gave up my job and we took the boys out of school. I hoped that would be an end to it. A new beginning.

Now we live on a new estate in a modern house with a tiny garden and neighbours who know nothing about our past. A vanilla life where no one knows our secrets, but if the police start asking questions about Leo and digging into his past, it's not going to take them long to discover his connection with Heather Malone. And then what? What's the obvious conclusion they're going to jump to?

'Leo? Are you home yet?' I shout, pushing the front door closed behind me and letting Biscuit off her lead.

I hear the creak of a floorboard. A door brushing against carpet as it's pulled open.

'Mum?' Casper appears on the landing at the top of the stairs. 'Do you need a hand with the shopping?'

'What? No. Where's your brother?'

Casper shrugs. 'Dunno. I haven't seen him.'

I growl in frustration before trying his phone again. That boy is going to be the death of me.

Voicemail. Again.

'Is there any more news about Olivia?' Casper asks, sitting on the stairs. 'Everyone's talking about it at school.'

'No, love. Nobody's heard a thing.'

'I hope nothing's happened to her.' His face creases with concern. He's such a sensitive soul.

'I'm sure she's fine. Don't worry about it.'

'Do you think someone's taken her?'

'I wouldn't have thought so. I'm sure the police will find her soon.'

'But what if they don't, Mum? What if she's—'

'Casper! Stop it. Nothing's happened to her, okay? She'll turn up in a day or two. It's nothing for you to worry about. Now, do you have homework to do?'

'A bit,' he groans.

'Then I suggest you get on and finish it.'

Casper slopes off back to his room, rolling his eyes.

I slip off my coat, kick off my boots and march into the kitchen with my head spinning and my shoulders knotted with tension. The thought of having the police in the house quizzing Leo fills me with dread, but there's nothing I can do about it. At least I'll know what to expect this time. It's just the thought of going through it all again, the suspicion, the repeated questions, the way they have of making you feel guilty when you haven't even done anything, is terrifying. And if they think Leo has anything to do with Olivia going missing, they're going to pursue him relentlessly, innocent or not.

I fling open the fridge and spot a bottle of Sauvignon Blanc in the door. I'm seriously tempted. My nerves are shot and I could really do with a drink. But I'd better not. I have a feeling I'm going to need to keep my wits about me, especially if the police turn up here asking difficult questions. I push the door closed again and rest my head against its cool, smooth surface.

When a key scrapes in the lock of the front door, I jolt upright. Leo, home at last. As I race into the hall to intercept him, his eyes open wide with surprise.

'Where have you been? You should have been home an hour ago.'

Leo shrugs nonchalantly as he heels off his shoes.

'Have you heard about Olivia?' I ask, blocking him from running up to his room.

'Yeah, everyone at school's saying she's gone missing,' he says, like it's an everyday occurrence that barely warrants a mention.

'Aren't you worried? I thought she was your friend.'

'Of course I am,' he says, his eyes narrowing. 'Why would you say that?'

'And you still maintain you weren't in Clover Wood with her yesterday afternoon?'

'Mum!'

'I know what I saw, Leo.'

'You don't know anything.' He raises his voice, his face clouding.

'I saw you fighting with her. I found a knife with blood on it, and now she's vanished. How do you explain that, because I have to tell you, it doesn't look good?'

He stares at me in astonishment. 'What, you think I did something to her?'

'Did you?'

'No.'

'So what were you doing with her? What were you arguing about?'

'I told you. I wasn't with her yesterday.'

'Don't lie to me, Leo. I can't help you if you don't tell me the truth.'

'I'm not lying to you. Why don't you ever believe me?'

He tries to push past, heading for the stairs, but I stand my ground. 'Don't walk off when I'm talking to you.'

'You think I've killed her, don't you?'

I'm momentarily stunned. 'What? No, of course I don't think that.'

'You think that after Heather, I must have killed Olivia. Well, thanks for the vote of confidence, Mum. You don't trust me, do you? You've never trusted me.'

'That's not true. I want to protect you.'

'But you're not. You want to blame me for everything,' he says, twisting what I'm saying. 'And if you're so keen on protecting me, why did you make us move house and schools? I hate it here. I wish we'd never come.'

'You know why. I did it for you,' I scream. 'If you hadn't been stupid enough to give drugs to a fifteen-year-old girl you didn't even know, we wouldn't have had to move house. Your father wouldn't have to spend half his week commuting to work. And your brother wouldn't have his whole life upended. God, you can be so selfish sometimes.'

'Me?' he says. 'That's rich coming from you. You only moved us because of what people were saying about you behind your back.'

'That's not true. How dare you.'

'You couldn't stand it, could you?'

'You don't know what you're saying.'

'I didn't lay a finger on Olivia, alright?'

'But you were with her? It wasn't only me who saw you. One of Olivia's friends says she saw you together, which probably makes you the last person to see her before she vanished.'

'Who said that?' he demands.

'I don't know. It doesn't matter. What matters is that the police know, so I think we can probably expect a visit from them some time soon.'

Leo's face pales. He clenches his fists and fidgets on the spot. 'The police?'

'Jerome's spoken to them. So you'd better get your story straight because when they start digging around and find out about Heather, how do you think it's going to look?'

'But I haven't done anything.'

'I need to know what's going on so I can help you, Leo. Just look at what happened the last time you tried to cover up the truth.'

We stare at each other for what feels like several minutes, both of us weighing up the other.

For a moment, I think he's on the verge of telling me something. To finally come clean. He wets his lips and lowers his eyes.

'Do you promise —?'

But his sentence is cut short by a knock at the door. My heart hammers against my ribs.

'Who's that?' Leo hisses, as if I have some kind of special powers to see through a locked door.

'You'd better answer it.'

His shoulders slump and the defiant, belligerent teenager who was squaring up to me moments before vanishes before my eyes, a lost little boy materialising in his place.

He turns and reaches for the latch. Pulls open the door.

Two uniformed police officers are standing on the doorstep, caps under their arms.

'Leo Sugar?' the shorter of the two asks. 'Can we have a quick word? It's about a friend of yours, Olivia Hunter.'

Chapter 11

Leo stands rooted to the spot, not saying anything. Awkwardly frozen.

'I'm Leo's mother, Sabine.' I ease my son out of the way with a faux friendly smile. No point in starting off on the wrong foot. 'Why don't you come in?'

The shorter officer, who's done all the talking so far, steps inside, wiping his boots on the mat. He and his colleague follow me into the lounge.

'What's all this about?' I ask, conscious of the nervous tremor in my voice.

The taller officer answers. I know it's a cliché, but he looks incredibly young, his chin still spotty with acne and his jet-back hair combed into a neat side parting. 'I'm sure you're aware, Olivia Hunter, your neighbour's daughter, is missing. We're trying to piece together her last movements.'

'Right,' I say. 'Why don't you sit down?'

As they both take a seat on the sofa, I inwardly wince that the cushions all need plumping up and the coffee table is covered in mess. There's a dirty glass, a couple of dog-eared magazines and a renewal letter from the insurance company that's been there for the best part of the week and needs dealing with.

'Can I get you a tea or coffee?' I ask politely, trying to behave as if we have nothing to hide.

'That won't be necessary. This shouldn't take long,' the shorter officer says. He looks as if he has some more experience under his belt. Dark bags under his eyes, leathery skin and an air of unshakeable confidence, like he's been here, done that, seen it all before.

Leo hovers by the door. 'Come in and take a seat, Leo. The officers just want to ask you a few questions.'

With a sulky pout, Leo shuffles into the room. He sits in an armchair and folds his arms defensively. We've both been here before and from the look on his face, Leo's relishing the inquisition about as much as having teeth pulled.

I wish he'd try harder, though. Would a smile really hurt? We can't afford for them to become suspicious and decide to run his name through the police computers, because once they find out about Heather Malone, it's going to be an uphill battle to convince them Leo has nothing to do with Olivia's disappearance.

'How can we help?' I ask breezily, as if having the police coming to our home is an everyday occurrence and not something I'm dreading with the heaviest of hearts.

'Can you confirm your full name, please?' the taller, younger officer says, turning his attention to Leo.

'Leo Sugar.'

'And how old are you, Leo?'

'Seventeen.'

'Okay, so we'd like to ask you some questions about your friend, Olivia,' he glances at me, 'if that's okay, Mrs Sugar?'

'Yes, of course.' I stop myself from saying, 'We have nothing to hide.' Only people with something to hide say they have nothing to hide.

'How long have the two of you been friendly?'

'We've not long moved to the area,' I explain. 'Olivia's really helped Leo to settle in at his new school.'

The older officer shoots me a look of irritation. 'If you could let Leo answer, please, Mrs Sugar.'

'Sorry. Yes, of course.'

'Leo?' he prompts. 'How long have you been friends with Olivia?'

Leo sniffs. 'A couple of months, maybe. Only since we moved here.'

I wish he'd sit up straight and not look so sulky. If he's going to be difficult and monosyllabic, this isn't going to go well. I bite my lip to stop myself jumping in and elaborating on his behalf.

'And what's the nature of your friendship?'

'We just hang out sometimes,' Leo says. He's not even looking them in the eye.

'Most mornings they walk to school together, don't you?' I say, unable to help myself.

'Mrs Sugar, please let your son speak for himself.' The older officer's getting cross with me now. 'Is that right, Leo? You walk to school with Olivia sometimes, do you?'

'Yeah, sometimes.'

'Is there anything more to your relationship than just being friends?'

'What d'you mean?'

'Is she your girlfriend? Or have you ever had any romantic relationship with her?'

Leo's cheeks flush bright red. 'No!'

'So just friends?'

'Yes.' He looks down at his hands and picks at his fingernails, fidgeting awkwardly in his seat.

'And when was the last time you saw her?'

Leo's eyes shoot towards the window, glancing into the garden. A heavy silence falls on the room as we all wait for him to answer. Work at the construction site behind the house has stopped for the day and it's the only time we get any peace.

'I'm not sure,' Leo eventually offers, clearing his throat.

'Try to think. It's important.' The younger officer leans forwards, notebook and pen poised. 'Did you see her at all yesterday?'

'Yeah, I called for her and we walked to school.'

'Right, and presumably you saw her during the day?'

'We had a biology lesson after lunch, but that's it.'

The older officer stares intently at Leo. He's being quite intimidating. I have the urge to yell at him that my son's not guilty of anything and that they're in our house as guests, but I need to hold my tongue.

'But you didn't see Olivia after your lesson?' the older one says, slowly and deliberately, almost like he's trying to trip Leo up. I will him not to lie.

'No.'

'And what time was your biology lesson?'

Leo's gaze flies to the ceiling. 'Dunno. About two-thirty, I suppose.'

'So you haven't seen Olivia Hunter since around two-thirty yesterday afternoon? Is that correct?'

'Yeah.'

'And how did she seem?'

'Fine.'

'How would you describe her mood?'

'Fine.'

'You need to help us here, Leo. You do want us to find your friend, don't you?'

'Yeah, course.'

'So, was she happy? Sad? Depressed? Quiet?'

'She was a bit quiet, I suppose,' Leo finally admits.

'Right, a bit quiet? And any idea why that might be?'

Leo grips the arms of the chair tightly, his hands balling into fists. 'I don't know.'

'So the last time you saw Olivia Hunter was in your biology lesson at around two-thirty yesterday afternoon when you thought she seemed a bit quiet?' the older officer summarises. 'And did you speak to her about why she was quiet? Did you ask her if there was anything wrong?'

'No.'

'Oh?' The officer's brow tightens into a ridge of thick lines. 'Didn't you think to ask if she was okay? I thought she was your friend.'

'Officer, are you accusing my son of something?' I say, unable to stop myself. They're badgering him, and I'm sure they're not allowed to do that.

'It's okay, Mum,' Leo says quietly. 'I didn't get the chance to speak to her. She was with her friends and they don't like me much.'

'Why's that, Leo?' the older officer asks.

He shrugs. 'Dunno.'

The officers make a note in their books. 'Did you see Olivia after school at all?'

Leo shoots me a worried glance. 'No.'

'Are you one hundred per cent certain? Take your time.'

'I didn't see her again,' he clarifies.

'It's just that one of Olivia's friends,' the older officer looks down at his notebook, flicking back several pages, 'says that she saw you and Olivia together later in the day.'

Leo swallows and stares at the carpet.

The officer lets a pregnant pause hang in the air and I will Leo not to say anything. Not to feel pressured into filling the silence.

'No, I didn't,' Leo mumbles.

'She says she saw the two of you together heading towards Clover Wood. She says you were arguing. Olivia was trying to run away and you were chasing her.'

Leo shakes his head but says nothing.

'Is that true, Leo? Were you with Olivia yesterday afternoon after school, arguing with her?'

'No,' he croaks.

'So why would her friend say it? Is she making it up?'

'Dunno.'

'What time was this?' I ask. 'You said it was after school, but can you be more specific?'

The older officer checks his notebook. 'Between four-fifteen and four-thirty,' he says.

'Ah, right, well, it couldn't have been Leo then, could it?'

Leo glances at me, eyes narrowed.

'Why's that, Mrs Sugar?'

'Leo was with me. I run a dog walking service and he was helping. He came in the van and wasn't out of my sight all afternoon,' I say with as much confidence as I can muster.

'And what time would this have been?'

'Let me think. Well, Leo was home just before four and we went straight out. Isn't that right, Leo?'

My son stares at me with incredulity and nods.

'So you see, there's no way anyone could have seen him with Olivia, because he was with me all that time.'

Chapter 12

Rory is already on his third pint and having more fun than he imagined he would with the people he's stuck working with every day. The young people who don't seem to suffer from hangovers, who don't have mortgages or children, who don't have to catch the train for a ninety-minute commute home into the suburbs. But actually, they're a good laugh.

'Right, my round,' Paul, one of the other designers, shouts over the noise of their over-excited table. Rory always assumed Paul was gay, but his girlfriend's just turned up and joined them, so it just goes to show what he knows. 'Rory, pint?'

Rory drains the last of his Guinness and bangs his empty glass down on the table. 'Yeah, go on then. I'll get the next one in.'

'Who knew you were such a party animal?' Toni nudges him in the ribs with a sly wink.

'I'm not quite over the hill yet, you know.'

He sneaks a glance at his phone on the table that's sticky with spilt beer and Pinot Grigio. It's gone seven-thirty and even if he left right now and ran, he'd miss the next train home. He might as well stay for another.

Among various other notifications cluttering his lock screen, he notices several missed calls from Sabine. She'll be wondering why he's not home yet. He probably ought to have called to let her know he'd be late, but he's not going to ring her now. Not from the pub, half-cut and surrounded by a rowdy mob who've been drinking since they left the office at five.

Marney, sporting a tin badge the size of a saucer, emblazoned with a colourful '21' on her lapel, and with a red feather boa she's acquired from somewhere wrapped around her neck, stands and downs a full glass of Prosecco to cheers from the table.

Cries of 'happy birthday' ring out for about the dozenth time this evening.

Rory composes a short text message under the table, letting Sabine know he's popped out with some colleagues and will be home later. He hits send.

Job done. He doesn't need to worry now. As long as he makes the last train, he can sober up on the walk back to the house. With luck, Sabine will be in bed and he won't have to explain himself.

'Better offer?' Toni asks.

'What?'

She nods at the phone he's trying to hide between his knees. 'Who are you messaging?'

'No one,' he says. 'My wife. Just letting her know I'll be back late.'

'Will she mind?' Toni shouts in his ear. Her warm breath grazes his neck, the smell of her perfume a heady mix of cinnamon and citrus.

'Probably,' Rory laughs. 'I forgot to tell her I was going to be late.'

'How long have you been married?'

'Eighteen years.' He grimaces. It sounds like a life sentence. There are people in the pub who weren't even born when he and Sabine started dating.

'Congratulations.'

'For what?' he shrugs. He doesn't want to talk about his marriage or to be reminded of the drudgery his life has become. He wants to know more about Toni. Her life's far more interesting than his.

'I can't imagine being married to someone for that long,' she says.

'Do you have a partner?' He'd never normally be so forward, but after a few drinks in the pub, it's okay to ask, isn't it? Technically, it's not a work situation if they're in the pub, but even so, he'd hate to be called out for asking inappropriate questions, and he never knows quite what's acceptable these days. It's a minefield.

She smiles enigmatically, her eyes roving across his face, taking in all the creases, the imperfections, the scars.

'No,' she says at last. 'I don't like the idea of being tied down to any one person.'

'Good for you.'

'It's not for everyone, but it suits me. You've got kids as well, haven't you?'

'Two boys. Seventeen and fifteen. I know, I don't look old enough.' He laughs, but it sounds hollow.

'It must be very rewarding.' Toni sips her espresso martini with its little brown coffee bean floating on top.

'It has its moments.'

'You don't regret having them, do you?'

'No. God, no. Of course not. They're the best thing that's happened to us. But, you know...'

'What?'

'They change your life, don't they? And they bleed you dry,' he tells her ruefully.

The fact is, he can't even remember the last time he went to the pub. He and Sabine rarely go out at all these days. When did they last have a meal out? Or go to a comedy club or see a band? Other than that stadium concert when they went to see Coldplay a few years ago when they sat up in the gods, sharing the experience with fifty thousand other people. They've not been to see a proper band in a sweaty hall where everyone stands, teenagers crowd surf and everyone throws beer for as long as he can remember. Probably since the boys were born.

Suddenly, he feels sober. Paul thumps another pint of Guinness down on the table.

'Cheers, Paul. Happy birthday, Marney.' Rory raises a glass in her direction.

'Are you okay? You don't seem very happy,' Toni says. Her thigh is pressed up against his and Rory can feel the warmth of her leg through her jeans.

'I'm fine. We've just been having some issues at home with one of the boys, that's all. That's why it's so nice to get out for a change.'

'You should do it more often.'

'Maybe I will.'

'Cheers.' Toni chinks her glass against his pint.

The cold, tarry stout is going down far too easily. He'll need to be careful. He doesn't want to end up so drunk he can't make it home. And besides, he needs to be at work tomorrow. They all do.

'Do you want to talk about it?' Toni asks as a cheer goes up from the other end of the table. Marney and a few of the others are playing a game of spoof, as if they need the encouragement to drink any more.

'Talk about what?'

'You said you were having some issues at home.'

Rory wipes the beer froth from his moustache and waves a dismissive hand. 'You don't want to hear about my problems.'

'I do, but only if you want to talk about them.' Toni bumps him with her shoulder. 'You don't have to.'

'It's nothing, really. Usual story. My eldest got in with the wrong crowd who led him astray and anyway...' He doesn't want to tell her about Heather and how she died after scoring drugs from Leo, or that he was arrested by police and has a caution to his name. Or that because of the fallout from Heather's death, they've been trolled mercilessly and Sabine's moved them all to a new town where they're trying to rebuild their lives, but it's all totally shit, and now it's starting to unravel all over again after the girl who lives opposite disappeared.

'I was a dreadful teenager,' Toni says. 'Always in trouble. My mother and I never saw eye to eye. All we ever did was argue. Until she chucked me out.'

'She threw you out?'

'I was only sixteen.'

'What did you do?'

'I stayed with an uncle for a bit, until I was able to get a job and afford a room in a shared house.'

'Wow. I had no idea.'

'I like your shirt,' she says. 'I love how you dress. So many men don't make the effort or have no idea, but you've got great style.'

'Thanks.' Rory glances down at his shirt, cut from a colourful, almost psychedelic cloth. He's always worn bright shirts and bold patterns. He'd shrivel up and die if he had to wear one of those plain, boring shirts from Marks & Spencer so many of his contemporaries wear. It's important to have a little style and individuality, especially working in a creative industry.

Appearances are so important. That's why he always wears a tailored three-piece woollen suit and a crumpled linen scarf matched with a decent pair of leather shoes to work. Today, he's wearing his favourite pair of mustard-yellow brogues. They cost a small fortune, but they're worth every penny and will probably last him a lifetime.

'Rory, you'll come, won't you?' Marney shouts from the other end of the table. Her eyes are glassy, and she's swaying from side to side.

'Where?'

'The karaoke bar,' she screams, her face lighting up.

Everyone around her punches their fists in the air and chants, 'Kar-a-oke! Kar-a-oke!'

Bloody hell. He's not been to a karaoke bar since before he and Sabine had kids. He doubts London's ready to hear him crooning in public, but he doesn't want to be a party pooper. Besides, he's not ready to go home yet. He's enjoying himself. Properly letting his hair down for the first time since forever. It's like being a student all over again. That's not a crime, is it?

'Are *you* going?' he shouts to Toni, who's nursing what's left of her cocktail with a smirk on her face.

'What, to karaoke? Of course I am. Didn't you know, I'm the karaoke queen?'

Something else he didn't know about her.

And so, twenty minutes later, Rory finds himself in a dingy room in Soho with his team, most of them hardly able to stand straight, nursing a ridiculously expensive bottle of lager, while Marney grabs a microphone and prepares to sing *Sweet Caroline*.

The words come up on a TV screen on the wall and everyone links arms as the music starts to play, swaying from side to side in time to the rhythm. Rory grins to himself, his stomach fizzing with pleasure.

Marney, still clutching her red feather boa, struggles with the lyrics, singing too slowly and dreadfully off key. But no one cares. They're all waiting for the chorus.

It hits them like a tidal wave, sweeping them up in a swell of euphoria. They stand and shout the words, arms swaying, heads thrown back. The room is a wall of sound. And all thoughts of home, of Sabine, the boys, Heather's death and Leo's troubles, evaporate and are forgotten.

There is only the here and the now. Rory sings for all he's worth, not caring whether he's in tune or not, or whatever anyone else thinks. He's lost in the moment. And he's loving it.

Toni grabs his hand and swings him around so they're facing each other, singing together. Their own personal duet. Even above the din, Rory can hear Toni has real talent. She can certainly carry a tune, even if the others can't. Maybe he'll suggest a song for them to sing together. *Islands in the Stream*? Too cheesy?

She pulls him closer and puts her mouth to his ear. Yells something he doesn't quite catch.

'What?' he screams.

'Come with me,' she says. 'I've got something to show you.'

She takes his hand and leads him from the room into a low-lit corridor, the sudden silence echoing in his ringing ears.

'Where are we going?' His voice is hoarse and strained.

'This way.'

Toni looks up and down the corridor and drags Rory into the ladies' toilets, giggling. He's too drunk to protest. Well beyond caring, even though he knows that whatever Toni's proposing, he'll regret it in the morning.

She pushes him into a stall, follows him in and pulls the door closed.

'Toni, I - I...'

She shushes him quiet. He stands there, nose to nose with her, with no room to move. Does she expect him to have sex with her? It's all a bit grubby. And what if someone comes in?

'Are you having a good time?' she asks with a mischievous grin.

'I am. Are you?'

'It's alright.'

She shoves a hand into a bag strapped across her chest and pulls out a small, clear plastic wrap of white powder.

'But I reckon it would be better with some of this, don't you?' she says, waving the bag under Rory's nose. 'What do you reckon? Are you game?'

Chapter 13

Rory wakes with a start. He blinks his eyes open and stares out of the window, momentarily confused. The train is coming to a gentle halt. A slight jolt. A squeal of brakes. He must have nodded off shortly after they left London, the warmth and rhythmic swaying enticing him into a drunken slumber. Home at last.

Or is he?

He doesn't recognise the station, the coffee shop on the platform, nor the row of empty bike stands.

His mouth is grainy and sour, his eyes sore, and his throat raw from all the singing. A couple behind him get up, giggling, and stumble off. He leans forwards, strains to make out the station name with his face pressed against the cold window.

That can't be right. A wave of panic washes over him, a prickly heat that rushes from his chest, up his neck and along his scalp like a swarm of cockroaches. It's three stops further on from where he was supposed to get off.

He jumps up, snatches his bag and his coat, and races for the doors. He thumps the button with his fist, willing them to open.

A guard on the platform looks left and right along the length of the carriages, raises a whistle to his mouth, then sees Rory as the door hisses open. He hesitates. Lets Rory gather himself and slink off the train in the nick of time.

He only closed his eyes for a second or two. Rory scans the departures screen suspended above the platform, desperately hoping there's another train due shortly that will take him back the other way.

There! A train bound for Waterloo. But what? It's not due until five-thirty. Oh god, it's the first commuter train of the day. That's not for another four hours. What's he going to do? He can't stay here. It's freezing and even the dingy waiting room's not going to afford much protection from the cold. And anyway, he needs to be back at work by nine.

He has no choice. He'll have to take a taxi, but god knows how much that's going to cost. It must be at least a twenty-mile drive. The alternative is to call Sabine and beg for a lift, but she'll be asleep by now and would hit the roof if he phoned her at this time in the morning, still drunk.

Resigned, he follows the signs towards the exit and shuffles wearily through the barriers which have been left open, so he doesn't need his ticket. Surprisingly, there's a short queue for taxis. Half a dozen people or so. Businessmen, mostly. Working people like him who've been stuck in their offices late or popped out for a drink after work. Plus a few couples returning home after a night out in the city.

After a five-minute wait, which feels more like forty-five minutes in the chill, damp air, he reaches the front of the queue and climbs into a white saloon. There's a sickly smell of vanilla inside from an air freshener hanging from the rear-view mirror.

He's conscious he must reek of booze. It's on his breath and probably leaking from every pore, an occupational hazard for every late-night taxi driver the world over.

Fortunately, the driver is in no mood for small talk. He has the radio on low playing some kind of high-energy, fast-beat bhangra. Rory puts his head back and closes his eyes as an unwelcome bloom of nausea ferments in his stomach. He should have eaten something. Grabbed a burger or at least a packet of crisps. He's going to pay for it later, especially as in a few hours he needs to be up and back on the train.

He's too old for this.

But it was fun. He's not thought once about the problems Leo's having at his new school or the trolls who've made their lives hell. He's felt young and free. And imagine ending up in a karaoke club, of all places. He chuckles to himself as he remembers Marney attempting *Wonderwall* and getting all the lyrics muddled up.

He should do it more often. They always used to ask him to join them when they went out, but he'd always been in too much of a hurry to get home to Sabine and the boys. And now they've stopped asking.

The taxi slows at a set of traffic lights. Rory checks the meter. The journey's already cost as much as one round of drinks in the club, which was pretty extortionate, and he's not even home yet. But what the hell? He's already spent a fortune this evening. What's another thirty quid? Sabine's going to be mad with him, but it was worth it.

Rory checks his phone. There's a text from Sabine he'd not noticed earlier.

Where the hell are you? Call me as soon as you can. S

Didn't she get his message saying he was going to be late? She's probably fed up that he's been out enjoying himself while she's been stuck at home. But he'll make it up to her. Buy her some flowers from Faith's florist or suggest a takeaway and a bottle of Prosecco at the weekend.

When the taxi finally drops him off outside the house, Rory notices lights on in the hall and their bedroom window. Sabine must have left them on for him. That's thoughtful of her.

He tries his best to be quiet as he slips his key into the lock and pushes open the front door, but he misjudges the step and trips, falling headlong into the hall with a loud crash. He winces.

'Rory? Is that you?'

He curses under his breath. He thought Sabine would be asleep and he could slip into bed without facing the third degree tonight. All he wants to do is get his head down.

He hauls himself to his feet, clinging to the wall, his head spinning.

'Sorry,' he slurs. 'I was trying to be quiet.'

'Where've you been all night?' Sabine hurries down the stairs, pulling on a dressing gown, her face taut with anger.

'Didn't you get my message? I went out for a few drinks to celebrate Marney's birthday.'

'Marney?' Sabine raises a suspicious eyebrow.

'One of the girls on the team. You know, Marney. She's the one I was telling you about who draws those caricatures of people around the office.' Rory's not sure why he's explaining this at two o'clock in the morning, but he doesn't want Sabine thinking there's anything going on. He's old enough to be Marney's father.

'Look at the state of you.' Sabine casts a disgusted eye over his crumpled suit.

'I didn't eat anything, which on reflection, was a mistake.' Rory feels himself swaying like a blade of tall grass in a gentle summer breeze.

'Did you even listen to my voicemail?'

Rory narrows his eyes, trying to remember. He recalls seeing she'd left one, but he's not sure he actually listened to it.

'Well, obviously not, because if you had, you'd have realised we needed you here tonight.'

'Why? What's happened?'

'The police have been here.'

'The police? Why?'

'Because they think Leo was involved in Olivia Hunter's disappearance,' Sabine says.

Rory shakes his head, trying to make sense of what his wife's telling him. 'Why would they think Leo was involved?'

'Because one of her friends said they saw him with her heading for Clover Wood yesterday afternoon, arguing.'

Rory puts a hand on the wall to steady himself. 'Hang on, didn't you say *you* saw them in the woods together?'

'I thought I did. I wasn't sure.'

'No, you were adamant. You told me last night. That's why you wanted me to have a word with Leo. You said you saw him fighting with Olivia, and then you found a knife.'

Sabine glances down at her bare feet. 'The thing is, when the police turned up, I panicked and told them it couldn't have been Leo because he was with me yesterday afternoon.'

Rory hears the words, but they percolate only slowly into his brain. 'You did what?'

'I told them Leo was helping me with the dogs, so he couldn't have been with Olivia.'

'You lied to the police?' he says, stunned. Why would she do something so stupid?

'I didn't know what else to do. If they think Leo has anything whatsoever to do with Olivia going missing, they're going to look into his record and they're going to find out about Heather Malone. And how do you think that's going to look?'

'But you lied to the police,' Rory repeats. How could she?

'What else was I supposed to do? I'm his mother. I was trying to protect him while you've been out getting drunk.'

She turns and flounces into the kitchen, leaving Rory clinging to the wall but sobering up fast.

'But you lied to the police,' he mutters under his breath.

That's not good. That's really not good at all.

Chapter 14

The one night I really needed Rory here, and he goes out and get drunk with people from work. People I don't know. He couldn't even be bothered to phone to let me know where he was or that he was going to be so late. I shouldn't have had to deal with this on my own. He should have been here, with us. With me and Leo.

'I'm sorry, it was a spur-of-the-moment thing,' he says, his breath rank with alcohol fumes as he follows me into the kitchen.

'You need to sober up.' I swat away his attempt to touch my arm. I grab the kettle and half fill it with water. He needs a coffee.

'I take it there's been no word about Olivia?'

'Do you think the police would have been around here interrogating Leo if there had?' I hiss. I can't help myself. Rory should have been here helping us through this. I can't believe he could be so selfish.

'Interrogating?'

'That's what it felt like.'

'Christ.' Rory climbs onto a stool at the breakfast bar and buries his head in his hands. 'How did he cope?'

'He was his usual monosyllabic self. He didn't exactly ingratiate himself with them. Honestly, I thought we'd left all this behind us when we moved. I don't know if I can go through it all again,' I moan.

'Are we one hundred per cent sure Leo's not involved? You said you saw him. And there was that knife...'

'Of course he's not involved! How could you even suggest it?'

I pour hot water into a mug with a spoonful of coffee granules and push it under Rory's nose with a glass of water.

'If you're so sure, why did you give Leo a false alibi?' Rory asks.

'Because I panicked. The moment they find out about Heather, they're going to assume the worst. He's nearly eighteen. They'll have him in a cell quicker than you can blink an eye. And I'm not letting my son go to prison.'

'Okay, let me think.'

Rory's eyes are heavy with tiredness and bloodshot with alcohol. He's in no fit state to think, but I need to talk about it. I didn't plan to lie to the police. It just came out. I could see the direction their questions were heading and how those two officers were thinking.

The last time, when the police turned up following Heather's death, I sat there mutely, letting them fire questions at Leo like he was a common criminal. I didn't say anything, and I've always regretted it. I let him down when he needed me, and I wasn't going to let history repeat itself.

I guess I was in shock back then. A girl had died and the police were on our doorstep asking awkward questions. About the party. About drugs. About Leo's relationship to Heather. We knew Leo was at a party and we'd been fairly relaxed about him drinking the odd beer, but I had no idea he was taking drugs. And not just a joint, which I might have turned a blind eye to, but LSD. It's a Class A drug. Serious stuff. Although he never told me who'd supplied it to him.

I sat there around the dining room table with them like I was watching myself from the ceiling and I had a weird sense of no longer being in my own body. We should never have let Leo speak to those detectives without a lawyer, especially when he confessed that Heather had scored the drugs from him, but we were caught totally wrong-footed. It was a beautiful Saturday morning. Rory and I had just finished breakfast and were planning to head off into town to go shopping. And then our whole world came crashing down.

Leo being arrested and taken to the station in handcuffs is a sight I'll never forget. It was a sickening, awful experience no parent should ever have to go through and one I never want to repeat. Which is why I guess I lied to the police this time. I don't want Leo to have to go through that again.

'Where's the knife?' Rory asks.

For a moment, I can't think. 'I put it in the dishwasher.'

'The dishwasher?'

'I didn't know what else to do with it. It had blood all over it,' I shout.

'Is it still in there?'

'No. I put it in one of the cupboards. In a water bottle.'

I open the cupboard, retrieve the knife, and show it to Rory.

'Get rid of it,' he says.

'What? Where?'

'I don't know. But it's best it's not in the house.'

There's a frantic look in Rory's eye.

'Why? You don't seriously think...?' I ask, lowering my voice to a whisper.

Rory shakes his head. 'I don't know. Do you?'

'I don't want to believe it, but...'

'But what?'

'I don't know him anymore. He won't talk to me, and he's always so angry, like the entire world is against him. I know he's not happy here and he blames me. Maybe it *was* a mistake moving, but I thought we were doing the right thing. I don't know. Have we? I'm worried about him. I think he's... troubled.'

Rory frowns.

'Maybe he's taking drugs again. The fact is, I feel like I don't know my own son anymore. Or - or what he's capable of.' I swallow a hard lump that forms in my throat. I don't want to believe he's hurt Olivia, but I have to accept it's a possibility. 'Please, will you try talking to him?' I beg.

'I don't think he'll talk to me.'

'You could at least try. See if he'll open up to you and find out what's going on inside his head. You promised we'd do it together tonight.'

Rory takes a deep breath and lets it out slowly. 'Okay, I'll give it a go, but I don't know what good it will do.'

I glance at the clock on the oven. In a few hours, I need to be up with the dogs. I have to get some sleep, although with all tonight's drama, I don't know if I'll be able to.

'I'm going to bed,' I say as Rory finishes his coffee. 'Make sure you lock up.'

'Okay, I'll be up shortly. Leave a light on for me.'

I turn in the doorway, wrapping my dressing gown tightly around my middle. 'I don't think so. You can sleep in the guest room tonight.'

'What?'

'I'm not having you snoring in my ear all night. And then maybe next time you'll let me know if you're going out partying with all your new work friends.'

Rory's face falls, but I mean it. I'm in no mood to share my bed with him tonight.

Chapter 15

When I did finally drop off, my dreams were anxious and stress-filled. I lost the dogs in the woods. My teeth crumbled in my mouth. Leo fell into a dark pit so deep I couldn't reach him. And now, I feel more tired than when I went to bed. My eyes are tender and puffy, my limbs leaden.

The house is quiet. Too quiet. Rory should be up by now and getting ready for work. Unless he's left already and I haven't heard him, he's overslept. I'm not surprised, the state he came home in last night. Well, if he has a hangover this morning, it serves him right.

I knock at the door of the guest room and let myself in. The curtains are still closed, and the air is rank with sweat and stale alcohol breath.

'Shouldn't you have left for work?' I say, deliberately loudly.

I walk around the end of the bed and throw open the curtains. Rory groans and rolls over.

'What time is it?' His voice is hoarse, and he sounds in pain.

'Ten to seven.'

'Shit.'

He throws off the covers and the mattress creaks as he struggles to get up, but my attention is on the street outside. For the first time in more than twenty-four hours, there are no police cars.

'Why didn't you wake me sooner?' Rory moans.

My heart skips. Maybe they've found Olivia and brought her home in the middle of the night. Perhaps she's in there right now, the family reunited. How fantastic would that be? And, of course, it would mean Leo's off the hook.

'I don't feel so good,' Rory says as he crashes back into bed and drags the duvet over his body. 'I think I'll call in sick.'

'Okay.' I'm not really listening. My mind's elsewhere, thinking about our son. Our future. For a moment last night, I actually started to believe that maybe he did have something to do with Olivia's disappearance. I should have known better. As if Leo is capable of hurting anyone.

'I'm going to have a shower and get going,' I say as I turn away from the window. 'Make sure the boys are up and get to school.'

'Yes, boss.' Rory groans again and buries his head under the duvet.

'The good news is that it looks as though they might have found Olivia.'

Rory shoots his head out from under the covers and cracks open an eye. 'Really?'

'Well, there are no police cars outside this morning.'

'Thank god for that.'

After a quick shower, I get dressed and grab some tea and toast, briefly reminded of the horrible dream I had where my teeth disintegrated as I bit down on a toasted slice of bread. I clear up my dishes, feed Biscuit and pull on my boots. Biscuit trots obediently at my feet as we leave the house and head for my van. She's already well-versed in our new routine, climbing into her cage and settling down on her bed, while I prepare to collect the rest of the dogs.

My first stop would normally be to collect Hank, but I don't want to intrude if the family is enjoying an emotional reunion, especially as during the last conversation I had with Jerome, he virtually accused Leo of being complicit in Olivia's disappearance. Or at least knowing more than he was admitting.

I bet there's a totally innocent explanation for why Olivia didn't come home on Monday night. She's probably been with a friend and forgot to let her parents know she was staying over. Or with a secret boyfriend. I hope Jerome and Faith aren't giving her a hard time. They should just be grateful she's home and safe.

I decide to leave collecting Hank until last and instead drive to Anthony and Zac's house and pull up at the end of their drive. There are no cars parked outside the house, so I assume they're both out. But as I hop out of the van, I hear a car approaching. Two short blasts of a horn make me jump.

'I didn't expect to see you this morning.' I smile at Zac as he pulls up in his Mini and climbs out wearing skintight jeans and an impossibly tight white T-shirt under a loose red hoodie.

'Thought I'd join Anthony at the gym this morning. A body like this doesn't look after itself.' He laughs as he pats his taut stomach.

'You still want me to take Tyson today?'

He puts his hands together in supplication. 'Would you be an angel? I'm at home today but I won't have time to take him out. And you're so good with him.'

'It's no problem. It's what you pay me for, after all.'

'Did you hear about Olivia Hunter?' he says, lowering his voice.

'I know. Shocking, isn't it?'

'The amount of police that were around yesterday, I thought there'd been a murder.' He puts his fingers to his mouth in melodramatic horror, his eyes widening.

'I think they might have found her overnight,' I say. 'At least there are no police cars outside the house this morning.'

Zac glances over my shoulder. 'You're right. I hadn't noticed. Well, fingers crossed.'

'She probably stayed over with a friend and forgot to tell her parents. You know what teenagers are like.' Or maybe he doesn't. I don't know if Antony and Zac will ever have kids of their own, but they're a long way off being parents to teenagers. I wouldn't wish it on anyone.

'Maybe.' Zac screws up his nose. 'Or maybe the truth is closer to home.' His eyebrows shoot up, but his forehead remains stubbornly smooth.

'What do you mean?'

'I shouldn't say anything. It's not like me to gossip,' he says.

If I've learnt anything about Zac and Anthony since we moved to the estate, it's that they're the biggest gossips. The first time I met them at a barbecue Jerome and Faith threw late in the summer, when we'd only been here a matter of weeks, they were falling over themselves to tell me all about the neighbours. They had an opinion about everybody. How they thought Hanna was lying about her age. Far older than her claimed forty-three years, they whispered in my ear. That Faith's floristry business was struggling, and she'd had to let two staff members go, and how Zahara had been married twice before settling down with Kwame. I took it all with a degree of cynicism, not sure how much of it to believe. I hate to think about what they say behind our backs. Hopefully, they won't find out the truth about us or the whole estate is going to know.

'You can't say something like that and leave me hanging.' I pat Zac's bulging bicep.

He glances up and down the street and leans towards me. 'It's just, don't you find Jerome a little creepy?'

'Creepy? How?'

'You know what I mean. He's just -' Zac shudders and clenches his fists, 'always acting a bit weird. Didn't you notice him checking you out at that party in the summer? Don't get me wrong, it was a nice dress, but he couldn't take his eyes off you.'

It *was* a nice dress. My green floral print dress with the plunging neckline that I was worried was a little too tight. I caught Jerome peering down my front a couple of times but didn't take offence. I was partly flattered and only partly outraged. I guess he has a wandering eye.

'I'm not saying you were the only one,' Zac continues. 'He was like a dog on heat that afternoon.'

'Was he?'

'Totally. Poor Zahara took the brunt of it, of course, but she is gorgeous, isn't she? She used to be a model, you know, but I'm not surprised with cheekbones like that. Anyway, Kwame had to warn him to back off. I thought at one stage they were going to get into a fight. Jerome was even all over Hanna.'

'What has that got to do with Olivia?'

'She's a pretty girl, isn't she? And you must have seen how he is with her. All a bit touchy feely if you ask me.' He shudders theatrically. 'It's not normal.'

'Come on,' I say. 'It's Jerome we're talking about. You can't seriously be suggesting...' I'm not sure exactly what he is suggesting, but it's not good.

Zac holds up his hands, palms out. 'All I'm saying is the guy's a bit odd. I'm not saying stranger danger isn't a thing, but how often do you read it's someone the victim knew?'

'No, not Jerome,' I gasp, appalled Zac could even suggest such a thing. 'I spoke to him yesterday. He was absolutely distraught.'

'Weirder things have happened.'

I shake my head. The idea of Jerome being involved in his own daughter's disappearance is utterly abhorrent. 'Sorry, I think you're wide of the mark.' Even if it's what Zac thinks, he shouldn't be sharing wild speculation with other people, least of all one of the neighbours. I have to look Jerome in the eye in a few minutes.

'Your eldest must know something. Leo, isn't it? I always see him and Olivia together,' Zac says.

My blood runs cold. 'No, I don't think so.' Do I sound defensive?

'I think he might have a crush on her.'

'They're friends, that's all.'

'If you say so, Mum,' Zac says with a lascivious laugh. 'Maybe the police should talk to him. If it's not the father, maybe it's the boyfriend?'

Zac thinks he's being funny, but if that's his idea of a joke, it's in poor taste.

'Shut up, Zac.'

'What? I'm only teasing.' He must notice me stiffen when he touches my arm.

'Are you going to fetch Tyson?' I ask coldly. 'Or do you want me to come in and get him?'

'No, you're alright. I won't be a tick.'

He lets himself into the house. The scratch of claws racing across their wooden floors is followed by a low, familiar bark.

While I wait, I stare down the road at the Hunters' house. It looks quiet. Nothing to give away what's going on inside, until a police car rolls slowly up the road and turns into Jerome and Faith's drive. For some reason, I stoop behind Zac's Mini, not wanting to be seen. Two officers climb out and knock at the door, but I'm too far away to see who answers. They disappear inside and the door closes behind them.

I stand up straight and glance down at the Mini, which is always remarkably clean and shiny, given the state of the roads at this time of year. It's why the dent over the arch of the front wheel stands out so prominently, the metal crumpled in a section about the size of my foot. Zac must have been mortified. He takes as much pride in the appearance of his car as he does himself.

A wet nose nuzzles my hand and Tyson jumps up to greet me with his stubby tail wagging.

'Someone's pleased to see you,' Zac says.

After a few moments rubbing the top of his head and down his haunches, the way he likes it, Tyson finally calms down and lets me clip on his lead.

'What've you done to your car?' I ask casually.

Zac's face tightens. 'I don't know. Must have been someone in the car park at the gym. It was like that when I got back to it.'

'Did they leave a note?'

Zac shakes his head. 'Of course they didn't. Nobody ever does, do they?'

'Hopefully it'll hammer out.'

'I hope so.' Zac nods down the road towards Jerome and Faith's. 'I see the police are back.'

'Yeah, they've literally just turned up.'

'Hopefully, with good news.'

'Hopefully,' I say. 'I guess I'll find out shortly.'

Chapter 16

Of all the dogs, Hanna and Fergal's beautiful Hungarian vizsla, Bertie, is probably the most striking. He's so placid with a gorgeous soft coat and big, floppy ears. He's a pedigree breed, though, and probably worth a lot of money. I'm utterly terrified something might happen to him when he's in my care.

Unusually, there's no one at home when I knock at the door, so let myself in. Bertie comes bounding up and almost knocks me off my feet. I love it when the dogs are so pleased to see me. It gives me confidence I'm doing something right.

'Down, Bertie. Sit!' He immediately sits at my feet with his tongue hanging out and his big, beady eyes staring at me expectantly. I toss him a treat from my pouch, which he gobbles up greedily.

He's an energetic dog, but he's been so well trained, he always obeys my commands. Not like Hank, who does his own thing, no matter how loudly I scream at him.

I look around for Bertie's lead. Hanna usually leaves it out on one of the kitchen worktops, but I can't find it anywhere.

I really don't want to call Hanna and bother her about it, especially as she's out, probably at a business meeting. It's bound to be here somewhere. And besides, it's a good excuse to have a poke around. I love seeing how other people live their lives, their tastes and proclivities. You can get a real sense of what they're about from the style of their homes, what they hang on the walls and put on display on their shelves. But it's what they don't put out on show, what they hide away in drawers and cupboards, that's the real eyeopener. The things they don't want anyone else to see.

Take Anthony and Zac's house. It's immaculate. They have next to no clutter. They've painted all their interior walls white, ripped up the carpets and replaced them with wooden boards, and have minimal, expensive furniture. When you peer under the surface in their house, it's exactly the same. Everything in their drawers and cupboards has its place. They even line up the labels of their tins in the kitchen cupboards and have the handles of the mugs all pointing in the same direction. Everything has its place and everything has to be just so.

Not like in Fergal and Hanna's house, I discover. It may look tidy on the surface, but their kitchen drawers look like a bomb's gone off in them, while in the lounge, the long oak sideboard is concealing a horror show of messiness. Old magazines, board games, tablecloths, DVDs and candles, among other things, all shoved in there on top of each other. How do they ever find anything? I'm no Marie Kondo, but this is a whole different level. I might never find Bertie's lead at this rate.

I'm on the verge of admitting defeat and calling Hanna after all, when I remember there's a cupboard under the stairs. Ours is an open space where Biscuit has her bed and where we keep our shoes, but Fergal and Hanna have boxed theirs in, no doubt to hide more of their junk.

When I swing open the door, there are a dozen coats and jackets hanging from three hooks and, sure enough, among them is Bertie's lead.

'You could have told me it was in here all along.' I scratch Bertie's ears and laugh as he nudges up against my legs.

I have to unhook a handful of coats to free it, but when I put them back, a lightweight cardigan slinks to the floor. It's not like anything I've ever seen Hanna wear before and besides, it looks too small for her. It's a silky, pastel green tight knit with a lace-trimmed collar, more like the sort of thing a younger girl would wear.

In fact, haven't I seen it before? It certainly looks familiar.

When I bend down to pick it up, I catch the faint scent of the perfume it's laced with. Vanilla with a hint of coconut that reminds me of warm summer days in Greece when the boys were younger. It's the perfume Olivia wears. I remember it from the times she's been to our house with Leo.

It must be Olivia's cardigan. Now I think about it, I even remember seeing her wearing it. She left it hooked over the newel post at the bottom of the stairs. It struck me at the time, and put a smile on my face, as it's so unusual to see anything so feminine around our house.

So if it's Olivia's cardigan, what the hell is it doing in Hanna and Fergal's house?

Chapter 17

There could be a million and one reasons Olivia's cardigan is hanging up under the stairs in Fergal and Hanna's house. Olivia's a sociable girl. At the party in the summer, she was chatting with everyone. So unlike my boys, who can barely manage a grunt if they're spoken to by an adult, let alone starting a conversation. She could have popped around to see Hanna for a chat and left it behind. Or perhaps Hanna found it in the street and didn't know who it belonged to, hung it up with the coats and forgot about it.

It doesn't mean anything. It's just that I've never heard Hanna talk about Olivia before, so it seems unlikely Olivia would have been a visitor to their house. It's not even as if they have kids and Olivia might have been babysitting for them. Which is why I find it so unsettling. But then, would I feel the same way if Olivia hadn't gone missing? No, I'm reading more into it than I should. It's not something I should trouble the police with, is it? Of course not. It's none of my business and, as Leo is fond of telling me, I should keep my nose out of other people's affairs.

Bertie sits and barks.

'Alright, alright, I'm coming,' I tell him, hanging the cardigan back up where I found it. I'm going to forget I ever saw it.

I march Bertie out of the house and put him in the back of the van with Biscuit and Tyson. Then it's off to collect Rosie from Kwame and Zahara's and, finally, I have to pick up Hank. I'm already twenty minutes late. They're probably wondering where I am.

Faith answers the door and if anything looks worse than she did yesterday. Wan and sallow, her eyes puffy from crying. Maybe I was wrong. Maybe they haven't found Olivia after all.

'Oh, Sabine,' she says, somewhat surprised to see me. 'I didn't realise the time.'

Hank charges out of the door, straight past me and into the garden where he finds a bush where he can cock his leg.

'How are you, Faith? Has there been any news?' I ask tentatively.

She shakes her head. 'No, nothing. The police are still looking, but they're as clueless as everyone else. I feel I should be out looking too, but they're insisting we stay here by the phone in case Olivia's in trouble and tries to call.'

'Is there anything I can do?'

I really wanted to believe Olivia had returned home overnight, and it had all been a big misunderstanding. That she wasn't missing but had simply forgotten to tell her parents she was staying out. But now she's been gone for two nights, it's looking more and more bleak. I wish there was something I could say to make it better. Some words of comfort and hope.

'Do you think she might have met someone?' I ask, floundering for something to say and instantly regretting opening my mouth. Faith doesn't need to hear my idle speculation.

'Why? What have you heard?'

'Nothing. I was just wondering if perhaps... I don't know. Maybe there was someone online she's been in contact with?' I will myself to shut up, but the words keep tumbling from my mouth. This isn't what Faith needs to hear right now.

She shakes her head. 'I don't think so, but the police are looking into all of that. They've taken her laptop, but her phone is missing and they can't trace it. They think it must have been switched off.'

'Oh, right,' I say. 'Well, it sounds as if they're doing everything they can.'

'Did you speak to your son?' she asks hopefully, her eyes lighting up as my heart sinks. 'What did he say? Anything that can help would be useful.'

'I don't think he knows anything, sorry.'

'Oh, it's just that Olivia's friend, Daisy, said she saw them together on Monday afternoon and that Olivia seemed upset.' She stares at me as if willing me to reveal the clue I'm hiding that's going to unlock the mystery of her daughter's disappearance.

'I'm afraid she was mistaken. As Leo told the police, he was with me on Monday afternoon, helping with the dogs.' I'm sure my neck and face are flushing, my body giving away my lies.

I hate lying, but I'm doing it for the right reasons. Leo has nothing to do with Olivia's disappearance, but if his name gets dragged into it, it'll only muddy the waters and distract from the search. And none of us want that. We all just want Olivia home, safe and well.

'I guess Daisy must have been mistaken,' Faith says. She looks crestfallen but continues to eye me suspiciously.

'I'll speak to Leo again and see if there's anything he might have remembered since last night.'

'Would you? Thank you,' she says, sounding genuinely grateful. 'Anything he can think of might help.'

'How are you both coping?'

'Not too good. Jerome's beside himself. He's been climbing the walls, so he's gone out looking for her. It'll make him feel better doing something useful rather than sitting here, waiting. Would you like to stay for a cup of coffee? Do you have the time?'

It's awkward enough standing here on the doorstep, wondering how long before I can make my excuses without seeming impolite. I don't want to stay for coffee and have to share in the misery of her daughter's disappearance. I can't think of anything worse. I know that makes me a bad person, but I don't know the family that well. They just happen to be the people who live across the road. We have nothing in common with them other than that.

I glance at my wrist out of habit, even though I haven't worn a watch in two years. 'Sorry, Faith, I've got the dogs.' I swing my arm towards my van, which I've left parked in the road. 'I can't leave them too long on their own.'

'Oh, gosh, no. Of course not. Let me fetch Hank for you.'

She seems to have forgotten that Hank escaped when she opened the door and is currently sniffing around the garden, but she's gone before I can stop her.

'Faith!' I call, but she doesn't hear me.

'It's only Sabine from across the road come to collect Hank,' I hear her saying, presumably to the unseen police officers in her house.

A deep, male voice replies, but I can't make out what he says.

I'm not sure what to do. Whether to take Hank or to wait for Faith to come back, having realised her mistake. In the end, I stand awkwardly at the doorstep, calling for Hank, who's suddenly become selectively deaf.

A nondescript dark saloon pulls up in the street. Two people climb out. A woman in a sombre trouser suit, her hair braided and pinned to the back of her head, marches up the drive with a man in an ill-fitting grey suit trailing behind. They don't need to flash their badges for me to work out they're plain clothes officers. Detectives, presumably.

'Hello?' the woman says in a gruff, masculine voice. 'Who are you?'

The question's so blunt and to the point, it momentarily catches me off guard. My cheeks flush.

'I - I'm just a neighbour,' I stammer. 'Sabine. I walk the Hunter's dog, Hank.'

The woman stares, dull grey eyes assessing me. There's no warmth to her expression when her lipstick-red lips curl into a forced smile. 'Leo Sugar's mother?'

I nod, guilt flooding my body. She knows who I am. Have they been discussing me? Does she know I lied about Leo being with me on Monday afternoon? I shouldn't have done it, but I wasn't thinking about the consequences.

'How is he?' she asks.

'Fine, thank you.'

'He must be terribly worried about Olivia. They were friends, weren't they?'

'They sometimes walked to school together,' I clarify, the insinuation in her question obvious. 'But yes, he's been quite upset.'

She continues to stare at me as if she's expecting me to fill the silence.

'Is there any news on the investigation?' I ask.

She gives me another tight smile. 'I'm afraid I'm not at liberty to discuss that.'

'No, right. Of course not. I hope you find her. Everyone is desperately worried.' I shove my hands in my pockets and hunch my shoulders, my whole body tense.

'That's understandable.'

The front door swings open and Faith reappears, looking confused. 'I can't find Hank—' she begins, before noticing the two detectives.

'Mrs Hunter? DS Lockyear and DC Caulfield,' the female officer says. 'We wondered if we could ask you a few more questions about your daughter.'

Hank bounds up, baring his teeth and growling at the two strangers.

'Hank, stop it,' Faith chides.

'Why don't I take him?'

Faith hands me his lead, which I clip onto his collar.

'You'll let me know what Leo says, won't you?' Faith asks. 'Sabine's going to talk to her son again in case there's anything more he knows,' she explains to the detectives.

'Good idea.' Lockyear narrows her eyes at me. 'And yes, let us know if he remembers anything.'

My heart's beating like a drum. 'Would you like me to keep hold of Hank for a few days? He can stay at ours while you're dealing with all this? I'm sure Biscuit would love it. It would be no trouble.'

'Oh, no, I couldn't ask you to do that,' Faith says.

'It really is no bother. And I'd like to help, even if it's something small.'

'Are you sure?'

'One hundred per cent. I'll bring him back when you've got less on your mind.'

'Thank you, Sabine. That's so kind.'

At least it makes me feel marginally better about having lied to her about Leo.

Chapter 18

Rory stands motionless under the steaming jets of the shower, letting the water soak into his hair, run down his face and off his chin. When Sabine woke him, his brain felt as though it was about to explode inside his skull and his stomach was cramping with nausea. But under the warm water, everything feels slightly better. He could stand here all day, enveloped in its restorative powers.

He's always suffered from hangovers, but not like this. This is debilitating. He can't think. He can't move. All he wants to do is go back to bed, pull the covers over his head and wallow in his own self-pity. It must be his age. Along with all the aches and pains of getting older, it seems a boozy night takes a heavier toll these days.

He should be on the train by now and halfway to the office, but he can't face it. Maybe after he's eaten something, he'll feel more human. He'll have to call in sick. Tell them it was something he'd eaten, although he didn't actually eat anything last night, which is probably why he feels so awful this morning.

Of course, they'll all know he isn't really sick and will probably laugh behind his back at the old man who can't handle a few drinks. The others are bound to be there on time, but they have the resilience of youth on their side. They're used to it. Plus, none of them has a long commute like Rory. Maybe he'll say he's working from home this morning and try to make it into the office after lunch.

Or maybe not.

He groans and runs his hands over his face and through his thick grey beard, snaking his fingers across his skull. He's never drinking again. At least not on a work night.

It was Marney's fault. She was egging everyone on. He wouldn't normally have gone, but last night he needed it. It was a release. An escape from the pressures that have been building and building in the last few months.

First, there was all that business with Heather Malone and Leo's arrest, followed by such an outpouring of anger and hatred towards them. And then the stress of the move. Selling the old house and moving to a characterless modern property on a soulless new estate where they don't know anyone. Finding a new school for the boys. Sabine kept reassuring them it was a new beginning, like rebooting a computer and eliminating all the old bugs and glitches that had blighted their previous existence.

But it hasn't worked. Leo has been withdrawn and sulky since the day they sold the old house. He's not enjoying his new school. He hasn't made many new friends, and he's become increasingly sullen and difficult. Sabine's talked about getting counselling for him, but Rory's not sure it's worth it. He'll come around, eventually. He just needs time to adjust.

And as if all that wasn't enough, Sabine has convinced herself Leo's somehow caught up in the disappearance of that girl from across the street and has given Leo a false alibi to the police.

It's no wonder Rory needed to drink himself halfway to oblivion last night. For a few hours at least, he didn't have to think about any of that crap. He didn't have to worry about Sabine. Or Leo. Or Heather. Or Olivia. He only had to think about himself and let off steam. It's been a long time since he's laughed or enjoyed himself so much. The hangover is a small price to pay.

'Dad? Are you nearly finished in there? I need to clean my teeth.' Casper hammers on the door like there's a fire.

'Just a minute.'

'I don't want to be late for school.'

Rory sighs. Is there ever any peace in this house? He turns off the shower and stands dripping as he reaches for a towel.

'Is Leo up yet?' he asks as Casper barges into the bathroom, wafting away the clouds of steam.

'Yeah, he's already left, I think.' At least that's one less worry. 'Aren't you going to work today?'

'Working from home this morning. I might head in later.'

Casper shrugs and turns his attention to his phone, which he's balanced precariously on the edge of the basin as he squeezes paste onto his toothbrush.

Rory pads across the landing and into the guest room where yesterday's clothes are dumped in a heap on the floor at the end of the bed. He picks up his trousers, all creased and crumpled, and notices as he straightens them out that there's something in the pocket.

He pulls out a beer mat that's been artfully shaped into a swan. He remembers now. Toni made it for him. He'd carefully folded it and put it in his pocket, promising in his drunken state that he'd treasure it forever.

He folds out its wings and pinches its beak back into place. Toni's like no one he's ever met before, with a lust for life and a devil-may-care attitude he envies. It was exciting to get to know her outside of work, where they could really talk. She's a few years younger than him, but she's already done so much with her life, visited so many incredible places. And he loves how she's not confined by convention. She doesn't see any point in marriage, and when it comes to sex, gender is a meaningless construct. If she likes someone, she'll sleep with them. It's exciting and liberating, although he could never be like that.

Mind you, what's she going to think of him when he fails to turn up for work this morning? Probably that he's a complete lightweight who can't handle a night out. No doubt she's already on her way in and will turn up looking as bright and as breezy as ever, hungover or not.

Rory shivers as water runs from his hair down his back. He lays his trousers over the end of the bed, scoops up the rest of his dirty clothes and drops his shirt and underwear into the laundry basket on the landing.

He grabs his phone and glasses from the table by the bed and takes a moment to look out of the window, depressed by what he sees. All the houses are identical. Modern, identikit homes of the same mock-Georgian design and with the same square of garden at the front. They're not ugly buildings, but they don't have any character to speak of. He hates it here. It's no wonder Leo is so miserable.

Across the road, movement catches his eye. A car pulls up and two people clamber out. Detectives by the look of them, heading for Jerome and Faith's. The woman, obviously in charge, strides purposefully up the drive, followed by a guy in a dull grey suit. Sabine's standing at the door.

They start chatting and Rory wonders what they're asking her. Whether they're talking about Leo. Sabine should never have lied to the police. She's asking for trouble. But then, trouble seems to follow them all wherever they go lately.

He watches them for a while. Sabine looks desperate to get away with Hank pulling at his lead. Faith's on the doorstep, her face knotted with anxiety. It must be horrendous for them, having a child go missing. They're a strange couple, mind you. She's harmless enough, but Rory finds Jerome difficult to connect with. All that tough guy, toxic masculinity bullshit. He's probably a closet racist. Almost certainly a misogynist, and with about as much sophistication as a cartoon hanging in an art gallery.

Rory hates how he treats women. Ogling them like they're pieces of meat on display for his pleasure. He'd even been at it with Sabine at their party in the summer when she wore that tight-fitting dress and Jerome kept trying to peer down her top. It's no wonder Kwame almost punched him, presumably because he'd been doing the same with Zahara. It was an unsettling few moments in what was otherwise a chilled afternoon, when Kwame squared up to Jerome, shoving him in the chest, and Jerome put on this innocent act, as if there had been a massive misunderstanding. It looked for a while as if things would turn ugly, and the men were about to get into a proper fist fight, but thankfully, it fizzled out and nothing more was said. But Rory knows what he saw, and he now knows what Jerome is really like.

After all, what kind of man brings out a shotgun at a party? Apparently, it was a family heirloom, handed down by his grandfather. But why parade around with it, showing it off? There's nothing big or clever about guns, especially at a barbecue, of all places. But he suddenly appeared with it, pretending to shoot pigeons out of the sky like that was supposed to impress people. The man's an idiot.

He feels sorry for Faith being married to someone like that. She's relatively normal in comparison. Why she'd be attracted to someone like Jerome is beyond him.

She must be going through hell with her daughter missing. Olivia's an attractive girl, growing into her looks as she matures into a woman. It's no wonder Leo's drawn to her, although she's well out of his league. He'd do well to forget about her and move on. There's no point moping about someone who doesn't feel the same way. Maybe that's what they were arguing about in the woods when Sabine saw them together the other day. Not that it would justify Leo pinning her against a tree. He thought he'd brought his son up better than that. That's why he finds it so hard to believe. There's no way Leo would act like that. Sabine must have been mistaken in what she thought she saw.

The chances are Olivia has run away from home and there's nothing more sinister about it than that. Kids do it all the time. He remembers a statistic he read in the papers once that more than a hundred thousand children go missing or run away from home every year. What's the betting Olivia's one of them, especially having a father like Jerome? Hopefully, she has friends or relatives who are helping her out and she hasn't ended up on the street somewhere. That really would be a tragedy.

A car appears from the opposite end of the estate. It's a dark blue Mini, its paintwork gleaming. He recognises it instantly. It belongs to Zac and Anthony, the couple with the boxer dog they hilariously named Tyson, without a hint of irony. One of them works in a gym and the other for an airline, although Rory can never remember which way round it is.

The Mini cruises slowly down the street, slowing to peer into Jerome and Faith's house. There's an unsightly dent in the car's front wing, right behind the headlight, over the wheel arch, which puts a smile on Rory's face. Anthony and Zac are always so immaculately turned out, their house pristine, and their car never dirty. He shouldn't find it funny, but whatever's happened, they must be devastated.

'Dad, I'm off,' Casper calls out.

Rory looks towards the door as the shadow of his youngest son shoots past. 'Have a good day. I'll see you tonight.'

When he turns back to the window, the car's gone.

Chapter 19

I've not been long home from walking the dogs when my phone rings. I don't recognise the number and, fearing a cold call and someone trying to sell me something I don't want, I answer suspiciously.

'Yes?'

'Mrs Sugar? It's Amy, Leo's form tutor.'

My heart sinks. What's he done now? It's not the first time the school's called me about his behaviour since he joined at the beginning of the autumn term. They've already warned me he's been repeatedly caught using his phone in lessons and hasn't been handing in assignments on time.

I had to remind them he's seventeen, not seven, and that I can't force him to do his homework. But I am worried for him. If he doesn't buck up his ideas, he's in danger of throwing away his future. He needs to knuckle down and get his qualifications if he's going to make anything of his life.

'What's he done now?'

'I'm afraid we've not seen him this morning. We've had to put it down as an unauthorised absence.'

This is exactly what I was worried about. Leo made it clear he didn't want to switch schools and my biggest fear was that he was going to start skipping lessons. That boy is going to put me in an early grave.

'I'm so sorry, I had no idea.'

'The thing is, it's not the first time we've had to reach out to you, Mrs Sugar. We all appreciate he's new here, and it's going to take time for him to adjust, but if his behaviour doesn't improve, we might have to consider his future with us,' Amy says in a monotone, almost as if she's reading from a script.

'Yes, I understand, but he's still settling in—'

'It's not fair on the other pupils who want to learn. Yesterday, he was involved in a fight with another student and was lucky not to have been sent home. We did try to call you.'

'Right, sorry, I didn't get your message.' A fight? Leo's never been in a fight in his life, as far as I know. He can be moody and difficult, but this is something on a different level. Even in the aftermath of Heather's death, when everyone turned on us, he wasn't getting into fights.

'It's something we take a dim view of, especially with sixth-formers who are old enough to know better. It doesn't set a good example to the rest of the school.'

His behaviour seems to be going from bad to worse. Next, she'll be telling me he's attacked one of the teachers. I hope he's not back on drugs. We had a long chat with him after Heather's death, and he promised it was a one-off and he wouldn't touch them again. Was I too trusting? Maybe I should have listened to my gut and sought professional help instead of thinking we could handle it ourselves.

'Obviously, you're aware that one of his friends, Olivia Hunter, is missing,' I say. 'He's taken it quite hard. She's our neighbour and they've become close, not that I'm trying to excuse his behaviour, but maybe you could make some allowances on this occasion?'

'All our thoughts are with Ms Hunter and her family at this difficult time, of course, but we can't turn a blind eye to disruptive behaviour nor unauthorised absences. You need to ensure Leo returns to school, or has a sick note, otherwise we'll be left with no choice other than to take further action.'

'I understand,' I sigh. She clearly doesn't have teenage children nor appreciate how difficult it is to keep control of them around the clock. Leo's virtually an adult. He turns eighteen next year and then he's free to do whatever he wants.

'We'll look forward to seeing Leo back tomorrow then,' she says and hangs up.

I slam the phone on the counter and let out an agonised scream. Where did we go so wrong with him? He was always loved as a child and never wanted for anything. We taught him right from wrong and encouraged him to take part in sport and other extra-curricular activities outside of school. He used to be so popular and friendly, rarely without a smile on his face, but he's a shadow of the boy he used to be.

We raised him no differently to Casper, but they couldn't be any less alike. And yet they've had the same opportunities, the same home life, the same upbringing, but while Casper is turning into a well-adjusted, likeable young man, Leo is fast becoming a delinquent.

I'm sure it's all connected to Heather's death. That's when we first noticed the change in him. Of course, it was a big deal for him. He was arrested, interrogated by the police and vilified by Heather's family and online, but if he's not careful, he's going to let it destroy his life.

'Who was that?'

Rory's voice makes me jump and sends my heart rate through the roof.

'Jeez, I forgot you were home,' I say, putting a hand to my chest as he appears at the kitchen door. 'Don't go creeping up on me like that.'

'Sorry,' he says sheepishly. 'Problems?'

'The school again. Leo's not turned up.'

'Terrific.'

'And apparently yesterday he was caught fighting. This has to stop, Rory,' I say. 'We can't go on like this. Maybe it's time we got some help for him after all.'

'Therapy?' Rory pulls a face. 'I don't know.'

'Well, he doesn't listen to me. If he's still traumatised, he needs to speak to a professional.'

'He just needs some space. He's growing up, becoming his own man, but you make out like he's some kind of freak.'

'And what if he has something to do with Olivia Hunter going missing after all?' I ask, my anger rising.

Rory puts a hand to his head and grimaces as I raise my voice. 'There's no need to shout.' He looks a mess. Pale and listless, but then he's never been able to handle his drink. 'Is that what you really think?'

'I don't know.'

'I wish you hadn't lied to the police,' Rory says. 'They could prosecute you for providing a false alibi, you know.'

'Yes, I know that! It was stupid. I shouldn't have done it, but I wasn't thinking, was I? I just don't want them digging around into Leo's past.'

'So where is he now?' Rory asks.

'I left you in charge this morning, remember? I thought you were going to make sure he left for school?'

'I did. He went while I was in the shower.'

'So where did he go?'

Rory shrugs. 'I don't know.'

'Let's find out, shall we?' I retrieve my phone, dial Leo's number and put it on loudspeaker. He'd better have a very good reason for skipping school.

The line clicks, rings once and goes to voicemail. Rory and I stare at each other.

'Leo, it's Mum. I've just had school on the phone. They tell me you've not been in today. I'd like to know where you are, so you'd better phone me as soon as you get this. Your father and I are not happy.'

I hang up and slam the phone on the counter.

'So if he's not at school and he's not at home, what's he doing?' Rory asks.

'I don't know, but I can't keep an eye on him twenty-four seven. You're going to have to have a word with him.'

'Me?' Rory looks horrified.

'Yes, Rory, you. You promised. He doesn't listen to a word I say.'

'I don't know, Sabine.'

'Just try, please.'

Rory pouts and shrugs. I might as well have asked him to shove his head in a bucket of molten lava. 'Do you really think it will do any good?'

'You won't know until you try, will you?'

'Okay. Fine.'

'We need to nip this in the bud. Will you do it as soon as he gets in?'

'Ahhh,' Rory says, looking shifty.

'What?'

'I was going to pop into the office later. I'm feeling better now and I shouldn't really take sick leave just because I'm hungover,' he says.

'You're kidding?'

'But I'll be back later tonight. I'll talk to Leo then.'

'You promise?' I ask.

'Absolutely.'

Chapter 20

Rory finally makes it into the office by late morning and it's already buzzing. Predictably, the entire design team, including Marney, who was throwing up in an alley around the back of the karaoke club the last time he saw her, is already in and everyone is at their desks.

'Sleep in, did we?' Toni asks with a twinkle in her eye as he pulls up his chair and slips off his coat and jacket.

She was knocking back shots of tequila at the club until at least midnight. It's not fair that she looks so fresh when he feels so rotten.

'Ha ha, hilarious.' Rory pushes his glasses up the bridge of his nose and switches on his computer. His brain feels as if it's been removed from his skull, passed through a blender and poured back in, despite the paracetamol he's washed down with a high-caffeine energy drink.

'Is the old man struggling? Can't handle a night out?' she smirks. It's supposed to be a joke. He's supposed to laugh and make light of his own failings, but her words irritate him.

'I guess I'm a bit out of practice.' He plasters a smile onto his face and concentrates on checking his emails.

'I reckon I only got about two hours' sleep last night,' she whispers, her eyes fixed on her screen, pretending to concentrate on her work.

'Well, I missed my stop on the train and nearly ended up in Southampton.'

She's not interested. 'I bumped into an old friend in a cocktail bar after you left, and you know, one thing led to another, and we ended up back at her place.'

Her place?

'Good for you.'

She glances at him, but he pretends not to notice. 'Was your wife cross you were so late?'

'Sabine? No, she was fine,' he says lightly.

'That's good.' She obviously doesn't believe him.

'How are you getting on with those social media posts you were working on?' he asks. He doesn't want to talk about his wife with Toni.

'Yeah, nearly done.'

'Can I take a look?'

'Sure.' She swings her screen around, but he can't .

He stands up and walks around to her side of the desk and places his hands on the back of her chair, her head inches from his face. She smells good. Fragrant. If Rory had gone back to a friend's for a wild night of sex after a night drinking and had only had two hours' sleep, he's sure he'd look, feel and smell like a bag of old crap.

'They're good. Really good.'

'Thanks.'

'I need a coffee. Want one?' If he's going to get through the rest of the day, it's going to have to be fuelled by caffeine.

'Can you grab me a green tea?'

Rory heads for the kitchen, where a couple of young women from the fundraising team are gossiping about one of their boyfriends. They give him an unimpressed once-over before turning their backs on him. Does he really look that bad?

While he waits for his coffee to brew, his mind wanders back to home. Why is Leo being so difficult? The last few months haven't been easy for any of them, but it's as if Leo is determined to cause the maximum fuss. He doesn't have to love his new school. He only has to endure it. And it's only going to be for another year while he gets his A levels under his belt. Then he can go off and do anything he likes. Getting into fights and bunking off isn't the answer.

Sabine's desperate for Rory to have a word with him, but what's he supposed to say? They don't have that kind of relationship, talking about feelings and emotions and that kind of stuff. He shudders. The only meaningful conversations he's ever had with Leo are about music and sport. Things that don't really matter. This business with his friend, Olivia, going missing obviously hasn't helped. It's destabilising for him. The school should make allowances for him.

Rory ambles back to his desk with the drinks, sets Toni's green tea down by her elbow, and returns to his computer.

But an hour later, he's beginning to flag. Concentrating seems such an effort today.

'You fancy grabbing some lunch?' Toni asks, pushing her chair back and standing. She pulls on a jacket. 'Come on, looks like you could use the fresh air.'

He shouldn't, really. He should use the time to catch up, but she's right. Some fresh air will probably do him good. They don't need to be long.

Outside, he turns towards the sandwich shop where he usually grabs a tomato and mozzarella panini and a bottle of sparkling water, but Toni slots her arm into his and pulls him in the opposite direction.

'Where are we going?' he asks, puzzled.

She takes him to a small square where half a dozen catering vans are serving street food. The smell is incredible. Garlic and ginger, lime and coriander. His mouth waters and his stomach rumbles.

'What do you fancy?' she asks.

'I don't know.' He's a bit overwhelmed, not sure what to choose, but he doesn't want her to think he doesn't know what he's doing. 'I think I might go for something Japanese.'

'Great choice.'

He heads off to a van serving a dizzying array of noodles, skewers and dumplings and orders a yakisoba with no real idea what it is, but it appears to comprise noodles, carrots and chopped spring onion, and looks the safest option.

Toni returns with a taco and they sit on a bench in the cold together to eat.

'Good?' she asks, her mouth full.

'Not bad.'

It's a far cry from eating a panini at his desk.

They sit for a while not speaking, Rory's thoughts preoccupied by his son's errant behaviour. Was it a mistake they made as parents? Did Rory not show him enough love when he was small? Casper's turned out okay, so why's Leo crashing off the tracks so spectacularly?

'Is everything okay?' Toni asks. 'You're quiet today.'

'Hangover,' he says, rolling his eyes.

'Are you sure that's all? You seem distant. Didn't you have fun last night?'

'Absolutely. I loved it,' he says, wiping his mouth with a flimsy paper napkin.

'Yeah, me too. What then? Still having problems at home?'

Rory sighs and pushes what's left of his noodles to one side. 'Is it that obvious?'

'You can talk to me, you know, if it would help.'

'You don't have kids, do you?' he asks.

She screws her face up in disgust. 'No.'

'Wise decision.'

'They giving you trouble again?'

'Just our eldest, Leo. He's having problems at school.'

'I hated school,' she says. That doesn't help.

'My wife wants me to talk to him, but I can't see how that's going to help. He won't listen to me.'

'Maybe it's a phase he's going through.'

'I hope so.' The throbbing behind Rory's eyes takes on a new intensity, like someone inside his head is trying to get out with a red-hot poker. He grimaces in pain.

'Are you okay?' Toni touches his arm affectionately.

'I don't think midweek drinking suits me.'

'Come on,' she says, jumping up. 'I know just the cure.'

She grabs him by the arm and pulls him to his feet.

'Where are you taking me now?'

She drags him down a side street and out the other side. They cross the road, dodging taxis and buses, and head towards an old-fashioned London pub tucked between an office block and a showroom selling pushchairs and buggies.

'Oh no, I can't face another drink,' Rory says, holding up both hands in protest.

'Honestly, it'll do you good and make you feel a million times better.'

Against his better judgement, he follows Toni inside. It's busy with a strange mixture of workmen in dusty, dirty overalls and businessmen in suits.

She pushes her way to the bar and orders two bloody marys, heavy on the vodka.

The thought of it turns Rory's stomach, but there's something else he feels, too. Excitement? It's only a lunchtime drink. Plenty of people do it. But not Rory. It feels... wanton, especially when he's got so much work on. But he loves being in Toni's company, captivated by the way she acts on a whim without thinking of the consequences. She's such a breath of fresh air.

Surprisingly, the tomato juice settles his nausea and he can hardly taste the alcohol over the bitterness of lemon and the sting of Tabasco.

They pull up two free stools at the end of the bar and have to shout to be heard over the noise.

'Our neighbours' daughter has gone missing,' Rory says, the alcohol freeing his tongue. He feels a sudden need to unburden himself and talk to someone neutral. And Toni offered a supportive ear. 'But because she and Leo are friends, Sabine thinks he must be involved.'

'Right.'

'I don't know what to do. I think Leo's just being moody. But Sabine's worried she saw the two of them together, fighting, shortly before Olivia went missing. I think she's being paranoid.'

'Oh?'

'She was a long way away, and it was getting dark. It could have been anyone she saw.'

'Probably.'

'I mean, it's been a couple days now since Olivia vanished, but Sabine's become obsessed about it. It's all she talks about. And she wonders why I stayed out late last night.' He grunts and takes another drink. 'Really, I'm sorry for the girl's parents, although her father's a bit of an arse, but it's not our problem.'

Toni nods and finishes her drink.

'We've even had the police around asking if we know anything,' Rory continues.

'Rory—'

'I just want a quiet life though, you know? We've had such an upheaval the last few months, and now we're living in suburban hell in this brand-new house that leaves me cold. Honestly, you'd hate it.' He sighs. 'I never thought my life would end up like this.'

'Look, I don't—'

'Be careful, Toni,' he says, ploughing on. He's on a roll now and it feels so good to talk so openly. 'Middle age creeps up on you and all the fun you used to have vanishes like that.' He clicks his fingers in the air. 'And you have no idea when or how it happened.'

Toni gathers her bag from the back of the stool and straps it over her shoulder as she stands. 'I've got to get back to the office,' she says coolly.

'Oh, really? So soon?'

'I'm sorry, but I didn't bring you to the pub to talk about how shit your life is. I'll see you back there.'

And before Rory can utter another word, she's gone. Out onto the street and marching off, and he has no idea what he's said to upset her.

Chapter 21

It's almost unheard of to see Leo without his phone. It might as well be surgically attached to his hand. He's always on it. At the table eating dinner. Watching TV or chilling on his bed. Even while he's playing computer games or finishing a school assignment. It's a distraction from everything else going on in real life.

Except when I want to get hold of him.

I've been trying his number all day, leaving increasingly exasperated messages, but he hasn't bothered to call me back.

Even more worrying is that he's revoked my access to the tracking app we all agreed to put on our phones last year, so I've no idea where he is.

As the hours tick by, I become increasingly irritable. Every little thing gets under my skin. Whether it's Biscuit whining at the back door to be let out, stubbing my toe painfully on a chair or the kitchen tap that won't stop dripping. My angry reaction to each is far out of proportion. It doesn't help that Rory's taken himself back to work. I'm sure it's only because I asked him to speak to Leo again. I don't understand why he's so reluctant. Leo won't listen to me, but Rory's always had such a good relationship with both boys, maybe he can get through to him and find out what's troubling him. I know Rory thinks I'm making a fuss about nothing, but he must be able to see Leo's on a slippery slope.

When Leo finally returns to the house late in the afternoon, I've worked myself into a frenzy, my anger with him simmering at boiling point.

'Where the hell have you been?' I yell as I catch him in the hall taking off his shoes. They're caked in mud, as are the lower legs of his jeans, and he's trailed dirt all along the floor. 'I've been trying to call you all day.'

He stares at me blankly.

'Why weren't you in school today?'

He shrugs. 'I didn't feel like it.'

'That's no excuse. I've had the school on the phone again,' I say, planting my hands on my hips. 'And what's this about you fighting?'

'It was nothing.'

'Clearly it was or the school wouldn't have mentioned it. You still haven't told me where you've been.'

'Nowhere,' he huffs.

'You must have been somewhere. What the hell is going on with you, Leo?'

'I just hung around, okay? I couldn't face school, so I gave it a miss.'

'You don't get to choose when you go to school. Your education's important. You need decent A levels or you're going to end up cleaning toilets for a living. How do you fancy that?'

'Don't be so melodramatic.'

'I'm telling you for your own good, because at the rate you're going, the school's going to kick you out and you can kiss goodbye to a place at university.'

'I don't care. I hate it there anyway. I wish you'd never made us move.'

I could throttle him. 'You know why we had to move.'

'I don't have to listen to this,' he shouts. He pulls his shoes back on but leaves the laces trailing as he storms into the kitchen.

'Don't you walk away from me, young man.' *Young man*? I sound like my mother. 'I've not finished talking to you yet.'

But he's not listening. He fishes out what's left of a granary loaf from the bread bin and shoves it in his rucksack. Then grabs two cans of Coke from the fridge and heads towards the front door.

'Where do you think you're going now?' I yell.

'Out!'

'No, you're not. You're grounded.'

He throws open the door, stomps out, and slams it in my face.

I growl in frustration and stamp a foot petulantly, but what can I do? I can't physically stop him. He's virtually an adult. That's why I need Rory here. Leo wouldn't talk to his father like that, I'm sure.

I rush to the door and yank it open. I'm about to yell that if he walks away now, he might as well not come back, but instead of finding Leo on the doorstep, I'm startled to find Hanna with a look of concern on her face. 'Everything okay?'

Oh god, she must have heard everything. How embarrassing. 'Yes, I'm fine.'

She glances down the drive towards Leo, who has his head down and his hands shoved in his pockets as he hurries away. Maybe it's just as well. Neither of us is in the right state of mind for a sensible conversation. The problem is we're too similar. Too hot-headed.

'It's just that I heard—'

'Teenagers,' I say, rolling my eyes.

Hanna raises an eyebrow, but I don't offer any further explanation. I don't want our private lives being gossiped about around the estate. We've been there before and it's not an experience I'm in a rush to repeat.

'Was there something I can help you with?' I ask, in no mood for house calls.

'I didn't mean to interrupt, but I wondered if you could put one of these in your window?' she says, peeling a sheet of printed paper from a stack she's carrying. 'And maybe one in your van?'

'What is it?'

She hands me a poster she's had printed up with a smiling picture of Olivia above an appeal for information about her whereabouts.

'I just wanted to do something to help, you know?' Hanna says. 'I feel so helpless, don't you?'

It's a touching gesture. I wish I'd thought about doing something similar and now I feel bad that I've not done more. At least I'm taking care of Hank, which is something, I suppose.

'Yes, totally.'

'Did you hear they ran a short piece on the local radio at lunchtime and the local paper has an article on its website?' Hanna says.

'No, I didn't, but that's good.'

'And I thought as a show of solidarity, I'd organise a vigil tonight around the Angel.'

The developers installed the bizarre stone sculpture in the centre of the estate when they finished the first phase of work. Obviously, it's supposed to be an angel, but it doesn't look much like one. It's a smooth lump of rock with what looks like two arms outstretched and no facial features, giving it a weirdly androgynous look. I've no idea what they were thinking when they came up with the idea, whether it was supposed to be a pretentious piece of installation art or a focal point for the community. No one really knows.

'Tonight?'

'Yes, I thought it might be nice if we all came together, said a few prayers and lit a few candles to let Jerome and Faith know we're thinking about them. You and Rory will come, won't you?'

She's caught me totally by surprise. It sounds like an awful idea, but I can't think of an excuse quickly enough. It's not that I object to Hanna organising something, but I can't see what use it serves. We'd be better off doing something practical, like convening a search party.

And then I remember the cardigan I found in her cupboard under the stairs, which I'm convinced is Olivia's. Is she doing this out of guilt? Is this her way of diverting attention from something she's done?

No, that's crazy. Hanna's too... nice.

'Yes, of course,' I say. 'We'll be there. Do we need to bring anything?'

'Just yourselves. We're going to start at seven, but be there in plenty of time.'

'That's very thoughtful, Hanna.' Biscuit nudges past my knee to see who's at the door. Hanna ruffles her head and Biscuit whimpers.

'Well, we have to stick together in times of trouble, don't we?'

'Do you want to take Bertie while you're here?' I ask.

'Oh, yes, I might as well, I suppose,' she says as if the thought hasn't occurred to her.

'Come in and I'll fetch him for you.'

I leave Hanna in the hall while I retrieve Bertie, who's curled up asleep on one of the dog beds in the lounge, tired out after his afternoon walk.

'I heard the police had teams searching the building site today,' Hanna says when I return. She points in the direction of the construction work going on behind the narrow strip of woodland at the rear of our house. 'And they've been scouring Clover Wood.'

'Yes, I've seen them. They're certainly being thorough.'

'And if Olivia's still...' Hanna lowers her head and scratches at the ground with her foot. She takes Bertie from me and clips his lead to his collar.

She can't bring herself to say the word. But it's what we're all thinking. None of us wants to imagine the worst, but we have to face the possibility something awful has happened to Olivia and she might not be alive.

'I'm sure they'll find her soon,' I say.

'Let's pray they do.'

It's what we're all hoping, me probably more than anyone else, because if Olivia's found, Leo will be off the hook.

Chapter 22

I'm surprised by the number of people who've turned out, especially on such a cold evening, but I suppose they want to show they care. We're all huddled up in thick coats and scarves against a biting north-easterly wind that's picked up. Most people have brought candles in jam jars at Hanna's request and stand in quiet contemplation against a low background murmur of polite and respectful conversation. I recognise most of the faces of our neighbours, even if I've not been introduced to all of them yet.

'What's the point of this again?' Rory hisses in my ear.

'To show support for Jerome and Faith,' I say out of the side of my mouth.

At least he's made it home on time tonight. Actually, he was earlier than usual, although it's probably because he's still feeling hungover and left work at five on the dot. He wasn't too happy when I dragged him straight out of the door before he'd barely stepped inside, but I promised Hanna we'd be here and I don't want anyone talking about us behind our backs, making disparaging comments about how we don't care.

At the stroke of seven, Hanna steps forwards with a grim smile.

'We've gathered here tonight, each of us holding a candle as a small but powerful beacon of hope in the darkness.' She speaks with a warm authority without the use of notes.

Flames flicker, illuminating hands and faces as everyone gathers closer in a tight semi-circle around the Angel to listen to Hanna's words.

'The disappearance of Olivia Hunter, a vibrant and cherished seventeen-year-old girl with a beautiful smile and a passion for life, has left a void in our hearts. She is not only Jerome and Faith's daughter, she is a part of our community and our extended family. Her absence is deeply felt by each one of us here tonight. And as we stand here this evening, let each flame be a reminder of the light Olivia has brought into our lives and let it symbolise our collective resolve to keep the light of hope burning, and that she will soon be returned safe and well to her family.'

It's a surprisingly moving speech. A lump swells in my throat and tears moisten my eyes. Rory reaches for my hand and squeezes it. I'm glad he could make it. I'd have hated to have been here on my own. Biscuit whimpers and lays down on my foot, the warmth of her body seeping through my boot.

'Let us take a moment to pray.' Hanna bows her head.

I'm not religious in the slightest, but it's a nice thing to do, and I lower my head out of respect.

Rory clears his throat and shuffles his feet. He's worse than me when it comes to religion. He screws his nose up in disgust at anything vaguely spiritual. In all the years I've known him, he's never once stepped inside a church, even for weddings or christenings.

'Oh, please, seriously,' he mutters under his breath.

I dig my elbow into his ribs. There's no need to be rude.

As Hanna wraps up, she invites everyone to place their candles at the base of the Angel where she's put a lovely framed photograph of Olivia. We all shuffle forwards, politely taking our turns.

After placing my jar on the ground and returning to find Rory, who's refused point blank to carry his own candle, I spot Jerome and Faith loitering at the edge of the gathering, clinging to each other. They must have come out during the vigil, not wanting to be the focus of attention. You can see how much they're suffering, their faces crumpled with grief and pain. They're usually the life and soul of any gathering on the estate, but tonight they're nothing more than shadowy figures hanging around on the periphery, like unwanted guests at a party.

I should say something. Offer my support and love. That's what a decent neighbour would do, but I'm not sure how welcome my approach would be. Clearly, Jerome suspects Leo knows more than he's letting on about Olivia, and I don't want to antagonise them or cause them any more suffering.

Thankfully, I'm saved from having to make that decision when Kwame and Zahara approach us.

Zahara presents two air kisses on either side of my head and the men shake hands.

'Isn't it awful?' Zahara says. She's wrapped in a beautiful, thick woollen shawl that covers her arms and hangs down over her waist. She looks as stunning as ever. Her skin blemish-free, her eyebrows perfectly shaped and thick, lustrous lashes frame soulful, grey eyes.

'I know. It's hard to get your head around, isn't it?' We take a step away from the crowd to talk.

'The town is absolutely crawling with police, but I don't think they have the first idea what's happened to her,' Zahara says.

'At least they're looking.'

'How are the boys settling in now?' Kwame asks. 'It must have been a big upheaval for them, especially starting a new school.'

Rory and I share a brief glance.

'Fine,' I say too quickly. 'They're settling in really well.'

'That's good. It can be tough for teenagers having to cope with such a big change.'

'And I guess Leo must be upset. He's friendly with Olivia, isn't he?' Zahara asks.

'Yeah, he is,' I agree. 'She's really looked out for him since we arrived.'

'Are the boys not here tonight?' Kwame looks around as if Leo and Casper might be loitering close by.

'No, they both have assignments that need to be in tomorrow,' I lie with a forced smile. I don't want to admit that I've not seen Leo since he stormed out earlier and Casper really didn't want to come, so I let him off the hook. 'Of course, they would have been otherwise.'

Rory grabs Kwame by the arm and leads him to one side to talk music. Ever since he found out that Kwame was a sound engineer, he's been falling over himself to impress him with his knowledge of these obscure bands he's been listening to. Honestly, it's like living with a third teenager sometimes.

'What do you think's happened to her?' Zahara asks, moving in closer and lowering her voice.

'I don't know. I thought perhaps she'd gone off with a friend and forgotten to let her parents know, but it's been two days now.'

'It doesn't look good, does it? What do they say, after the first forty-eight hours, the chances of finding someone alive drop to virtually zero.' Zahara shakes her head sadly.

'Oh god, don't say that.'

'You'd think someone must have seen something.'

'I know. How can someone just disappear without a trace?'

'It's freaky.' Zahara frowns. 'Did I hear Leo was with her just before she vanished?'

'No,' I say firmly. 'I don't think so.'

'Oh, I thought one of her friends had seen the two of them together? I wondered if she'd said anything to him.'

'Mistaken identity. Leo was with me, helping with the dogs.' I hate spreading the lie, but I can't have people speculating about Leo, although they've obviously been talking.

'You know what I heard?' Zahara lays a hand on my arm and glances around to make sure no one else is listening. 'I heard she was seeing an older man.'

My hand flies to my mouth. 'Seriously? Where did you hear that?'

'I can't remember now. Someone round here told me. Anyway, that's where I would focus my investigation if I were the police.'

'How much older?'

'Like in their thirties. Someone who really ought to know better. I mean, she's only sixteen, isn't she?'

'Seventeen.' I glance around at the crowd and the little pockets of our neighbours standing chatting. 'Do you think it could be someone from the estate?'

The fact is, it could be anyone, if it's true. Maybe that would explain why I found Olivia's cardigan at Fergal's house. What if it was Fergal she's been seeing? What a shocking thought. But then, didn't Zahara say that Olivia often popped in to see Kwame and that she thought Olivia was infatuated with him? No, that's not the word she used. Starstruck, she said. Same thing, isn't it? Maybe he took advantage, although why Kwame would choose to have an affair with a seventeen-year-old girl when he's married to someone as stunning as Zahara is beyond me.

'Maybe,' Zahara says, looking around the crowd. 'So who's not here and who's acting suspiciously?' she asks, like she's Miss Marple.

But the only person I can think of who's not here, apart from Casper, is Leo. I've tried calling, but he's switched his phone off again and I've no idea where he is. I'm sure he'll come home eventually, when he's calmed down a bit. And then maybe Rory can have that chat with him.

'Hello, everyone. Can I have your attention for a minute?' Everyone stops talking and looks up as Jerome steps out of the shadows.

Hanna rushes to his side. 'Don't feel you have to say anything. We just wanted to show you we're thinking of you in our prayers.'

He takes her hand in both of his and smiles through sad eyes. 'That's very kind of you, Hanna. I just wanted to say how thankful we are to you all for your support during this difficult period.'

It's horrible to see him so distraught, and so brave of him to stand up and talk in front of a crowd.

Conscious that everyone's now staring in his direction, I glance away, looking up the street towards our house. Unexpected movement catches my eye. A figure stalking along the pavement in the shadows, head down, moving silently.

'Please keep looking and praying,' Jerome continues as I squint into the gloom. 'And thank you all again for your kindness.'

The figure heads towards our house and darts into the garden, disappearing from view.

'I'm sorry, I've got to go,' I say to Zahara. 'I really need to get home. Something's just come up.'

Chapter 23

'Sabine, where are you going?' Rory shouts after me as I hurry towards the house with Biscuit at my feet.

Everyone's probably wondering what the hell's going on, but I don't care. I'm not letting Leo sneak back into the house without an explanation about where he's been all day.

His shoes have been kicked off and abandoned haphazardly in the hall. A door upstairs slams shut.

'Leo? We need to talk.'

I'm not having him speaking to me the way he did earlier and thinking he can treat this house as a hotel, swanning in and out whenever he feels like it.

'What's going on? Why did you run off like that?' Rory asks, panting, as he catches up with me in the hall.

I let Biscuit off her lead and she skulks off into her bed under the stairs, sensing trouble brewing.

'Your son,' I fume. 'I'm not having any more of his nonsense. You need to talk to him. Tonight.'

'What's he done now?'

I've not had the chance to bring Rory up to date on Leo's outburst earlier. Or how he stormed out of the house when I told him he was grounded.

'Apart from skipping school? Getting into fights and speaking to me like I'm dirt on his shoe, you mean?'

'Okay, let's take this down a notch, shall we?'

'You should have heard the way he spoke to me earlier. I told him he was grounded, and he stormed out. I can't take much more of it, Rory.'

'Alright, let me talk to him.'

'Now?'

'Yes.'

Finally. It's all I've wanted.

Although, the way Rory trudges wearily up the stairs, it's clear he's only doing it to pacify me.

I should leave him to it. Let them have a chat, man to man. But I can't. I want to hear what Leo has to say for himself, and perhaps if Leo sees we're a united front, it'll make him realise his behaviour is totally unacceptable.

'Mum? Dad?' Casper sticks his head out of his bedroom door. 'What's going on? What's all the shouting about?'

'Nothing. Go back into your room and finish your homework,' Rory says.

'I've finished it already.'

'Then find a book to read,' Rory snaps.

'A book? Yeah, right.' Casper disappears back into his room.

Rory hesitates on the landing and I almost bump into him.

'What are you doing?' he hisses when he realises I'm right behind him. 'I thought you wanted *me* to have a chat with him?'

'I thought it would be better if we spoke to him together. Go on, knock.'

Rory sighs, rolls his eyes and then taps on Leo's door.

'What?' Leo grunts.

Rory lets himself in and we stand side by side. Leo's slumped on his bed, his head propped up on his pillows. He looks tired. There are puffy black bags under his eyes and his skin is grey. Wisps of pubescent stubble are growing unevenly from his chin. I really hope he's not back on the drugs. I trusted him when he said he wouldn't touch them again, but maybe we should start testing him, to be sure.

'Can we have a word?' Rory asks.

Leo shrugs, his face taut and sulky.

'Your mother and I are worried about you. You don't seem very happy at the moment.'

'I'm fine.'

'Are you? You don't seem fine. Why weren't you at school today?'

'Didn't feel like it.'

Rory glances at me. 'I don't care whether or not you feel like it. You have to go to school. It's not an option,' he says.

'I hate it there. The teachers are all useless and all the other kids are idiots.'

'I'm sure that's not true.' Rory leans casually against the doorframe with his hands in his pockets, like he's having a chat with a mate.

'What would you know? You're never here.'

'Don't speak to your father like that.' I can't help myself. Leo never used to talk to us like this.

Rory holds up a hand to quieten me. 'Where were you tonight?'

'Out.'

'Out where?'

'I dunno. Seeing a friend.'

'What friend?'

'You wouldn't know him.'

'Try me.'

'I said you don't know him.'

'Well, what's his name?'

'Donald Duck.'

Rory breathes in slowly and lets it out through his nose.

'Leo, please,' I say. 'We're on your side.'

'Yeah?' He arches his eyebrows in disbelief.

'Yes, believe it or not, we are. I want the truth. Do you know what's happened to Olivia?' I ask.

'No!'

'Are you sure? Because you've been acting strangely ever since she went missing.'

'You still think I killed her, don't you?'

'Don't be so stupid, Leo. But I think you might know something you're not telling us.'

'Well, I don't.'

Rory pushes himself off the doorframe and crosses his arms. 'If you're in some kind of trouble, you need to let us know.'

'I'm not.'

'But you were with Olivia on the day she went missing?' I press. 'You can't deny it because I saw you. What were you arguing with her about?'

Leo picks up his phone and begins stabbing at the screen, deliberately ignoring me.

'Leo!' I yell, my blood pressure rising. 'Put that damned phone down and talk to us.'

'Why?' he screams, throwing the phone across the room in a fit of temper. It bounces off a wall with a thud and lands on his desk. 'You've already made your minds up. You think I did something to Olivia, and it doesn't matter what I say. You don't believe a word I tell you. Okay, fine. I was with her and I attacked her with a knife. I didn't mean to kill her, but I panicked. And then I buried her body in the woods. There, you happy now?'

Rory and I are stunned into silence.

'Leo,' I gasp after a few moments. 'Don't say that.'

'Why not? It's what you think's happened.'

'Come on, we just want the truth.' Rory runs a hand over his beard.

'You wouldn't believe the truth!' he screams.

'What's that supposed to mean?' I ask.

'It doesn't matter.'

'If there's something you need to tell us, it's best we find out now.'

'Can you just leave me alone? Please?'

'Not until we sort this out. We want to know where you've been all day, when you should have been at school, and where you were this evening.' I put my hands on my hips and plant my feet firmly on the floor. I'm not leaving until I have some answers.

'Why are you always on my back?'

'Why do you think, Leo?'

'I made one mistake and you keep on holding it against me,' he says.

'One mistake? A girl died, in case you've forgotten. She was fifteen years old. You gave her drugs and she jumped off a bridge.'

'And how many times do I have to say I'm sorry?' He drags his arm across his face, wiping away a tear that's trickled down his cheek.

'Your mum was wondering if you might need some help. You know, whether it might help if you saw a professional.'

'What do you mean?'

'Well, maybe a counsellor or a therapist,' Rory says. 'Someone who could help you process your feelings.'

'I'm not mental. I don't need therapy.'

'There's nothing to be embarrassed about,' I say. 'Lots of people have therapy to help them deal with trauma. We just think it might be a good idea to help you come to terms with what happened.'

'No,' he says firmly. 'I don't need help.'

'Are you taking drugs again?' I ask.

'No.'

'Are you sure?'

'I just said no, didn't I?'

'Alright, calm down. Because if I suspect you're using again, you'll leave us no choice but to start testing you.'

'*Using*? You make it sound like I'm a junkie or something. I'm not on drugs and I don't need help. I just need you both to get off my back for five minutes,' Leo shouts.

Rory glances at me and shrugs.

'It's only because we care.' I lower my voice and moderate my tone. I'll try anything right now to get through to him.

'Yeah, right. Whatever. Can you just go now?'

'I want you at school tomorrow,' I tell him. 'And no more reports about your behaviour, got it? Get your assignments in on time. Stop being disruptive in class, and if I find out you've been fighting again, I'll get you signed up to the local boxing club. How do you fancy that?'

'Have you finished?' Leo says, shooting me a look of pure disdain.

'Last warning,' I say. 'You're skating on very thin ice.'

Chapter 24

Jerome stirs, stretching out his legs. His foot knocks over a bottle that skittles to the floor and rolls across the carpet. His neck is stiff and his skin cold. He pulls a thin blanket over his shoulders and groans, wondering why he's not in bed. He must have fallen asleep on the sofa and Faith draped the blanket over him. His head is thumping and his mouth is sticky and dry, the smokiness of whisky clawing at the back of his throat.

And then it hits him all over again, like he's standing under a rockfall of heavy boulders. His precious little girl is missing and hasn't been home for three nights now.

Sleep and alcohol bring a temporary respite from the pain, but every time he wakes or sobers up, the memory floods back and the agony sinks its teeth in deeper.

They've contacted all her friends, spoken to all the hospitals, repeatedly tried her phone, but it's as if Olivia has vanished in a puff of smoke. No one's seen her or heard from her in days. The police keep assuring them they're doing everything they can, but why haven't they found her yet? They don't have a clue. And how long before they lose interest and he and Faith are left to deal with this alone?

He tries not to think the worst, but it's hard. She can't just have vanished. Someone must have taken her. So where is she? And what are they doing to her? If they've hurt her, Jerome swears he'll find them and he will kill them. He'll make it a long, drawn-out death and he'll enjoy every second.

'You're awake then?' Faith shuffles into the room in her pyjamas and dressing gown, although it doesn't look as though she's slept much.

She picks up the half-empty bottle of whisky Jerome kicked over and sets it upright on the table next to his empty glass. He's pretty sure the bottle was full when he started on it in the hollow hours of the night.

'I need to get up,' he says, throwing off the blanket and sitting too quickly. His head swims and for a moment he thinks he's going to be sick.

Faith slumps in the armchair by the TV, her gaze vacant and unfocused. 'Do you want me to make you some breakfast?' she asks, her voice devoid of tone or emotion.

'No, I'll just grab a quick shower and get going.'

'Where?'

'Where do you think?' he snaps, running a hand through his thinning hair. 'I'm going out to look for her.'

'You shouldn't. The police said we should stay here in case she calls.'

He stares at his wife with disgust. 'She's not going to call,' he growls. 'They just want us out of the way.'

'You should stay.'

Jerome sighs. He has to do something. He can't sit around waiting for news. Doing nothing. Hoping for a miracle. At least if he's out there, he's doing something positive and practical. He's always been a practical man. Good with his hands. He was never so great at school, but he's done okay. He runs his own business, lives in a big, fancy house, and has the kind of comfortable life he could only have once imagined.

He never dared to dream he'd be living in a modern house like this on a brand-new estate. It has five bedrooms, three en suites and a double garage. Not bad for a self-made electrician. He just wishes the neighbours weren't so snooty. They look down on him because he doesn't have an important job in an office or wear a suit to work. But he's every bit as good as them.

'It would be nice if our useless neighbours did something to help,' he moans. 'Never mind holding a bloody candlelit vigil. How's that going to find Olivia?'

'They just wanted to show their support.'

'They could show their support by getting off their arses and looking for her,' he says. The more eyes out there searching, the better chance they have of finding her.

She can't have vanished. Someone must have seen or heard something.

'Don't be so tetchy, Jerome,' his wife says.

All he wants is for his little girl to come home. Is that too much to ask?

'Did you see the Sugars last night, pretending like they cared? That woman, Sabine, looking all tearful and glum, like she gave a shit? And where was that boy of theirs? I notice he didn't turn up.'

'Jerome, don't.'

'They lied to the police, Faith. We know they did. You heard Daisy. She was adamant she saw Olivia with that boy on Monday afternoon. So why did Sabine tell the police he was with her? If I find out he's laid a finger on my little girl, I swear I'll tear his fucking head off.'

'Jerome, stop it. Don't say things like that.'

'Why not? It's true. I don't trust them. They're hiding something. And then to have the nerve to turn up last night, it makes me sick.'

Faith's chin falls onto her chest and she sobs. She's been crying a lot the last few days. Jerome would like to cry as freely as Faith seems to be able, to let out all the hurt and the pain, but he can't. He feels numb. And angry. And frustrated. But he can't cry, because real men don't.

'We don't know anything about them, do we?' he says.

'Who?'

'The Sugars. They're an odd family, don't you think? Her husband, what's he called?'

'Rory.'

'Yeah, Rory, that's right. He's weird. What's with that stupid beard and those poncy shirts? Like he's a fucking dandy or something.'

'He's a designer,' Faith says. 'I think they tend to be flamboyant like that.'

'It's odd if you ask me.'

Faith sighs. 'Sabine's nice.'

'Mmmm.'

'What's that supposed to mean?'

'I don't trust her either.'

'Hank likes her.'

Jerome stares at his wife. 'Hank's a fucking dog. He likes anyone who feeds him or scratches him behind his ear. Have you seen her, always poking her nose around other people's houses? You know she has the keys to half a dozen houses round here?'

'So she can collect the dogs.'

'Right,' he says, 'but I bet she has a good nose around while she's there, don't you? I bet she's been through all our cupboards and drawers. Nosey cow.'

'Jerome, stop it. Please.'

'And as for those kids...'

'I think Olivia's fond of Leo,' Faith says, wiping her eyes with a tissue she plucks from a box on the side.

'Well, I don't like him. I've no idea what she sees in him. And why did he lie about being with her on Monday, unless he's got something to hide?'

'You don't know he lied. Daisy could have been mistaken.'

Jerome shakes his head. No, he has a feeling about that family. Where have they come from, anyway? When he asked them at the barbecue he put on for the neighbours at the end of the summer, they were both vague and evasive, like they didn't want to talk about it when he asked where they'd been living before.

'What do we really know about them?' Jerome asks.

'Who?'

'That family. The Sugars. There's something not right about them.'

Faith glances out of the window, staring across the street at Rory and Sabine's house. 'I think something must have happened to them before they moved here,' she says. 'Sabine mentioned something in passing. I think their move here was all sudden, but she wouldn't say why.'

It's the first Jerome's heard of it. Now his interest is piqued.

'Are you going to have that shower? The police will be here any minute,' Faith says.

Jerome groans. He hates the house being overrun with cops. He'd rather they were out looking for Olivia rather than being here with them, asking questions and making them endless cups of tea. Do they really need liaison officers here holding their hands?

'Where's your laptop?' he asks.

'I thought you were going out?'

'I am,' he says, 'but this is important. 'I want to see if there's anything about them online. Aren't you curious?'

'It's not really any of our business.'

'It is if they know what's happened to Liv.'

Faith gets up with an exaggerated sigh. She wraps her gown around her waist and trudges off, returning with the laptop she uses to run the business. Jerome snatches it out of her hands.

He switches it on, asks her to remind him of her log-on details, and opens a search engine.

It's nowhere near as difficult as he thought it would be to find out about the Sugars' recent history. In fact, there's heaps of it, more than he could have ever imagined, plastered all across several news sites and social media.

He skim reads post after post, hardly able to believe his eyes. It's no wonder they had to move and have tried to keep a low profile. He remembers hearing something on the news at the time about that girl falling to her death, but didn't think any more about it. He certainly didn't imagine the boy who killed her would end up living opposite and befriending his daughter.

'Faith,' he says, unable to tear his eyes away from the screen. 'I think you'd better look at this.'

'What is it?' she asks wearily.

'I know why the Sugars had to move.' Finally, he glances up. Faith's glaring at him, puzzled. 'It's their son. Liv's so-called friend.'

'What about him?'

Jerome runs a hand over his mouth, his stubble thick and coarse. 'They reckon he killed a girl.'

'What?' Faith splutters. 'Let me see.' She spins the laptop around.

'It's all there,' Jerome says, stunned. 'He killed a girl but got away with her murder. Can you believe they let him go scot-free?'

Faith shakes her head, eyes wide.

'And now he's living on our street, in the house across the road?' He looks at Faith and arches his eyebrows. 'I don't think it's any coincidence that Olivia's gone missing and I think Leo Sugar knows exactly where she is.'

Chapter 25

A light drizzle of rain starts to fall as I pull into our drive. At least I avoided it while I was out with the dogs. There's nothing worse than having five wet animals in the house, leaving mud smears all across the kitchen floor. Plus, there's the smell. Is there anything more nauseating than the smell of wet dog?

I kill the engine and peer up at the leaden skies. Hopefully, the rain will have passed by the time I need to take them out again later this afternoon. I hop out of the van, hurry around to the back, and throw open the doors. Five pairs of expectant eyes stare at me. Biscuit jumps to her feet and barks twice, as if telling me to hurry.

At least having the dogs has taken my mind off Leo. I'm not sure the chat we had with him last night had any impact at all. I keep hoping it's just a phase he's going through, like Rory said, and that in time he'll grow out of it. Temporary teenage angst.

I read about it last night. There are lots of reasons teenage behaviour takes a turn for the worse as they develop. Partly it's chemistry and a change in their hormones, and partly it's a desire for independence, which I guess makes sense.

Leo's nearly eighteen now and, as much as it pains me, I have to accept he'll soon be ready to fly the nest. He's not a little boy anymore, although it doesn't seem that long ago I was holding him for the first time, a helpless bundle of wrinkled, pink skin. I fell in love instantly and have enjoyed almost every minute of motherhood.

I suppose we're just going to have to learn to give him space and more freedom or we risk pushing him away forever. And hopefully, in time, he'll come back to us. I have to accept both boys are growing up. Life moves on and as much as I've fought to keep our family together, one day soon, they're both going to be gone, and it's going to be me and Rory on our own.

'Where's Leo?'

I spin around, startled by the voice, and come face to face with Jerome, his brow furrowed and his body tight with tension. His hands are balled into fists at his side.

'I beg your pardon.'

'You heard me, Sabine. Where's your son? I want a word.'

His tone takes me by surprise. I know he's going through hell right now, but there's no need to be so brusque. Hank barks, but Jerome ignores him, his attention entirely focused on me.

'He's at school.' At least I hope he is. He promised last night that he wouldn't skip any more lessons, although my trust in him and his word is running at an all-time low.

Jerome's breath is rank and his eyes bloodshot. He's probably been hitting the booze hard. Not that I'm judging. I think in his shoes I'd be self-medicating, too.

'What did you want to talk to him about?' I ask, my heart beating fast. There's something in Jerome's eyes that scares me.

'You lied for him. Why?'

'Excuse me?'

'Don't play dumb with me. Why did you tell the police Leo was with you on Monday afternoon? Are you protecting him?'

'Hang on a minute—' I splutter. He might be going through a hard time, but he can't talk to me like that, especially not on my own drive.

'What do you have to hide?' Spittle flies from his mouth and lands on my cheek.

'Nothing. Jerome, I—'

'Liar!'

'Please don't speak to me like that.'

'If you know anything about what's happened to my daughter, you'd better start talking.'

'Of course I don't.'

'If he's got my daughter involved in drugs,' he hisses, 'I'll kill him.'

'What?'

'I know why you came here. What you were running from.'

My heart's racing like a steam train now. What exactly does he think he knows? 'Seriously, I have no idea what you're talking about. If you'll excuse me, I need to get the dogs inside.'

I turn to tend to the animals, but Jerome grabs my arm roughly and spins me around.

I scream as his fingers dig into my bicep.

'If anything's happened to her and I find out Leo was involved—'

'I don't know what you think is going on but Leo has nothing to do with Olivia's disappearance,' I yell in his face with a courage that materialises from nowhere. 'I know you must be incredibly upset and frustrated, but please leave my family alone and stop making such ridiculous accusations.'

'If you're covering for him, that makes you just as guilty.'

'I'm not.'

'Really? So, tell me why you moved here, Sabine. I know all about Heather Malone.'

I'm sure my heart misses a couple of beats. He's been looking us up, prying into our lives. How dare he. 'I don't know what you're talking about.'

'Don't insult my intelligence,' he screams in my face, shoving me up against the van. 'He killed that girl and got clean away with it.'

'That's - that's not true,' I gasp.

'So why's it all over the internet? I know all the seedy details about what your filthy junkie son did to that poor girl.'

'He's not a junkie. And he didn't kill her. It was an accident. Leo didn't mean her any harm.' I'm shaking now. 'The police investigated and concluded it wasn't Leo's fault.'

'He supplied her with drugs though, didn't he?'

'Only because she begged him for them.'

'And that makes it alright?'

'No, of course it doesn't, but it's not his fault she died.'

Jerome sniffs, his lips curling into a nasty snarl. 'That's not what her parents think. Or a lot of other people who knew her. It's no wonder you wanted to hide. Did you think no one would discover your little secret here?'

'It's not like that.'

His hand shoots out and grabs me by the throat, forcing my head backwards. I gulp a breath of air and my lungs feel like they're going to burst.

'What's he done with my little girl?'

'I - I don't know,' I choke, struggling for breath as he lifts me clean off my feet. I hammer at his shoulders with my fists, but there's a wild, faraway look in his eyes.

'Let me make it clear. If I find out your boy has hurt my princess or had anything to do with her going missing, I'm going to rip his throat out. Understand?'

I try to nod and finally he releases his grip. I fall to the floor, clutching my neck, stunned that I've been physically attacked outside my home.

He jabs an angry finger in my direction as he backs away. 'Tell him I want Olivia back! Otherwise, there will be hell to pay.'

Chapter 26

I struggle to hold back my tears as I stagger into the house with the dogs. I slam the door and turn the key in the lock. Although I wouldn't normally bother locking the door during the day, I'm still shaking. I can't believe Jerome attacked me. Had me pinned up against the van by my throat. The man's insane.

I stumble to the stairs and collapse on the bottom step with my head in my hands, my tears flowing freely. Nobody's ever laid a hand on me like that before. And the look in Jerome's eye. It was like he wanted to kill me.

Moving here was supposed to be a reset, a place where people wouldn't judge us or hate us, but now it's as if we're back to square one. If Jerome knows about Leo's past, how long before it's around the estate like a wildfire out of control?

I wish Leo had never gone to that party. Hadn't been experimenting with drugs. Had never met Heather Malone. Then none of this would be happening. We'd have our lives back. Our dignity.

There was always a risk people would find out, but I never expected it so soon. I don't want the upheaval of moving and starting over yet again, although I doubt I could persuade Rory or the boys to agree to it, anyway. But the thought of staying here with everyone knowing about us is about as palatable as sticking my hand in a shark's mouth. We've been through it before. I know how it'll start. The staring. The curtain twitching. The finger pointing and people crossing the road to avoid us. And eventually, it'll escalate into vitriol and abuse. Maybe even attacks on our property and ourselves. Just look at how Jerome reacted. Do I really have the strength to go through it a second time?

Another thought hits me. A body blow that sets the adrenaline racing through my veins. How long before Jerome tells the police about Leo? The moment he does, I can guarantee they'll be back at the door with their suspicions levelled at my son. They'll think he's responsible for Olivia's disappearance, even though there's not a shred of evidence against him.

I have to let Rory know. I can't keep this to myself. It's too big. He hates me calling him at work, but it can't wait. I dry my tears and, with my hand still trembling, pull out my phone. But before I can make the call, there's a knock at the door.

I freeze, a chill running down my spine. Is it Jerome back to have another go at me?

I remain motionless, hoping he'll go away. I don't want to get the police involved, but if he continues to intimidate me, I'll have no choice.

Another knock.

'Who is it?' My voice wavers.

'Sabine? It's Hanna.'

My body slumps with relief. I drag myself to the door and after smoothing down my hair, unlock it and throw it open.

'I saw the van in the drive and wondered if you fancied a coffee?' She has a beaming smile across her face.

I'd rather be on my own to process what's just happened, but I'm so relieved that it's not Jerome back again that I find myself inviting her in.

'Are you okay?' she asks, peering at me with concern.

'Yeah, yeah, I'm fine.' It must be obvious I've been crying.

We wander into the kitchen and I fill up the kettle, surreptitiously wiping the tear tracks from my cheeks.

'What did you think about last night?' Hanna asks, climbing onto a stool at the breakfast bar. She looks at me expectantly.

'What?'

'The vigil?'

'Right. Yes, it was really moving,' I say. She's clearly come looking for praise. 'Well done again for organising it.'

'It was good to see so many people turn out, wasn't it? Especially as it was so cold last night.'

'I think everyone just wants to let Jerome and Faith know we're thinking about them.'

'I'm so worried about Olivia, aren't you? I keep thinking the worst.' She clasps her hands anxiously, her thumbs pressed together, knuckles white. 'You've heard the rumours, have you?'

'No. What?'

'Well, you've not heard this from me, but apparently Olivia was seeing an older man.'

'Oh, yeah, that,' I say, heaping spoonfuls of instant coffee into two mugs as the kettle comes to a boil.

'You knew?' Hanna looks crestfallen, like I've just given away the twist in the thriller she's reading.

'Zahara mentioned it last night.'

'I couldn't believe it. Shocking, isn't it?'

'If it's true.'

'You're right. I suppose we shouldn't be gossiping about something like that, but it makes you realise, doesn't it, how little you know about what's going on in other people's lives.'

Bertie, hearing Hanna's voice, rushes into the kitchen and cocks his head.

'Hello, buddy.' Hanna drops to the floor and beckons him over. 'Are you having a good day with Sabine?'

He yawns, then turns and ambles away again.

'Sorry,' I say, not sure why I'm apologising. It's not my fault he isn't pleased to see her. 'Are you not working today?'

'I'm snatching a few minutes of me time between meetings. I have a forty-minute gap until my next one, but I needed to get out of the house, otherwise all I do all day is stare at a screen.'

It's not something I have to worry about, but Rory's always complaining about the hours he spends at his computer and the strain it puts on his eyes.

'Did you get all your posters put up?' I've said it before I notice the poster Hanna gave me still lying on the side under a pile of opened post. I meant to put it in the window but clean forgot.

'All the neighbours have been so supportive,' Hanna says, 'but I'm going to pop into town later and see if some of the shops will display them, too. I could always do with a hand if you're not busy.'

'Can I get back to you?' I ask in a panic. The last thing I want to be doing is trawling around town handing out posters. I have more important things on my mind. 'It's a lovely photo you've used of her.'

Hanna looks pleased with my compliment. 'Faith sent it to me. It's one of their favourites. She looks so happy, don't you think?'

'Which makes it all so much more heartbreaking. I don't know her that well, but she seems like a lovely girl,' I say. 'And bright. I heard she's trying for Oxford.'

'Oh, incredibly bright, I'm told. Like you, we don't know her well, but you know, we see her around. And, of course, she was at the party in the summer. So chatty. She was asking me all about the business and I how I started it.'

I'm desperate to ask about Olivia's cardigan and how it found its way into their house, if she doesn't know her that well. But there's no way of asking without making it sound like an accusation. It would also mean admitting I'd been snooping around.

'Any idea who this mystery older man is?' I ask.

'I don't have a clue.'

'Maybe someone on the estate?' I suggest.

'No!' Hanna's eyes widen with shock. 'Do you really think so?'

'I don't know.' I'm not sure I believe the rumour. It sounds like salacious tittle-tattle to me, but it's a distraction from people talking about Leo. 'I wonder if Jerome and Faith have any idea.'

'God no! Can you imagine Jerome's reaction? He'd probably, how do you say, blow a basket or something.'

'A gasket.'

'What?'

'The expression is blow a gasket.'

'Okay.'

She's right though. All fathers are protective of their little girls, but I can't imagine Jerome tolerating his daughter seeing someone older, and having experienced his nasty temper first-hand, I'd hate to be in their shoes if he ever found out.

'I was surprised to find out Olivia's friendly with Kwame and Zahara,' I say.

'Is she?'

'Yeah, according to Zahara, she's taken a shine to Kwame, ever since she found out he works in the music industry.'

Hanna's eyebrows arch upwards.

'She told me Olivia was always dropping around to hang out at theirs,' I add.

'Oh, my god. You don't think...?'

'Olivia and Kwame? No. I don't think so.'

'But it could be—'

'Well, anything's possible, I suppose,' I say, a nibble of guilt gnawing at my gut. The poor girl's missing and I'm spreading gossip. It makes me no better than Anthony and Zac. I'm not proud of myself, but my priority has to be protecting Leo, and I'll do whatever it takes.

I can almost see the cogs turning in Hanna's head. I've sown a tiny seed of suspicion and now I need to let it germinate and grow. Not that I have anything against Kwame or Zahara. Nor do I really think Kwame would be so stupid as to get involved with Olivia. She's so young, after all. But I'm acting on a mother's instinct to protect her child, and that's one of the most powerful forces in nature.

Hanna glances at her watch. 'Oh damn, I didn't realise the time. I'd better get back. I have another call in five minutes.'

That's funny. I thought she said she had a forty-minute window between meetings.

'You've not had your coffee.' I push a mug across the counter.

'Another time, maybe? I'm sorry.' She hops down from her stool and scurries for the door, all in a fluster.

I wave politely as she hurries down the drive.

I have absolutely no doubt that the moment she's back at home, she'll be straight onto the phone with her latest titbit of gossip.

I smile to myself and close the door.

Chapter 27

Faith is waiting for Jerome when he walks back into the house. Maggie, their police liaison officer, has already turned up, but Faith's still not dressed.

'Well? What did she say?' Faith asks impatiently.

'What do you think? She's still lying, pretending Leo was with her on Monday when he was with Olivia all along.'

'Morning, Jerome.' Maggie appears from the kitchen. 'Would you like a tea?'

'No.'

'Faith?'

She shakes her head and lowers her gaze. 'Are you going to tell her?' she whispers.

Maggie cocks her head. 'Tell me what?'

Jerome stares at his wife. He *was* going to tell Maggie. In his own time. When he was ready. 'It's about Leo Sugar,' he says.

'What about him?'

'He lied to you. He *was* with Olivia on Monday afternoon.'

'Are you sure?'

Jerome pulls his phone from the back pocket of his jeans and finds one of the news articles about that girl who fell to her death from a bridge while high on LSD. He hands the phone over.

Maggie frowns as she reads. 'What's this?'

'That boy across the road was responsible for her death,' he says, but the police should be aware of this. Why's he having to spell it out to them? What have they been doing all this time?

Maggie shakes her head. 'I don't understand what this has to do with Leo.'

'Look up his name. It's all over social media. He supplied her with the drugs and should have been charged with murder but was let off with a caution. Why don't you know this?' he shouts.

'Okay, Jerome. Keep your voice down. I'm sure we're already across it.' She hands his phone back, takes out her own and stabs at the screen.

'You're sure, are you?' he grumbles.

'It doesn't mean he has anything to do with Olivia's disappearance.'

'So explain to me why his mother lied, unless she's trying to protect him. I know he has something to do with Olivia going missing. You need to arrest him and get him to tell you the truth. This is my daughter's life!'

'Alright, let me speak to someone in CID,' she says. 'Don't worry, we're leaving no stone unturned.' She smiles, but there's no warmth in it. He can tell she's anxious, that he's turned up something they don't know about and should have done. It's total incompetence. Utterly unforgivable.

Jerome watches Maggie scanning her phone, flicking through pages on the internet, the furrows on her brow deepening.

'Would you excuse me for a minute?' she says and disappears into the kitchen.

A moment later, Jerome hears her on the phone, although her voice is low, barely audible. She's calling it in to her superiors. It's a scandal. Leo Sugar should be in a police cell by now, the detectives putting the squeeze on him.

'Are you okay?' Faith asks.

'Not really.'

'Why doesn't he just tell us the truth?' Faith wails.

When this nightmare started, he and Faith took comfort in each other. They held each other. Cried together. Supported each other. But now Jerome's just angry. It's gone on long enough. It's been three days since they've seen Olivia, and every passing minute is another torment. He feels so helpless. So lost. So numb.

Faith reaches out to him, but he brushes past her, heading for the stairs. He's not been in Olivia's room since she vanished. It's been too painful, but now he needs to be in there, the only way he can be close to her again, until she's found.

He wraps his hand around the handle of the door, and as he always does, hesitates a moment before silently pushing it open.

The bed, with its fairy lights that coil around the headboard, has been left unmade. Clothes are strewn across the floor. Make-up bottles and tubes left uncapped. Her desk is covered in school textbooks and papers, her laptop closed.

A peace lily wilting. A string of Polaroid photos of teenage girls pulling silly faces strung across the wall.

It's as if she's popped out and will be back at any moment.

A surge of emotion swamps Jerome. In here, her cheap perfume and hairspray linger on the curtains and the carpet. His legs are weak and his chest tight. If anything's happened to her, he doesn't know how he'll cope. Life won't be worth living. She's his everything.

He collapses on the bed, the springs of the mattress creaking, and hangs his head in his hands. The thought she may never come home kills him. She's his princess. His reason for living. A daddy's girl who only had to flutter her eyelashes and Jerome would be there to do her bidding. From the day she was born, he made a solemn vow to himself that she would never want for anything and that he would always protect her from the evils of the world.

But he's failed.

He topples sideways, burying his face in her pillow, inhaling the intoxicating scent of her hair. He curls up into a ball, his legs pulled up to his chest, and lets his tears soak into her bedclothes.

His fingers tease out the pyjamas under the pillow. A pink rabbit-print cotton vest top and shorts. He grasps them tightly and pulls them to his face, the cotton cool against his skin.

The door swings open.

'Jerome?'

He startles. 'What is it?' he snaps, angry at the interruption.

'What are you doing in here?'

He slides Olivia's pyjamas back under her pillow, sits up, and wipes away his tears. 'Nothing.'

'Moping about in her room's not going to bring her back, is it?' Faith says.

No, but it helps him feel close to her. 'I'm going out,' he announces, standing suddenly. He knows what he has to do now.

'Where?'

'I'm going to find her.'

He's said it before, but this time he means it, and he knows exactly how he's going to do it.

Chapter 28

Leo strides purposefully out of the school gates, glad to see the back of another day. He wasn't kidding when he told his parents he hates it. It's an awful school. The teachers are all arseholes and the students are no better. The day he walks out of here for the last time can't come quickly enough.

He almost didn't come today, but his mother would have killed him. She was furious he skipped school yesterday. Two days in a row would have been pushing his luck.

He doesn't mean to upset her, but she really has an irritating way about her. He can't even explain it. It's just something about the way she talks to him like he's a child that gets under his skin and makes him mad. He can feel the irritation building before she's even opened her mouth.

It doesn't help that she's always on his back. Always going on at him about Heather's death, like it doesn't haunt him enough. Is she ever going to drop it? If he'd known it was going to be like this, he'd have handled things differently. Made a different choice, but it is what it is, and now he has bigger worries on his mind.

He adjusts one of his earbuds and turns up the volume, getting lost in the music. It's his escape, where he can lose himself and find solace while everything around him is falling apart.

Some of Olivia's friends have gathered at the end of the street, but by the time he notices, it's too late to cross the road without making it obvious. He puts his head down and marches on, avoiding eye contact with them. Silly little girls with their fake eyelashes and stupid pouts. Can't they see how ridiculous they look? What does Olivia see in them? Every one of them vacuous and vain. She's far smarter, and prettier, than any of them.

One of them sticks out a foot and tries to trip him as he passes, but he sidesteps and carries on walking, pretending it didn't happen. He won't give them the satisfaction of reacting.

They've never liked him. They've never even given him a chance. From his first day, they made that clear. It must drive them mad that he and Olivia are friends.

'Weirdo.'

'Freak.'

He hears their taunts over his music and pretends he doesn't. It's just names. They're trying to bait him, but he's not going to waste his energy. He has plenty of other things on his mind, like why his mother lied to the police for him. Is he supposed to be grateful or something? He's old enough to fight his own battles without his mother thinking she has to protect him all the time. He's sick of it.

He's surprised the police haven't been back. They must have checked her story and discovered it wasn't true by now. There are so many CCTV cameras all over the place, it's like living in a police state. They're bound to discover the truth eventually. He saw a YouTube video the other day about how people are captured on cameras up to seventy times a day in some cities. It's obscene when you think about it.

It's a forty-minute walk home, but Leo doesn't mind. It gives him time to think and to plan. It also helps with his anger. He's always so angry these days. About everything. His parents. His brother. School. His teachers. The injustices of the world. His helplessness to do anything meaningful about it.

At first, he doesn't notice the van slowing to a crawl alongside him, until a window winds down and a voice from inside calls out.

'Hey, Leo.'

He stops and bends down to peer inside, removing an earbud from one ear.

'Oh, hey, Mr Hunter.' Leo's palms are clammy and his heart thuds loudly against his ribs.

'You walking home?'

Leo nods. 'Yeah.'

'Want a lift?'

'No, that's fine. Thanks anyway,' Leo says. The last thing he wants is to spend time with Olivia's father.

'Come on, get in. I'm going that way and it looks as though it's going to rain.'

Leo looks up to the sky, shrouded in light-grey cloud. It doesn't look as if it's going to rain.

'Really, I'm happy walking.' He smiles and pops his earbud back in.

'Leo, I'm not going to ask you again. Get in the van,' Jerome says, raising his voice. It sounds more like an order than a request.

Leo looks up and down the street, uncertain. He doesn't want to cause a scene. 'If you're sure?' he says.

'Just get in, will you?'

Jerome clears off a clipboard stuffed with paperwork from the passenger seat and clicks open the door.

Reluctantly, Leo climbs in and pulls on his belt.

'How was school?' Jerome asks. His tone's turned pleasant again. Friendly even as he pulls away, accelerating aggressively.

'Yeah, fine. Thanks.'

'What did you have on today?'

Leo casts a sideways glance at Jerome. This is worse than being interrogated by his own parents. Why does he care?

'English, history and a couple of free periods this afternoon.'

'And are you hoping to go to university like Olivia?'

This is definitely weird. He's acting like Olivia isn't even missing.

'Maybe. I'm not sure.' Leo keeps his eyes on the road ahead, bracing himself as Jerome drives far too fast.

'Olivia's hoping she'll get a place at Oxford.'

'I'm sure she will. She's really clever.'

'Will she?' There's an edge to Jerome's voice suddenly. A coldness that wasn't there a moment ago.

Leo's stomach tightens. Something's wrong. 'Can I get out now? I'll walk the rest of the way, thanks,' he says. They're approaching a set of traffic lights and as Jerome slows down, Leo contemplates jumping out and making a run for it.

'Sit where you are,' Jerome orders.

'But—'

'I said sit,' Jerome yells. 'Now, tell me where she is.'

'Where who is?'

'Don't play games with me, sunshine. Where's Olivia?'

Leo's mouth is dry. 'I don't know,' he mumbles.

Jerome takes a deep breath, as if he's trying to calm himself. 'I'll ask you one more time. Where is she?'

The lights ahead turn from red to green and Jerome accelerates, pressing Leo's spine into his seat.

'I - I don't know. I promise I don't know anything,' Leo stammers as an icy chill runs through his body.

'Don't lie to me! I know you were with her on Monday. Where were you going? What were you arguing about?'

'Nothing. I saw her at school, but not after that.'

Jerome hits the brakes so violently, Leo is catapulted out of his seat and only saved from going straight through the windscreen by his seatbelt that locks across his collarbone and sends his head whiplashing onto his chest. Behind them, a car blasts its horn.

Jerome grabs Leo by the collar, twisting a handful of hoodie and T-shirt in his meaty hand. He puts his face right up to Leo's and stares him in the eye.

'What have you done to her? Where is she?' he screams.

Leo can't move. He can't speak.

Jerome raises his fist as if he's going to punch Leo in the face. Leo flinches.

'I know all about Heather Malone.' Jerome grits his teeth and a vein on his forehead pulses furiously.

'W - who?'

'Don't play smart with me.' Jerome jerks his fist towards Leo's face but pulls up short.

Leo trembles. He wants to get out. The man's insane.

'You sold her drugs and let her fall from a bridge to her death,' Jerome snarls. 'You killed her!'

'No!' Leo protests. 'It's not like that.'

'Is that what happened to Olivia? Have you been giving her drugs?'

'No, of course not.'

'Then where is she?'

Cars pull out around Jerome's van, blaring their horns and shooting him filthy looks.

'I don't know.'

'You're lying!'

'I'm not. I promise.'

Jerome narrows his bloodshot eyes. There's a sourness on his breath and his jaw is tight. For a moment, Leo thinks he might kill him here and now. He certainly looks as if he wants to.

But then he releases Leo's collar and shoves him back into his seat. Leo takes a deep breath.

'Let's go for a little drive and a chat, shall we?' Jerome says, putting the van in gear. He glances over his shoulder and pulls away violently. 'And see if we can jog your memory.'

Chapter 29

Rory attaches the designs for the social media posts he's been working on for a new fundraising campaign to an email and hits send. He hopes the marketing team won't come back with too many changes, although there's always something.

Can you change the font?
Can you make the image bigger?
Can you alter the colour of the lettering?

Everyone's a design expert in this place. Well, if they're such experts, maybe they'd like to do it themselves next time and see how that goes. He didn't spend three years at art college for nothing.

He leans back and stretches his arms above his head, yawning. Toni glances up from her computer. She's been so engrossed in what she's doing, it's the first time she's looked up in the last couple of hours.

'Finished?' she asks.

'Until the marketing team decide to tear it apart and send it back in pieces.' He laughs, but it's not funny. Maybe it's time for a change. A new job. A new challenge.

'That girl you were telling me about who's missing, she's from around your neck of the woods, isn't she? I read about it this morning.'

Rory sighs. He knew she wasn't really listening when he unburdened himself in the pub, but now news of Olivia Hunter's disappearance has finally been picked up by one of the national newspapers and it's caught her attention. They didn't have anything new to report, but they've used Olivia's photo, the one the local press has been showing for a few days, and a quote from her father, Jerome, appealing for information. The police still don't have any idea what's happened to her, but stories about young girls who go missing, especially ones as pretty as Olivia, from good homes and privileged backgrounds, don't tend to end well, do they?

'Actually, she's one of our neighbours,' he says. He's already told her this.

Toni's mouth drops open. 'No, seriously? You know her?'

Rory shakes his head. 'Sort of. She lives opposite, but yeah, apparently she left school on Monday and nobody's seen her since.'

No need to mention that his son might have been with her in the woods in the hours before she vanished and that they'd been seen arguing, that Sabine herself might have seen Leo with a knife, struggling with her.

'Her parents must be worried sick,' Toni says with a look of genuine horror.

'You should have seen it last night. The neighbours organised a vigil when I got home,' Rory says. 'But it was all a bit cringe, like she was already dead. Everyone had to carry candles and one of our other neighbours made a sickly speech.' He pokes his fingers into his mouth as if he's making himself sick. 'Honestly, I could have crawled up and died. I mean, it's not like that's going to do anything to bring her back, is it?'

'I think it's a nice thing for the community to do.'

'Well, I thought it was all a bit odd.'

'You must know her parents, then?'

'Jerome and Faith? Yeah, although not well. Olivia's friendly with our eldest, Leo.' The words slip out before he can stop himself.

'Wow. I guess you've had front row seats to whole thing.'

Rory shrugs. He doesn't want to talk about it. He comes to work to get away from it all.

He glances at the clock in the corner of his monitor. It's almost five. Hardly worth starting on a new project so late in the day when he's tired, but the thought of heading home early fills him with dread.

'So, Mr Party Animal, are you joining us for drinks again tonight?'

'Where are you going?'

'The usual.'

He hasn't been asked to join the design team's Thursday evening after-work drinks at the Wellington for a long time.

He takes precisely half a second to decide. 'Yeah, why not?'

'Seriously? Who is this impostor who's taken over Rory Sugar's body?' Toni laughs.

'I can't stay long.'

'Just the one?' She smiles, her eyes twinkling mischievously.

'Alright, don't take the piss or I won't come at all,' he says, with a mock sulky pout.

Last time, just the one turned into an absolute skinful that ended in that eventful night in the karaoke bar. He's not going to make that mistake again. He still hasn't totally recovered.

'Don't be like that.' She clicks her mouse and powers down her computer. 'Come on, grab your coat. We can get there early and I can have you to myself for a bit. The first round's on you.'

Chapter 30

Icy fingers of fear run down Leo's spine. They've missed the turning for home and he has no idea where Jerome's taking him.

'Where are we going?' Leo asks nervously as Jerome turns off the main road and onto a narrow lane.

'Somewhere quiet.'

The lane becomes not much more than a track, what's left of the tarmac cracked and broken with deep potholes filled with dirty rainwater. Of course, they're heading for Clover Wood. Not to the car park where the dog walkers, families and ramblers congregate, but to the quieter side where hardly anyone ventures.

Jerome pulls into a muddy layby churned up by car tyres under a thick canopy of crooked tree branches. Leo's breathing has become shallow and ragged. What is Jerome playing at? What's he going to do to him?

'Give me your phone,' Jerome demands as he switches off the engine.

'Why?'

'Just give it to me.'

Leo reluctantly hands over his mobile. There's no point making him any angrier than he already is.

Jerome glances at it, grunts, and shoves it into his pocket. Then reaches into the door and pulls out a knife. It's one like his dad has in his toolbox, with a sharp, triangular blade that slides out from the handle when you press a button with your thumb. Leo's father almost took his finger off with his when he was opening a box of flat-packed wardrobes a few weeks ago.

'I don't want to hurt you, Leo. I just want the truth about my daughter.' Jerome's tone is calm and controlled.

'I've told you the truth.' Sweat beads on Leo's forehead, a prickly heat of panic running across his scalp. He glances out of the windscreen at the dark, foreboding woodland beyond. Could he jump out and run away? Leo's always been quick. One of the fastest sprinters at his old school. And Jerome's older. Much older. He could probably outrun him, couldn't he?

Jerome sighs. 'One last time, Leo. Where's Olivia?'

Leo shakes his head, his gaze fixed on the blade Jerome is pointing at his chest.

'I don't know where she is. I promise I'm telling the truth.'

'Last chance. Where is she?'

'I don't know.'

'Right, get out.' When Leo doesn't move, he yells. 'I said, get out of the van!'

Leo stiffens as Jerome jabs the knife towards his face.

'Okay, okay.'

Leo's fingers tremble as he feels for the handle. The door creaks open. He slips a leg out and finds the soft ground.

'Slowly,' Jerome warns.

It's now or never. This could be his only chance. Ten, maybe fifteen seconds of pure, all out, eyeball-popping effort and he could be in the cover of the trees and away to safety. His instinct is to grab his rucksack in the footwell, but it'll only slow him down. He'll have to leave it.

He takes a step back and pushes the door of the van closed.

Jerome turns away briefly to let himself out.

Leo turns and runs.

He aims for a dense patch of trees just off the footpath where the undergrowth is thick with bushes and brambles. He puts his head down and pumps his arms and legs. But the path is slick with mud after all the rain they've had recently and the soles of his trainers slip and slide. His lungs burn and his thighs ache with the effort, but he's quickly up to speed and doesn't dare look back.

'Stop!' Jerome yells after him. A fraction of a second later, he hears the heavy thud of feet running behind him.

Ahead, the path forks and in the gathering gloom, Leo hesitates for a fraction of a second, unsure which way to go.

He jinks left, but he can already hear Jerome closing on him. His front foot hits a patch of mud so slick it's like ice. His trainer slides out from underneath him, his left foot forced in the complete opposite direction to his right, his legs splitting.

When he recovers his balance and finds his footing again, Jerome's heavy breathing is in his ear. A hand snatches the back of his coat and pulls him roughly to a stop.

Leo tries to wrestle free, but Jerome has a firm grip on him and is physically much stronger.

'Stand still,' Jerome orders, bringing the knife up under Leo's chin. 'If you so much as move a muscle, I'll cut you.'

Leo stops struggling and holds up his hands in surrender.

Jerome spins him around and marches him back to the van, shoving him roughly in the back. 'Why would you do something so stupid?' Jerome pants. 'You're going to regret that.'

'I'm sorry,' Leo whines. 'Please, don't hurt me.'

'Open the door.' Jerome points to a sliding door in the van's side. Leo grabs the handle and rolls it open on slick rails, fully expecting Jerome to throw him inside. And then what?

It's full of work tools. Coils of electrical cables. Boxes of sockets and switches. And something else Leo wasn't expecting.

'Take it out,' Jerome instructs, pointing to a long wooden crate that takes up most of the floor.

It's a packing crate made from roughly sawn, pale wood, about six feet long and two feet wide and stamped with faded writing that looks like Chinese. Leo assumes there's something inside it, but when he drags it out of the van, it's lighter than he expected, and when he drops it on the ground, it sounds hollow.

'Grab that end,' Jerome orders, pointing to a rope handle on one end of the crate.

Leo does as he's told and between them, they carry the crate deep into the woods, off the footpath and through the thick undergrowth that snags at their feet and slows their progress, until soon Jerome's van is far out of sight.

'This will do,' Jerome says, dropping his end next to the trunk of a tree, under a low-hanging bare branch. 'Put it down here.'

Leo's imagination has been running amok, wondering what's inside and what Jerome is planning.

Jerome takes a hammer from a tool belt around his waist and tosses it towards Leo. 'Open it.'

The hammer lands in a patch of scrub, and Leo has to scrabble around to find it, scratching his arms and hands on spiky brambles.

'What are you waiting for? It's getting dark,' Jerome grunts.

It takes a moment or two, but when Leo finds it, he holds it aloft triumphantly, wrapping his hand around its rubber encased handle and glancing at the iron, clawed head. A potential weapon. He can't believe Jerome has just been stupid enough to hand it to him so willingly.

He'll have to wait for the right moment to use it, though, when Jerome is distracted and Leo is close enough to strike him. At least it gives him some hope of escape, even if Jerome has a knife.

For the moment, Jerome's keeping his distance and a cautious eye on Leo's every movement. Leo takes a breath and kneels at the side of the crate.

There are a dozen nails securing the lid in place and each screeches in protest as Leo struggles to prise them out, methodically working his way around the crate until the lid finally comes free and he flips it onto the ground.

Inside, he's surprised to find there's nothing but a few wood shavings, a scrap of old newspaper and a dirty fleece blanket.

He glances at Jerome, confused. 'What is this?'

'I knew it would come in handy at some point,' Jerome says with a sly grin.

Leo stares at him, confused.

'I kept hold of it after the move, but it's been taking up space in the garage. Now, get inside.'

'What?'

'Don't be difficult, Leo. Get in and lie down, there's a good boy.'

Leo stands slowly, not sure if Jerome's serious or not. He's not really going to make him get in, is he? This is crazy. Leo's stomach knots and churns as panic washes over him.

'You obviously need some more time to think about what you've done with my daughter, so you can stay in the crate while you try to remember.'

'But I told you, I don't know anything,' Leo wails.

'Leo, get in.' Jerome speaks so coldly, it sends a chill down Leo's spine.

'I can't. I'm not good with enclosed spaces.'

'I guess it won't take long for your memory to come back to you then, will it?'

'Please, no.' Leo glances around, looking for an escape, but there's nowhere to go. He can't outrun Jerome, and anyway, Jerome has a knife.

All he has is the hammer. He tightens his fist around the handle, sizing up its weight and where to hit Jerome. He doesn't want to kill him, but he'll only have one chance. He'll have to make it count.

He charges, screaming, swinging the hammer, hoping to catch Jerome by surprise.

But Jerome sidesteps calmly to his left, as if he was expecting it, and as Leo sails past, the hammer flying harmlessly through the air, he loses his footing, slips and tumbles to the ground.

Jerome's on his back in an instant, his knee pressed painfully between Leo's shoulder blades.

'Stop trying to play the hero, Leo,' he snarls in his ear. 'Now get up and get in the box.'

Tears of anger and frustration, humiliation and despair spring from Leo's eyes. He really doesn't want to get in the crate, but he knows he has no choice as Jerome tickles his throat with the sharp blade. He doesn't want to die out here alone in the woods.

Slowly, he pulls himself to his feet as Jerome backs off. He can't bring himself to look Jerome in the eye as he staggers back towards the crate, lifts one leg, and steps into it.

He's shivering now, ashamed of his tears. Ashamed he's showing so much fear.

'Lie down.'

Leo takes a deep breath, looks at his feet, and sits with his knees pulled up to his chest. The floor of the crate is rough and hard. Slowly, he lowers himself backwards until his spine is flat against the bottom. Then he straightens his legs and clasps his arms over his chest. He imagines it's what it must be like lying in a coffin. He sobs silently, wishing his mother was here to save him. She'd know what to do.

Jerome reaches for the fleece blanket under Leo's legs, pulls it out, balls it up and drops it onto Leo's stomach. 'Here, you're going to need this.'

'You're not leaving me?'

'You can make it stop any time you want. Just tell me where she is.'

But he can't. Leo bites his lip, focusing on the pinprick of pain as he closes his eyes. He had no idea Olivia's father could be so cruel.

Jerome heaves the lid off the ground with one hand and drops it back in place with a thud, trapping Leo inside.

In the sudden darkness, Leo freaks out. He kicks and punches, shouting and yelling, desperate. He doesn't want to be entombed in a wooden box like a corpse. He gasps for air and tries to sit up, pushing the lid off, letting the light back in.

In a flash, Jerome has the blade of his knife at Leo's throat again, his face contorted into a twist of anger and determination.

'Lie down!' he yells. 'Now we can do this the easy way or the hard way. It's up to you. If you'd rather I tied your arms and legs and put a gag in your mouth, I'm happy to do that. Otherwise, shut up and lie down!'

Leo lets his body go limp, giving up the fight. He thought nothing could be worse than being imprisoned in a crate, but it would be unbearable if he couldn't move his arms and legs, and couldn't breathe because he had a gag in his mouth.

As Jerome slides the lid back into place, Leo's plunged into terrifying darkness. He lies rigid, staring through the blackness at the wooden lid inches above his nose and listens to the painfully loud thump-thump-thump of Jerome nailing it back into place, sealing him inside.

He works quickly and efficiently, every hammer blow causing Leo to jump and whimper.

As the hammering stops, Leo has an unexpected and desperate need to empty his bladder. He doesn't want to wet himself like a toddler, but what other option does he have? The embarrassment stings his cheeks as the warmth spreads down his thighs.

He wants his mum.

He wants to go home.

But how long's Jerome planning to leave him in here? An hour? Two? Even that feels like an eternity, trapped in a wooden prison where he doesn't even have the room to turn on his side. His backside's already numb, his shoulders ache and his jeans are soaked through with urine. No, he can't survive in here for two hours. He'll go crazy.

His only hope is that someone will find him. It's a possibility. They're not in the middle of nowhere. The woods are always busy with dog walkers like his mum, or people out enjoying the fresh air. It'll only take someone to spot the crate amongst the trees and they're bound to come to investigate. After all, a wooden packing crate left abandoned in the middle of the woods is going to look incongruous. He just needs to wait and pray for a miracle.

But then there's another sound.

Leo strains his ears, trying to work out what Jerome's doing now. A rustling sound. And then what could be gravel being thrown onto the top of the crate, unnaturally loud in Leo's ears.

What is Jerome doing?

And then he understands. His blood runs cold and any hope he had of being rescued vanishes.

Jerome is covering the crate, trying to hide it, probably with fallen branches and leaves.

No one's going to spot him now and the chances of being rescued are virtually zero.

There is only one way he's getting out of here, and that's by telling Jerome the truth. But he's determined he's not going to give that up easily. He promised Olivia he wouldn't. And he'll do whatever it takes to protect her.

Chapter 31

Rory lies on his back, sober now, peering at the cracks in the ceiling with the bedclothes gathered around his waist and the jaws of regret snapping at his conscience. Next to him, Toni is asleep, her head buried in his shoulder.

Oh god, what was he thinking? This should never have happened. How could he have been such a fool?

On the floor, under a heap of discarded clothes, his phone buzzes. What if it's Sabine checking up on him? He hadn't even told her he was staying out and now she'll be worrying he's dead in a ditch, but he can't deal with her right now, so ignores the call.

She can never find out what happened. It would kill her and she's been through so much this year already.

It's not as if he'd planned it. When he told Toni he'd join them for just the one, he'd meant it. He was going to stop for a quick pint and then leave the team to it, but he should have learnt his lesson after Marney's birthday. After one, someone had bought him another, and by the time he was on his third, any ambition he'd had of making it home on time had flown out of the window.

People were laughing at his jokes, engaged in his stories, egging him on when he started spilling the gossip about some of the charity's senior management team, some of whom he'd worked with for years. He didn't once think about home and the problems his family was going through. Leo getting into trouble at school. Sabine worrying he was involved in Olivia's disappearance and lying to the police. Last night, all he had to worry about was himself. And he loved it. It was liberating having a proper laugh for a change.

And anyway, he deserved to have some fun once in a while, didn't he? He worked hard. He paid the mortgage. He put food on the table and a roof over their heads. But ever since Leo became caught up in that girl's death, there hasn't been much fun at home.

The team had all moved on to a cocktail bar at around eleven. It was Toni's idea. A quiet place she knew in Soho. Although it wasn't exactly quiet when they got there. The place was heaving, but they found a table at the back and all squeezed around it. He sat next to Toni, their thighs pressed together, and when she took his hand under the table, it seemed like the most natural thing in the world.

He was drunk, but he didn't care. He wasn't even worried that he'd probably miss the last train. He'd find a way home somehow.

He insisted everyone should have a gin martini with a lemon twist, which in retrospect had been a bad idea, not least because he'd offered to pay. The bar bill had been eye watering, and on a stomach full of beer, it pushed him over the edge. When they finally left the bar, he could hardly stand.

When it was time to leave, he remembers stumbling over his own feet, bouncing off a wall and falling into Toni's arms, both of them giggling like teenagers.

'What's your wife going to say when you turn up in this state?' she said, laughing.

He pressed a finger to her lips and shushed her quiet. He didn't want to be reminded of Sabine.

'I've had a lovely evening,' he slurred, clinging to her.

'Yeah, me too.'

'I don't want it to end yet.'

'Me neither.'

He stared at her face, noticing how beautiful she looked. He'd always thought she was attractive, but being so close to her under the orange glow of a neon sign, he saw she was stunning. Her skin was flawless and her eyes sparkled with life.

He leant closer and put his lips to hers, half expecting her to pull away and slap him. But she didn't. She met his kiss and dragged him into a side alley, pulling him closer, as hungry for him as he was for her.

He had no idea where the others went. They must have all drifted off home and not noticed they were missing.

'Come back to mine?' she whispered breathlessly in his ear.

He knew it was wrong. So, so wrong. But in that instant, he wanted her more than he wanted anything in the world, hungry for the taste of the forbidden fruit.

He nodded and pressed his forehead against hers, his breath fast and shallow. 'Only if you're sure?'

She snatched his hand and pulled him away. He remembers there was a taxi. More kissing. A lot more kissing. And he abandoned himself to her.

He has no idea where the taxi brought them. He recalls spilling into a Victorian terraced house, but there are thousands of those in London. She has a room on the first floor with a window overlooking a small garden. A TV on a chest of drawers in the corner.

She produced a white powder from her bag, and they made urgent, frantic love on her bed, with the unfamiliar scent of her sheets filling his nostrils.

He has no idea what time it is. Late. Or early, depending on your perspective. Too late to get home, anyway. There will be no trains at this time in the morning.

He should have called Sabine. Or at least sent her a message. She'll be going out of her mind with worry.

Toni groans in her sleep and rolls over onto the other side of the bed, pulling the covers over her naked shoulders.

How's he going to face her in the morning? At work? What are the rest of the team going to think? They'll have to keep it a secret. He can't risk Sabine finding out. It would destroy her. Toni will understand, won't she?

What the hell was he thinking? How could he have risked his marriage and his family for this? It's not as if he's in love with Toni, any more than he supposes she's in love with him. She lives like a student in a shared house with all her belongings crammed into one room, for pity's sake.

He sits up, cold air chilling his shoulders and his chest. What an idiot. He swings his feet onto the floor and buries his throbbing head in his hands.

Last night might just have been the biggest mistake of his life.

Chapter 32

It's so cold. Even with Leo's coat buttoned up to his chin and the fleece blanket draped across his chest, it penetrates his bones and dulls his brain.

It feels like forever since Jerome sealed him inside the crate, and he's still not come back. Hours must have passed, although time, without his phone, is just an illusion. Leo's toes and fingers are numb, his back and hips ache from lying in one position on the hard wooden floor, and he no longer has the energy to shiver, as if his body has decided it's better to conserve its resources.

Is Jerome even planning to return? Or has he left him here to die? It must be getting on for midnight. Hours and hours since Jerome abandoned him. Occasionally he hears an owl in the trees and the sound of scratching in the undergrowth. Animals of the night hunting for food, terrifyingly loud as he lies listening with nothing else to do.

He's tried everything to get out. His knuckles are sore and wet from where he attempted to punch a hole in the lid, and his knees are bruised and tender from kicking. The lid's not budged a millimetre, although Leo's not really surprised. He knows how tough it was to prise it off earlier, how tightly the nails had been hammered into the soft wood.

He's yelled until he's hoarse and his throat throbbed, and he's banged and thumped. But nobody's come. Why would they? No one knows he's here. And he has no way of raising the alarm. It's hopeless. The only person who can set him free is Olivia's father, and it seems increasingly unlikely that he's ever going to return.

Leo is embarrassed about crying, but all he wants is to be back home, in his bed. Warm and free. As if the cold wasn't bad enough, he can hardly move. The space is so narrow, he has to stay on his back, even though it's agony and all his muscles are complaining. He can just about bend his knees but not enough to release the tension in his thighs and hamstrings, and although he's tried rolling over onto his side, the crate is too narrow and his shoulders too wide.

The blanket helped keep him warm for a little while, but now it's next to useless. The cold is like an insidious, creeping poison that's spread throughout his body. He's never known such pain and discomfort. He's already promised himself that if his parents could just find him, he'll never ever give them grief again.

He's starving too and wishes he'd eaten more at lunch, rather than just grabbing a bag of chips from the takeaway around the corner from school. His stomach is rumbling, and he feels the desperate hollowness of hunger gnawing at his insides.

How long is this going to go on? All night? The smell inside the crate is already sickening, and it's only going to get worse. And what if Jerome doesn't come back in the morning? What if he's stuck in this crate for days? He's not sure how long he can survive without food and water, but he knows it's not long. And it's likely to be a prolonged and agonising death.

Surely his mother will raise the alarm when he doesn't come home? She'll call the police and they'll have to come looking for him, like they've been looking for Olivia. But where would they begin? He's pretty convinced no one saw him getting into Jerome's van, and anyway, who's going to suspect him? He's not going to be found soon. At least not while he's still alive.

Leo closes his eyes and concentrates on his breathing, slowing it down and imagining he's lying on a sandy beach with the sun warming his skin and the balmy waters of a crystal clear sea lapping at the shore. It's the only way to control his panic and regain some control. It's hard when he's in so much pain, fearing death, but if he thinks too much about his predicament, he'll drive himself mad.

He clings to the hope that he won't be stuck in here forever and that Jerome is only punishing him because he's upset about Olivia. That he'll be back soon, demanding answers. Because if he really believes Leo is involved in her disappearance, what's the point in letting him die?

The whole reason for this crazy torture is to scare Leo into telling him the truth, isn't it?

He can't keep protesting his innocence. Jerome doesn't believe him, so he'll have to tell him something. Maybe he could tell him Olivia has run away, and that he helped her buy a train ticket out of town. Or that he overheard her discussing with her friends about meeting an older boy, and that's what he was arguing with her about. There are so many lies he could tell. He just needs one that is guaranteed to convince Jerome to let him free.

There's something on his face. The tickle of tiny feet on his cheek. He freezes, his breath snagging in his throat. It's so dark that even if he could put his hand in front of his face, he wouldn't be able to see it. His imagination blooms. What is it? An enormous spider? It moves slowly, tentatively, heading towards his nose. He tries to reach it with his hand, but he can't stretch his fingers that far. He flicks his head one way and then the other, but whatever it is resolutely refuses to budge.

He tries blowing it off, pursing his lips to shoot a blast of air across his cheek, while his heart gallops with fear. The thing changes direction, heading now towards his mouth. He clamps his lips shut and squeezes his eyes closed, praying it will leave him alone.

He's not usually afraid of bugs and spiders, but when you're confined in a tight space and you can't use your hands, they take on a monstrous terror.

He feels the thing tiptoe over his lips, onto his chin and drop off. Presumably onto his chest, but he doesn't care, even if it's gone inside his hoodie. As long as it's not on his face anymore.

Leo forces his mind back to the problem of Jerome. What's he going to tell him when he returns that's going to get him out of here? He could lie, but of course, there is an alternative. He could just tell the truth.

Leo sighs. Is he really ready for that? He made a promise to Olivia and there's no way he's going to let her down.

He's doing this for her and all his suffering is nothing compared to what she's been through. He should be more courageous. Less self-centred. He owes it to her, even if it means being stuck in this coffin forever.

Chapter 33

Rory can't hide in Toni's house forever. He needs to go home and face the music. He's due in the office, but he can hardly turn up in yesterday's clothes smelling of stale alcohol and sour sweat, especially as they're currently strewn across Toni's bedroom floor.

He creeps out of bed, slips on his glasses and gathers up his suit, shirt and underwear, hanging Toni's discarded dress and tights over the back of a chair in the corner. She's still sleeping, her hair fanned out across the pillow. He doesn't want to wake her, let alone face her this morning. He's embarrassed about last night. He wishes it had never happened.

Oh god, what a pathetic fool. What a mess.

His phone has fallen out of his trouser pocket and is lying on the carpet face up. Suddenly, it lights up, revealing several missed calls from Sabine.

He picks it up like it's a bomb liable to go off in his hand, and collapses on the edge of the bed, staring at it, engulfed in a tidal wave of guilt, shame and self-loathing. How could he have done this to Sabine?

What with the fallout from Heather's death, the trolling and the hatred, and the house move, they've not had much time for each other lately. Both of them have stopped putting in the effort, although it's not as though he doesn't love her. It's just... It's just what? There is no excuse for his betrayal.

His thumb hovers over the call button. He ought to listen to at least one of the half a dozen messages she's left, but the thought turns his stomach to mush. He's let her down in the cruellest way. Hearing her voice isn't going to make him feel any better, especially sitting here naked with Toni sleeping a few feet away.

'Hey,' Toni moans as she rolls over and prises open her eyes. 'Good morning.'

'Oh, hi,' Rory says, glancing away as she sits up and the duvet falls from her chest, exposing her nakedness.

Last night, he couldn't get enough of her. A vision flashes through his mind of peeling her out of her clothes, his tongue exploring every inch of her body. But now the sight of her makes him feel awkward and ashamed. His cheeks flush and a lump hardens in his throat.

'Fancy finishing what we started last night?' she purrs, reaching for his arm.

He flinches and pulls away.

'I'm sorry. I need to get home,' he mumbles.

The lascivious grin on her face drops as covers herself. 'Something I said?' she asks, frowning.

'I shouldn't be here.'

'Nobody forced you.' There's a cold edge to her voice.

'I know. That's not what I'm saying. I shouldn't have taken advantage.'

She snorts. 'Nobody took advantage of anybody. It's just sex. It doesn't mean anything.'

Rory cringes. Sex. That's all it was. So why does it feel so much more?

'I'm married.'

'You didn't seem too worried about that last night.'

'Nobody can ever find out,' he says.

She shrugs.

'I mean it, Toni. If Sabine finds out...'

'Relax, she's not going to find out unless you tell her.'

Should he tell her? Is that the grown-up, mature thing to do? Explain to Sabine that he was drunk and made a terrible, terrible mistake and that he'll do whatever it takes to make it up to her?

God, how can he? It'd kill her. What difference does it make whether or not he was drunk? He's lied and cheated. How can he ever expect her to trust him again? No, he can't tell her. After everything she's been through these last few months, he can't put her through this. His torment and shame will be punishment enough. And he will make it up to her. He'll be the most loving, attentive and supportive husband you can imagine. And he'll never do it again.

He's confident Toni will keep their secret. Why wouldn't she? Like she said, it was just sex to her. And it's not as if Sabine's ever going to meet Toni, is it? And no one else knows. At least, not yet. It'll be the skeleton in their closet.

Something that maybe in time he'll be able to forget ever happened.

If he keeps his cool and sticks to a story that he got drunk and had to stay in a cheap hotel when he missed the last train home, there's no reason for Sabine to suspect anything. It means lying to her, of course, but it's for the best.

'Can you pass me my robe from the back of the door,' Toni asks.

'What? Oh, yes, sure.'

He stands, conscious of his nudity, and shuffles across the room. He plucks a silk robe adorned with red roses and spiralling, thorny stems from a hook on the door and hands it to her, averting his eyes like a prude. He wishes the floor would open up and swallow him whole.

'I'm going to have a quick shower and then I'll rustle us up some breakfast.' Toni slips out of bed and shrugs on the robe.

Rory shoots her a thin smile.

As she brushes past, she runs her fingers across his forearm. It makes him shudder.

And then she's gone. He hears a door open and close along the hall and the rush of water from a running shower. He dresses quickly, pulling on yesterday's sullied clothes. If only he'd had the strength of mind to stick to his intentions, to only have one drink and head home. But he's weak. And pathetic.

He finds his shoes, one kicked under the bed and the other, inexplicably, on the windowsill, and heels them on, wincing at the stiffness in his back as he bends to tie them.

He needs to get the hell out while Toni's still in the bathroom. To grab some fresh air and clear his head. His eyes are gritty, his head dull and throbbing, and his mouth tastes like a sewer.

But first, he needs to man up and listen to Sabine's messages. With a sigh of despair, he eyes his phone.

He dials his voicemail, holds the phone to his ear and waits for it to connect.

The first message is the last one she left, at around one twenty in the morning. What the hell was she doing still awake? His heart sinks. Probably worrying he was dead.

'Rory? Are you there? Oh god, where the hell are you? I'm going out of my mind here. Call me as soon as you get this. It's urgent.' A spike of adrenaline burns through his veins. Urgent? 'It's Leo. He's not come home tonight and his phone's switched off. I don't know what to do. Please, just call me, will you?'

Rory stands up too quickly, the blood sinking to his feet. He grabs the wall to steady himself and closes his eyes as his blood pressure equalises.

There's always something to worry about with Leo these days. So he's stayed out overnight. Probably to punish them after the row they had with him. He'll be back, his tail between his legs, when he's hungry.

But Sabine sounded so frantic, so worried. He should be there with her. Supporting her. Talking her down off the ceiling before she works herself up into a real frenzy. Not here, in Toni's bedroom.

He needs to get home.

He hurriedly pulls on his jacket, checks he has his wallet and flies out of the room. He virtually tumbles down the stairs, almost tripping over his feet as he loses his balance at the bottom. He grabs his coat hanging on the newel post and runs out.

Upstairs, the shower's still running. He feels bad for abandoning Toni, like an alley cat slinking off after having his fun, but he'll explain it to her later.

Right now, he needs to be with his wife and family.

Chapter 34

Jerome waits until Faith is in the bathroom before heading for the kitchen to fill up a plastic bag-for-life with a bottle of water, an apple and a packet of stale croissants that should have been thrown out days ago. Things that Faith won't notice are missing. He tiptoes to the front door, silently lets himself out, and dumps the bag in the van.

Leo's rucksack is still in the footwell. He meant to get rid of it. He can't risk the police finding it. He'll have to do it later.

Across the street, Sabine emerges from her house with Hank and that stupid cockapoo. Jerome freezes, pressed up against his vehicle, hoping she won't see him. He watches as she throws open the back doors of her van and ushers the dogs inside. Does she even realise Leo's missing? She's certainly not behaving like a mother whose son has vanished.

She must have been suspicious when he didn't come home last night, but it's not the same as when Olivia vanished. She's a good girl who never goes anywhere without letting them know where she is and who she's with. Not like Leo. He's a bit of a tearaway from all accounts, always in trouble at school. No respect for his parents, or anyone else for that matter.

Jerome hopes he's had a truly awful night inside that crate and that he's finally come to his senses and is ready to tell the truth. Of course Leo knows what's happened to Olivia. But if he's hurt her, another night in the crate will be the least of his worries. He'll be begging Jerome for mercy by the time he's finished with him.

Sabine slams the doors of her van shut and climbs in behind the wheel. Jerome scurries back inside the house, heads into the lounge and stands at the window where he has a better view of the street. He watches Sabine's van roll out onto the road and drive the short distance to Anthony and Zac's house.

He's convinced she knows more than she's letting on. Otherwise, why would she lie about Leo being with her on Monday? Why try to protect him unless she knows what he's done? The bare-faced cheek of the woman to stand on their doorstep and plead ignorance. It makes Jerome sick. And if that wasn't bad enough, she even had the gall to turn up at the vigil the other night, pretending she cares. What are they doing, letting her look after Hank? He's going to put a stop to that. They'll find someone else to take care of the stupid dog. He's not going to carry on paying her when he doesn't even trust her.

'What are you doing?' Faith appears behind him, her hair still wet from the shower. She peers out of the window, following his gaze. 'She'll be home soon. Don't worry, love.' She runs a hand up and down his back. 'We'll find her.'

'It's been four nights now,' he grumbles, watching as Sabine climbs out of the van and marches up Anthony and Zac's drive.

'We can't give up hope.'

Jerome shrugs her hand off his back. Faith's hurting as much as he is, but in the last twenty-four hours she's found an unexpected strength. A hope among the doom. She's crying less and started talking about all the things they're going to do when they're back as a family. It's driving him crazy. How can she talk like that while their little girl is still missing?

At least he's doing something, not just sitting at home twiddling his thumbs, putting blind faith in the police. They've tried to convince him they know what they're doing, but they don't have a clue. Four nights she's been missing now and they're no closer to working out what's happened to her. Well, he's done with waiting passively while they search yet another section of the river, or comb another patch of scrubland. They're not going to find her like that, relying on a random slice of luck. A piece of clothing. A shoe. A hopeful sighting.

If there were clues out there, the police would have found them by now. But at least it gives him hope that Olivia's still alive. He feels it in his bones. Such is the strong bond between them, he's sure he'd know if she was dead.

No, it's obvious. Leo Sugar has taken her. He's certain of it now, although he's not sure of the boy's motives. Or where he's hiding her. He's probably drugged her to subdue and control her. But she can't be far away.

'I'm going out. I'll be back later,' he says, barging past Faith.

If you want something done properly, do it yourself. And he wants to be gone before that liaison officer, Maggie, turns up again. He really can't bear that woman's platitudes and fake concern. If she really wanted to help, she'd be out there looking for his daughter, not holed up in their house, drinking their tea.

Outside, he heads for the garage and digs under a pile of dust sheets he uses for decorating. Hidden beneath them is an old leather case with two combination locks still set to his grandfather's date of birth. Jerome hasn't had the heart to change them since he left him the gun when he died three years ago.

He flicks the catches open and lifts the lid. It's not been fired in years, but it's been kept in good condition. Not that he plans to use it. It's only for show. In case Leo Sugar still needs any convincing.

Nonetheless, he loads it with two cartridges, puts it back in the case and locks it shut. Then he puts the case in the back of the van.

It's time to find out whether a night in a crate has loosened Leo Sugar's tongue. It's time to finally find Olivia.

Chapter 35

The train journey home gives Rory time to plan what he's going to say to Sabine, as guilt and worry eat at his insides. He's pulled up Sabine's number on his phone several times but has stopped himself dialling while he straightens out in his head how he's going to explain his absence last night. He needs to sound convincing, but he knows how easily she can tell when he's lying.

He doesn't want to get caught in the weeds of a convoluted lie that will trip him up later, so he'll tell her he had too much to drink at the pub after work and that he crashed at a hotel near the station after missing the last train home. He won't mention Toni and will have to hope she doesn't check the bank statements to see how much he spent on a non-existent hotel room.

It's a problem he could do without with their errant son still causing issues. Why is there always so much trouble with that boy lately? Hopefully, he'll grow out of it soon, rather than needing therapy, which is what Sabine seems to want. As if they could ever persuade Leo to see a counsellor.

Sabine's convinced that Heather Malone's death, the police investigation and the backlash they all faced is the cause of Leo's problems, but what good is a therapist going to do? They'll end up labelling him. They'll say he has ADHD or complex PTSD or something they can tick off in their book. But the fact is, he's a teenager. And teenagers play up. Rory was certainly no angel at his age.

Plus, Sabine virtually accused Leo of being involved in Olivia Hunter's disappearance the other night, so it's no wonder he took some time out. Rory would probably have done the same in his shoes. They shouldn't have gone to his room mob-handed. Leo's obviously unhappy, so what was the point in reminding him about Heather? It's all a hot mess, but he's going to make things right. He'll talk to Leo again, maybe take him out to the pub or somewhere they can spend time together. Sabine would appreciate that, and it's the least he can do to make it up to her.

The train pulls into the station. Rory pulls himself wearily to his feet and jumps off with his palms clammy and the blood pounding in his head. The short walk back to the house makes him feel marginally more human. He lets himself in and braces himself, biting his lower lip as he slips off his coat and jacket and hangs them on the newel post at the bottom of the stairs.

'Sabine?'

He finds her hunched over her phone at the dining room table, her hair scrunched up in her hands.

She turns to him, her eyes red. 'Where the hell have you been? I've been worried sick.'

The heat rises to Rory's cheeks. He clears his throat. 'I'm so sorry, I missed the last train.'

'And lost your phone too, did you? Why didn't you call?'

She has every right to be mad at him. He looks at his feet. 'I was drunk,' he confesses. 'I know I should have called. I'm sorry.'

'You could have been dead, for all I knew.'

'I know. I booked into a cheap hotel by the station. I didn't know what else to do.' The lie rolls off his tongue with remarkable ease.

'Didn't you get my messages?'

'Not until this morning, but I'm here now. Any news on Leo?'

Sabine sighs and her shoulders slump. 'No,' she says. 'And he's not turned up at school again.'

Rory's eyebrows shoot up. 'When did you last hear from him?'

'I've not seen him since Wednesday night. I was out with the dogs before he left for school yesterday and he never came home for dinner last night.'

'You've obviously tried calling him?'

Sabine shoots Rory a withering look as he pulls up a chair. 'That's all I've been doing since about seven o'clock last night, but it just keeps going to voicemail.'

'What about his friends? Has anyone heard from him?'

'What friends? Apart from Olivia, I don't think he has any.'

'Right,' Rory says. His head is still throbbing and thick with the fog of his hangover. He should never have had that martini, although that's the least of his regrets about last night.

Sabine peers at him through her fringe. 'I was about to call the police,' she says quietly. 'I was going to report him missing.'day

Rory blinks twice. 'Do you think that's wise?'

'He's the second teenager in the street to vanish this week,' she says. 'I don't think we have any choice.'

'Okay,' Rory says, nodding. He hadn't thought of it that way. 'If you think that's the right thing to do.'

'What do you mean? Of course it's the right thing to do.'

'He's a troubled teenager. He's just had a massive row with his parents. He's probably taken himself off to cool down a bit.'

Sabine pushes her tongue into the side of her mouth, her eyes narrowing. 'You're worried because I lied to them, aren't you?'

'No,' Rory says. 'Well, maybe. I don't know. I'd just be careful about getting them involved, that's all. Maybe give it twenty-four hours and see whether he turns up?'

'You know he has nothing to do with Olivia going missing, don't you?' Sabine says. 'That's the only reason I gave him an alibi. I didn't want the police suspecting him.'

'You still shouldn't have done it. But look, teenagers run away all the time for all sorts of different reasons. You shouldn't jump to conclusions. Give him some time and some space, and he'll be back. I'm sure.'

Rory leans across the table and wraps his arms around Sabine's shoulders. She sinks her head into him and he pushes the guilt away. This is where he belongs. At home. With Sabine. He's going to make everything right, and she never needs to know what an idiot he's been.

They stay like that for a moment, silently hugging, until Rory's back begins to complain, and he pulls away. Sabine wipes a tear from her eye.

'You really don't think I should be worried?'

'No more than usual.' He gives her a grim smile.

She frowns. 'What are you doing home, anyway?'

'I could hardly go to work in this state,' Rory says, pointing to his crumpled shirt. He's not even had a shower this morning and feels squalid in yesterday's clothes. 'And it's a Friday, so I thought I'd work from home.'

Sabine wrinkles her nose. 'You'd better have a shower and get changed then. I'm going to ring around the hospitals, just to be sure.'

Rory raises an eyebrow. 'Sabine, don't torture yourself,' he says.

'Just a few phone calls, that's all.'

Rory sighs, but he can tell Sabine's not going to be talked out of it, and frankly, he's just grateful she hasn't pressed him further on where he was last night.

He's not proud of himself, but he might have got away with it after all, thanks to Leo.

Chapter 36

It's been the longest night of Leo's life. He's slept for maybe ten or fifteen minutes at most. Every time he dropped off, he awoke suddenly in a panic, fearful and jittery. Everything aches and he's numb to the bone with cold. And as the long hours ticked slowly by, he's been through every emotion imaginable. Fear. Anger. Despondency. Determination. Hope. Despair. Resignation. Defeat.

But he's made it through. The utter darkness he'd experienced through the night has given way to a dull, diffused light that creeps in around the narrow gaps where Jerome has nailed the lid to the crate. Finally, Leo can see his hands, his knuckles bloodied and battered, scarred by his failed attempts at escape.

He should be grateful he's still alive, even if it's been the worst torture imaginable, but his mouth is so dry, all he can think is cool, fresh fountains of water. He'd kill for a drink right now, and although his stomach's been rumbling, liquid is what he craves. Something to wet his mouth and ease the sting of his cracked lips. There's so little moisture in his body he can barely swallow, while his mind incessantly wanders, transporting him to faraway lands and weird waking dreams.

He's become to every noise around him, his hearing supercharged. Scurrying in the undergrowth. Scratching on the crate. The flap of wings in the air. The creak of a tree branch. And now, somewhere in the distance, the bark of dogs?

He thinks of his mother with Biscuit and the others. She often brings them to Clover Wood. Could that be her now? He tries to call out, but his voice is no more than a strangulated croak and when he attempts to bang on the crate, his hands protest in pain.

He wishes more than anything that he could be home again with his mum. If only she could find him, he'd never raise his voice to her again or snap at her when she asked about his day.

She must be worried about him. What did she think had happened when he didn't make it home last night? Has she called the police? Or does she think he's sulking somewhere, making her pay for yelling at him?

He regrets that the last words he had with his parents were ones of bitterness and anger. They'd come to his room and as good as accused him of killing Olivia. As if Leo has it in him to hurt anyone. They just don't understand. How could they? They still treat him like he's a ten-year-old kid, but he'll be eighteen next year and free to do whatever he wants.

He's not sure he'll go to university, although Olivia thinks he should. She even suggested he should apply to Oxford and they could go together, but she was probably joking. Even if he could achieve the grades, which would be a tall order, it would kill him to be that close to her, watching her with other boys. She doesn't like him like that. She made that abundantly clear, but he can't help the way he feels about her. She drives him crazy.

He might go travelling instead. Get a job, save enough for one of those round-the-world tickets and visit all sorts of far-flung places. Vietnam. Cambodia. India. South America. Australia. When he's eighteen, he can go where he wants, whenever he wants.

A dull pain throbs behind his eyes. He really needs a drink. If only he'd remembered to bring the burner phone he'd bought from that shop in town, he could have called for help. Instead, in his hurry to leave the house yesterday, he'd left it under his mattress where it's hidden from his parents.

He bought two identical phones. Not expensive smart phones, but cheap, plastic Chinese pay-as-you-go models with new SIM cards and different numbers. He gave one to Olivia and kept one for himself. Then he'd made Olivia hand over her old phone. He'd removed the SIM, stamped on it until it stopped working, and threw it in the river. He's seen enough crime dramas to know that he couldn't risk the police using it to track Olivia down.

The sound of barking dogs fades. They're moving further away, not closer. Leo squeezes his eyes shut and sobs tears of self-pity. He just wants to go home. He doesn't want to die here, cold and alone.

Time has lost all meaning. Minutes may have passed, although it could have been hours, when he detects the low rumble of an engine. The squelch of tyres through mud. He holds his breath.

The engine dies. A door slams shut. And then silence... until he hears someone approaching, crashing through the undergrowth, fallen twigs cracking underfoot. His heart races and hope builds in his chest.

'Hey! Help!' he cries out, his voice strangulated and weak.

'Shut up,' Jerome's gruff voice bellows back.

Finally, he's back. Leo's going to be free. It feels like a miracle.

Slowly, the lid lifts, the wood creaking so loudly as the nails come loose, it's deafening after the silence of the night. The bright morning light stings Leo's eyes. A hand grabs him by the collar and hauls him up and out of the crate. Jerome thrusts a bottle of water in his hand and he drinks greedily, spilling it down his chin and over his coat as he barely takes a breath. Water never tasted so good.

'I brought you something to eat.' Jerome hands Leo an apple and two croissants.

He eats ravenously. It feels so good to stretch his arms, his legs, his back.

'Did you get much sleep?' Jerome asks.

'Not really.'

As his eyes become accustomed to the light, he notices Jerome has a shotgun hooked over the crook of his arm. Even if Leo had the strength to run, there would be no point now.

After surviving the night, he doesn't want to get shot.

'I don't suppose it was much fun, was it?' Jerome asks.

'No.'

'Fancy another night in there?'

Leo shakes his head.

'There's no reason you have to, Leo.' Jerome's tone softens. He steps back and rests against the trunk of a tree. 'All you need to do is tell me where I can find Olivia, and you can go home.'

'I don't know—' Leo croaks, but before he can finish his sentence, Jerome leaps up and hits him across the face with the back of his hand. The force of the blow knocks Leo backwards and off his feet.

He lands in the undergrowth and groans.

'Stop lying to me,' Jerome yells. 'You know where she is, so why don't you just tell me? Is she hurt?'

'No,' Leo gasps.

'Is she dead?'

Leo pulls himself up onto his knees and stares at Jerome with contempt. He hated him before, but now he despises him with every bone in his body. He'd kill him if he could. Maybe he should have done when he had his chance.

'You're beginning to test my patience.' Jerome lifts the gun and aims it at Leo's head.

Leo holds Jerome's gaze and feels an unexpected calm. He's done the right thing and if it means paying for it with his life, he can go to the grave with a clean conscience.

'I will make your life a misery,' Jerome snarls, stepping closer. He presses the barrel of the gun against Leo's forehead.

'Like you made Olivia's life a misery?' Leo says, emboldened. 'I know what you are. You're a creep and a bully.'

'Shut your mouth.'

'You're sick. I know what you've been doing and you need help.'

Leo's reactions are too slow, dulled by a lack of sleep and food, and he fails to see Jerome take a swing with the gun until the butt hits him across the temple.

A blinding flash of pain explodes in Leo's head and for a split second, everything goes black. He clings desperately to the edges of consciousness as his body is sent sprawling.

He clutches a handful of dead leaves as his hands ball into fists. Then pushes himself up and drags himself to his feet, swaying on the spot.

Everyone knows there's only one way to deal with a bully and that's to stand up to them. Don't show any weakness. That's why he was caught fighting at school, standing up against the bullies making fun of him, although his parents would never understand. They think he's a delinquent who enjoys getting into trouble for the sake of it. They don't get him at all.

'You can do what you like to me, I'll never tell you how to find Olivia,' he says, coughing. Defiant. A trickle of blood runs from a cut on his head, down his cheek and drips off his chin.

'I knew it,' Jerome spits. 'I should have known not to trust you. Where is she? Just tell me, or help me god, I'll break every bone in your body!'

'You'll never find her.' Leo shoots him a gleeful smile, taunting him. It feels good. If he's going to die anyway, he might as well keep his mouth shut. If only Olivia could see him now, she'd be so proud of him.

Jerome's eyes flicker with something that could be panic. Or fear. He's uncertain what to do. He obviously never expected a seventeen-year-old to call his bluff. In fact, Leo's probably the first person who's ever stood up to him.

Jerome bares his teeth as his finger tightens on the trigger of the gun. Leo closes his eyes and takes a deep breath. He's utterly terrified. He doesn't want to die, but he's not going to give Jerome the satisfaction of begging for his life.

'Last chance. Tell me!' Jerome screams.

'No.'

A deathly silence falls. Neither of them moves an inch. Leo listens to the blood rushing in his ears and the shallowness of his breath wheezing from his lungs. His only regret is that he's caused so much trouble for his parents and hasn't told them he loves them as often as he should. He wishes their last conversation hadn't been a blazing row and hopes they'll forgive him when the truth comes out. That they'll understand why he did what he did. That he was only ever acting in good faith. That he was trying to do the right thing.

'Go on, then, do it,' Leo says. 'What are you waiting for?' He grabs the end of the gun and holds it to his head, praying his death will be swift and painless.

Jerome yanks the gun out of his hands. 'Don't think it's going to be that easy,' he says. 'Get back in the crate.'

Panic builds from Leo's chest until it takes over his whole body. 'No, please, don't make me go back in there.'

'I said, get back in the box. Now!'

Chapter 37

I keep imagining something awful must have happened. That Leo's been knocked down by a car or mugged for his phone and left for dead, although Rory says I'm worrying unnecessarily and that he's probably just sulking with us. Punishing us. I wish I shared his confidence, but there's something niggling in my gut. Maybe it's a mother's intuition, but I can't help feeling something's seriously wrong and Leo is in deep trouble.

I've tried calling everyone I can think of who might know where he is, although it's a short list. I've not reported his disappearance to the police yet, though. Rory thought it was a bad idea and I don't even know if they'd take me seriously. Leo is almost eighteen, after all.

While I'm tearing my hair out, Rory doesn't seem in the least bit concerned. He's become more and more distant in recent months, our relationship increasingly under strain. But this week, things seem particularly bad. Twice he's been out after work and drunk too much. It's bad enough having a son go missing without my husband being absent, too.

I know it's a long commute, and he's probably letting off steam, but he's picked his moment. With Leo going off the rails and now missing, I need my husband here, at my side, showing a united front. We need to nip Leo's bad behaviour in the bud or who knows what will happen to him. But I can't do it on my own.

At least I have the dogs as a distraction from all the other stresses in my life. Something to keep my mind occupied when otherwise I'd only be worrying. Although they're currently all crashed out on their beds, asleep after their morning walk.

The walls feel like they're closing in on me, crushing me. I need to get out of the house again. I need some time on my own to think, to bring my blood pressure back down.

Rory's in his study supposedly working from home. I push open the door and stick my head into the room. He's showered and dressed, but his hair's still wet. He has his back to me, concentrating on the screen, but I can tell from the way he's slumped over his desk that his heart's not really in it. He's probably hungover again. I could certainly still smell the alcohol on his breath when he walked in this morning. Really, he's old enough to know better.

'Do you mind if I pop out for half an hour? Can you keep an eye on the dogs?' I ask.

He spins his chair around. 'Why? Where are you going?' There's a note of suspicion in his voice, which is rich given that he didn't even come home last night and I had no idea where he was.

'Out,' I say, curtly.

'What am I supposed to do with the dogs? I'm working.'

'You don't have to do anything. Just be here with them.'

I walk out and slam the door. Serves him right if he has a banging headache.

I grab my coat, pull on my boots and head out with no idea where I'm going. I just need some space to gather my thoughts.

Across the street, Jerome and Faith's house looks all quiet. There's a police car on the drive, but no sign of Jerome's van. He's been taking himself out and about in recent days, I've noticed, presumably looking for Olivia, but there's still been no word. It's been getting on for nearly a week now since anyone's seen her. That can't be a good sign. Poor Jerome and Faith. They must be going through absolute hell. I wish there was something more I could do.

As I head down the drive, a car roars up the street and the driver toots his horn. Zac's husband, Anthony, winds down the window of their Mini.

'Aren't you supposed to be at the gym?' I ask.

'I had a couple of cancellations this morning, so I thought I'd pop home and catch up on some paperwork rather than hanging around.'

I nod at the polished paintwork over the wheel arch. 'They've done a good job repairing that dent.'

Anthony's jaw tightens. 'Cost an arm and a leg, mind you. That'll teach Zac to be more careful when he's driving.'

'Oh, I thought he said it happened in the car park?'

Anthony rolls his eyes. 'Yeah, well,' is all he says. 'Have you heard anything more about Olivia?'

'No, have you?'

'Nothing. I hope she's okay. Listen, were you heading somewhere? Do you fancy a coffee? I've got a couple of hours to kill.'

'Sure,' I shrug. 'Why not?'

We sit in his airy lounge drinking strong coffee he brews in a fancy machine in their immaculate kitchen. I'm careful not to spill or drip mine all over their pristine white sofa. Who has white sofas? If they were in our house, they'd last about five minutes before they were covered in mud, ketchup or dog hair.

'Is Zac working?' I ask.

'Yeah, but he's back tonight. It's horrible, isn't it, this business with Olivia? You never think it'll happen in your own back yard.'

'I feel awful for Jerome and Faith. I can't imagine how they're coping.'

'Thank god we decided to never have kids. Mind you, we're both too selfish. And the thought of changing nappies...' He pulls a face in disgust.

I laugh. 'It doesn't get any easier when they grow up, either. I sometimes wonder if they're more trouble than they're worth.'

I'm joking, at least partly, but Anthony tilts his head to one side and asks sympathetically, 'Problems?'

I sigh. 'It's just my eldest, Leo. I guess he's at a difficult age, but I can't say anything right to him at the moment. He seems to be constantly in trouble at school and a couple of nights ago we had a massive row. Then last night he didn't come home.'

Anthony frowns.

'And he's not at school today, either. Honestly, I don't know what to do for the best.'

'My god, I'm sorry. I had no idea.'

'Rory says I'm overreacting.' I glance out of the window at their beautifully manicured rear garden. It's the same size and shape as ours, but while ours has been given over to a large lawn where the dogs run free during the day, theirs has been landscaped and planted like an exhibit at the Chelsea Flower Show. I'm so envious.

'You're totally not. I'd be beside myself with worry.' He puts a hand to his chest melodramatically.

'I'm sure he's just off somewhere licking his wounds,' I say, although I'm anything but sure.

'Well, I'd be worried if it was my child. Have you reported it?'

'To the police? No, Rory thinks I'd be wasting my time. Leo's almost eighteen. Legally an adult next year.'

'Yeah, but after what's happened with Olivia, don't you think you ought to at least speak to them? What if it's—'

'Connected? I thought about that, but I don't know. I don't want to waste their time.'

'You should definitely call them. Do it now. What's the worst that could happen?'

'You think so? You don't think I'm making a fuss?'

'Absolutely not. Come on, where's your phone?'

Reluctantly, I pull my mobile from the pocket of my coat. It's not an emergency, is it? I can't dial 999. So instead, I look up the number for reporting non-emergencies.

Anthony watches me, sipping from his mug of coffee as I dial. Eventually, I reach a cheery call handler who asks how she can help.

I glance at Anthony. He nods, eyebrows arched.

'It's my son. His name's Leo Sugar. He's gone missing.' An icy shiver spirals down my back. Memories of the hours we spent in that police station with Leo as he was questioned about Heather Malone's death come flooding back. It's left me nervous about dealing with the police.

'When did you last see him?'

'Two days ago. Wednesday night.'

'And how old is Leo?'

'Seventeen.'

'And have there been any cross words between you recently? Any arguments?' she asks, like she's reading from a prepared document, running through a list of questions to check off.

What am I supposed to say? I can't lie, but as soon as I tell her about the row we had with Leo on Wednesday evening, I know what she's going to think. The same as Rory, that he's run off to punish us and that he'll be back when he's calmed down.

'There was a minor argument, but it was pretty trivial. Nothing major. Leo's been playing up at school, you see, but he's never stayed away from home without letting us know before,' I say, trying to make her understand how out of character it is for Leo to behave like this.

'Does he have a mobile phone? Have you tried calling him?'

Does she think I'm stupid? 'Yes, but I can't get through. I must have left a dozen messages.'

'Well, you've done the right thing. And have you tried his friends?'

'Yes.' It's hard to keep the exasperation out of my voice.

'And are there any places you can think of where he might go?'

'No. He's never done this before,' I tell her.

'He's never gone missing before?'

'Never.'

'Okay.' I hear her taping on a keyboard, hopefully registering my report. Putting it on the system. At least that's something, I suppose.

She asks me a few more questions about Leo's mental state and whether he has any health issues.

Anthony mouths something animatedly at me. I frown at him and realise he's prompting me to mention Leo's connection to Olivia.

'I don't know whether it's relevant, but Leo's friend, Olivia Hunter, went missing on Monday. I'm sure you're aware of the case. Olivia's our neighbour.'

'Olivia Hunter?' The call handler's typing becomes louder and more urgent. 'And how well would you say they know each other?'

'Like I said, they're friends. They attend the same school. Olivia and her parents live opposite,' I explain.

'Okay, what I'm going to do is pass all this information onto a police officer who will be in touch shortly. In the meantime, I'd urge you to keep your phone on and don't stray too far from home in case Leo comes back.'

'Of course.' The fact she's taking me seriously and hasn't told me to stop wasting their time brings tears to my eyes, my emotions catching me by surprise.

Anthony reaches out a hand and squeezes my arm.

'We'll do our best, don't worry.' The woman takes a note of my name and number and hangs up, but while I feel better for doing what I'm sure is the right thing, I can't believe they're actually going to put any resources into finding Leo. Not like they've done with Olivia. Why would they? I bet they get reports of teenage boys going missing all the time. I'm certainly not going to hold my breath for a police patrol car to turn up outside the house any time soon.

'What did they say?' Anthony asks.

'They're going to look into it, but I need to get back, you know, in case Leo turns up.'

I jump off the sofa, gathering my coat, and almost knock over my half-drunk mug of coffee, but catch it before it spills over their lovely cream carpet.

'If there's anything we can do, you must let us know,' Anthony says, giving me a friendly hug.

It's kind of him to offer, but what *can* he do? I just have to pray that Leo comes home soon with a mumbled apology and life can go back to normal. Or at least as normal as it has been in recent weeks. It's about the best I can hope for right now.

Chapter 38

Rory pushes the keyboard to one side and lets his throbbing forehead fall onto the desk, his body hunching over in the chair. He's physically and mentally a wreck, his mind not on his work at all. All he can think about is Toni and what an idiot he's been. He's a liar and a cheat and he's betrayed Sabine in the worst possible way. How could he have done that to her? She's done nothing to deserve it.

Although he's had a shower and scrubbed his body from head to toe, he still feels grubby, but no amount of washing and cleaning is going to alter that. He can't turn back time and change his mind about going out for a drink. He can't undo getting blind drunk and making a move on Toni, kissing her in a back alley like a rampant teenager.

Even if he'd come to his senses at that point, made his excuses and left, it wouldn't have been that bad. He could have excused it as a drunken fumble. A momentary lapse in the heat of the moment. Of course he'd have felt guilty, but would it have been the end of the world?

But he didn't. He made a conscious decision to go back to Toni's flat and spend the night in her bed. It's tawdry and cheap, and honestly, he thought he was better than that. He's disgusted with himself.

At least Sabine's taken herself out of the house for a while. How she didn't see that he was lying to her about the hotel is beyond him. It must have been so obvious. He was sure it was written all over his face and in the strain in his voice. But she'd believed every word. It's lucky she had other things on her mind.

She's completely overreacted about Leo staying out last night, but then what did he expect? She's such a worrier. He's been telling her for weeks that Leo needed more space and she shouldn't keep going on at him, nagging him all the time. He's bound to be hiding out at a friend's house, but he'll be home when he's cooled off. It's what teenagers do. Everything's a drama when you're seventeen.

Would she have been so anxious if that girl across the road, Olivia, hadn't been missing? What's the betting she's fallen out with her parents as well, and taken herself off, completely oblivious to the fuss she's caused?

Rory did the same when he was fifteen, after he'd had a fight with his father who'd pushed him against a wall and threatened to punch him. He can't even remember what the fight was about. Rory ran off and stayed with his best friend, Spencer, for a night. No one called the police or worried he'd been abducted.

These days everyone's such a snowflake, worried the sky is falling down.

He really should get on with some work to take his mind off it. If he can get through today, he'll do something special for Sabine at the weekend. Nothing too over the top. He doesn't want to raise her suspicions. But something to make her feel loved and appreciated. Something to help assuage the ache of his guilt.

He groans when his phone rings. It'll be the office either checking up on him or, worse, coming to him with a problem.

'Hello?'

'Rory? It's Toni, just checking to see how you are. You ran out kind of quickly this morning.'

He sits upright, sending his head into a spin.

'Toni,' he says. 'Yeah, hi.'

Oh god, she's the last person he wants to talk to this morning, her voice a reminder of every bad thing he did last night.

'What happened?'

He runs a hand over his brow, teasing out the tension in his forehead. 'My eldest son didn't come home last night. His mum... Sabine... my wife... she was worried.'

'Oh, right.' He can tell by her bored tone that she really doesn't care. 'I thought you might have been feeling guilty and run home to your wife to make it up to her.'

'No, course not. Sorry. That was rude of me.'

'Yeah, it was, Rory.'

He wishes she'd stop saying his name. If she's in the office and someone overhears, everyone's going to know.

'I should have been here for my family,' he says.

'That was your choice.'

'Look, about last night—'

'Yeah, yeah, save it. I've heard it all before. What is it with you married men? It was just a bit of fun. No need to feel guilty.'

'The thing is, it should never have happened,' Rory mumbles. He struggles to find the right words, to articulate what he's trying to say, let alone what's going through his head.

What *does* he think?

That he's an idiot who's risked not only his marriage but his entire family on a ten-minute instantly forgettable tryst with a junior colleague from the office? He wants to tell her he regrets every single second, but he doesn't want to upset her. More to the point, he doesn't want her running off to HR and making a complaint about how he took advantage. He's a senior member of the team. She's quite a few years his junior. That wouldn't look too good framed in a certain light. The shame of losing his job over something like that would be unbearable. Everyone would know.

He lowers his voice. 'I mean, it was amazing and everything. Of course it was, but it can't happen again.'

She laughs bitterly. 'Trust me, Rory, it ain't happening again, especially after the way you legged it this morning without even saying goodbye. That's just rude.'

'I know. I panicked. I'm so sorry.'

'And will you stop saying sorry?'

'Sorry.'

'How's your head?'

Rory groans. 'Awful. Yours?'

'Fine. So I take it you're not coming in today?'

'No.'

'Alright. I have a couple of designs I need you to sign off. I'll email them over.'

'Sure. And I'll see you on Monday, yeah?'

'Whatever.' She hangs up, leaving him unsure how things are between them. It doesn't look good though.

He sighs. Just another mess to mop up next week.

The email from Toni pops into the top of his unread messages, but he can't bring himself to read it. He'll deal with it later. He wants Toni out of his head, and besides, he really needs a coffee.

When she hears Rory in the kitchen, Biscuit comes snuffling out from her bed under the stairs, followed by Kwame and Zahara's spaniel, Rosie. He makes a brief fuss of them both, but when it's apparent he's not offering them any food, they soon lose interest and head off again.

What possessed him to behave like he did last night? Probably because he's been thinking about Toni for weeks. Months. Fantasising what it would be like, catching himself watching her when she wasn't looking, feeling that sharp pang of jealously when she told him about her various lovers she'd entertained at the weekends. In the end, the sex wasn't even that great. Perfunctory, at best. And afterwards, he was filled with a debilitating self-loathing. How could he have risked his family for that? Was it worth it? Absolutely not.

Rory makes himself a coffee and drifts upstairs, drawn to Leo's room. It wasn't so long ago that all his eldest son wanted to do was grab a football and drag his father to the park for a kickabout, dressed in his England football kit. Or settle down with him in front of the TV and the fire with a big box of Lego, building tower blocks and space rockets.

He misses those times. If he'd known then how fleeting they would be, he'd have savoured them, instead of dragging himself back to his computer or allowing himself to be distracted by his phone.

The air in Leo's room is a fug of stale sweat. His bed's not been made and there are dirty socks and pants strewn across the floor. He picks up a photo in a frame. In it, Leo's holding a silver cup, a delighted smile plastered on his face and grass stains all over his football top. He was so pleased when his team won the league, in no small part because of Leo, who'd been their top goalscorer that year. He was so happy back then. But things have changed so much.

Elsewhere in the room, there are all sorts of mementos and reminders of Leo's fading childhood. The *Star Wars* models on the shelves. The cross-country medals hanging from a corkboard. A bookcase full of his favourite books he's not read for years.

With a sigh of regret, Rory sits on the bed, cradling his mug. He's sure Leo is fine. By tonight, he'll probably be home and all will be forgotten and Sabine will be so pleased to have him back, she'll treat him with kid gloves and insist on ordering in a curry.

He leans back, resting on his elbows. Maybe they can do something together as a family this weekend. A trip to the cinema or pizza at that Italian that's newly opened on the high street.

It'll be a chance for them all to reconnect. He can put it to them tonight and it'll be something for them to look forward to.

In the meantime, he should get back to work. Apart from anything else, he needs to deal with that email from Toni.

But as he stands, he notices the mattress isn't flush with the frame of the bed and that it's slightly higher on one side, as if there's something underneath it, holding it up.

Instinctively, he lifts it by one of its corners and pushes his hand under it, feeling around. He's surprised to find a mobile phone, one he doesn't recognise. It's certainly not the smartphone they bought Leo for his birthday. It's chunky and plastic-looking. The sort of phone you see drug dealers using in those TV crime dramas Sabine likes to watch.

He turns it over in his hands. There are a dozen missed calls, all from the same number. He ought to put it back and mind his own business, but curiosity and fear get the better of him. Leo's promised them faithfully he's not back on drugs, but what if this is a phone he's been using to score? Or worse, to deal?

He prays it's not what it looks like. But there's only one way to be sure. Rory taps the number pad and is asked for a four-digit passcode. He tries 0-0-0-0, but it's not that. Nor 1-2-3-4. In desperation, he types in Leo's birthday, the seventh of April, 0-7—0-4, more in hope than expectation.

And suddenly he's in.

He feels bad for snooping, but if Leo's dealing drugs using a phone he keeps hidden in his bedroom, he needs to know so he can deal with it. So he can fix it.

There's only one number in the contacts folder, listed enigmatically as 'O'. It's the same number that appears numerous times in the call log over the last few days.

He hits the dial button and puts the phone to his ear, the blood pumping furiously through his veins.

There's a momentary pause before the call connects.

It rings twice and is answered by a female voice Rory recognises instantly.

'Leo? Thank god,' she says, breathlessly. 'Where've you been? I was worried out of my mind when you didn't call.'

A wash of relief spreads across Rory's body.

'Olivia?' he says.

Chapter 39

Rory's sitting at the breakfast bar in the kitchen when I return to the house. He glances up and stares at me silently. I don't like the look in his eye, like that time he took a phone call from the care home when my gran had passed away.

'Rory?'

He glances at the two phones on the counter. One is his iPhone, a web of trailing cracks extending from one corner from the time he dropped it on the kitchen floor. The other is a small, plastic handset with a chunky number pad and a small, scratched screen, which I've never seen before.

He pushes it towards me with one finger. 'I found this in Leo's bedroom earlier,' he says. 'Hidden under the bed.'

I frown. Why would Leo have a phone hidden in his room? Unless... 'Oh god, you don't think he's back on the drugs, do you? Please tell me he's not dealing.'

'No, it's not that.'

'How can you be so sure?'

'Because I dialled the one number it's been used to call. Olivia Hunter answered.'

'Olivia? But—'

'She's fine.' Rory sighs and runs a hand through his hair. 'She says Leo helped her to run away, and now she's hiding.'

'Run away? Where?'

'She wouldn't say, only that she's safe and not to worry about her.'

'Oh god, I knew it. I told you, didn't I? I said Leo knew more than he was letting on. Have you called the police yet?'

Rory shakes his head. 'She doesn't want to be found. She says she doesn't want to go home.'

'Rory! You have to.'

'No,' he says, his brow furrowing. 'I promised I wouldn't.'

'The Hunters think she's been abducted or... or worse. You have to let them know she's safe.'

'I can't.' He slides two fingers under his glasses and rubs his eye. 'She doesn't want to see her father. She's terrified of him.'

'I don't understand. What are you talking about?'

'Look, I don't know exactly what's been going on in that house, she wouldn't say, but all I know is that she's refusing to go home. I could hear in her voice how scared she was, and she begged me not to say anything.'

'But it's not your job to decide. She's only seventeen. What if she's in danger?'

'I think she's fine.'

'You don't know that.' I still don't understand why she'd be so afraid of her own father. Jerome's a bit of a creep, for sure, but I never picked up any sense that he and Olivia didn't get on.

'No, I've made my decision. But look, you're missing the point. I think something *has* happened to Leo.'

'What makes you say that? I thought I was overreacting?'

'Olivia's not heard from him in almost twenty-four hours. She was expecting to see him yesterday afternoon after he'd finished school, but he didn't turn up. And obviously he's not been answering this phone either.' Rory holds up the unfamiliar mobile.

I stare at it with my heart hammering. 'So where is he?'

'I don't know, but I'm worried about him. I think we probably ought to involve the police after all.'

I run my tongue over my front teeth and glance down at my feet. 'I've reported him missing.'

'What? When?'

'I saw Anthony earlier, and he convinced me to call the police, not that they took it particularly seriously, mind you. Sorry, I didn't mean to go behind your back.'

'So they're not going to look for him?'

I shrug. 'They told me I should speak to his friends, check places he might have gone, and that someone would be in touch.'

'Right, okay,' Rory says, frowning. 'Well, I think you did the right thing. Did you try the hospitals? The school again?'

I nod. I've called everyone I can think of.

'What about Casper?' Rory asks. 'Have you spoken to him? He might know something.'

'He doesn't. At least not that he's saying.'

'So what do we do now?'

'I don't know,' I admit. I've run out of ideas.

'Has he taken any clothes with him? Are there any bags missing?'

'Not that I could see. I know you think he's run away because we had that fight, but I have a really bad feeling about this,' I say.

Outside, a car pulls up. Two doors bang shut, but I don't pay any attention to it. We've become used to the comings and goings of police patrols in the street this week.

'I don't think he's run away at all,' Rory says. 'He would have taken his phone, and the fact Olivia's not seen him either is a concern. I don't think he'd abandon her if there wasn't something else going on.'

A knock at the door causes the dogs to go crazy, barking and howling as if intruders are trying to force their way in.

'Who the hell's that?' Rory asks irritably.

'How the hell do I know?' I close the dogs in the lounge and march to the front door.

'Mrs Sugar, may we have a word?' The two detectives who came to speak to us earlier in the week are standing on the doorstep. Their names are seared into my memory, like a second-rate variety club comedy duo. Lockyear and Caulfield.

'What's this about?' I ask, my throat so dry my words come out as a high-pitched squeak, which makes me sound as if I have a guilty conscience. Have they finally established I gave Leo a false alibi and have come to arrest me?

'You reported your son, Leo, as missing earlier?' the woman, Lockyear, says.

'Oh,' I say, surprised. 'That was quick. I only called an hour ago.'

Lockyear shoots me a thin smile. 'We were in the area.'

'You'd better come in.'

They politely wipe their feet on the mat and I direct them into the kitchen.

'DS Diane Lockyear,' the female detective says, introducing herself to Rory. 'And this is my colleague, DC Steve Caulfield. I don't believe we've had the pleasure.'

'Rory Sugar. Sabine's husband.'

'Leo's father?' Lockyear asks.

'That's right. Thank you for coming,' he says.

I glance at the counter where Rory was sitting, but the phone he found under Leo's bed has gone.

'No problem.' Lockyear's smile is as cold and steely as the one she gave me on the doorstep. A woman not used to suffering fools gladly, I suspect. 'So, you'd better tell me all about Leo. When did you realise he was missing?' she asks.

Chapter 40

Lockyear, the female detective, is attractive in a handsome kind of way. She's lean and athletic and has sharp, penetrating eyes that sit above prominent, chiselled cheekbones that she's accentuated with make-up. Her hair's wild and untamed and looks as if it's been dyed so many times in so many colours, it's almost impossible to work out her natural colouring.

By contrast, her male colleague is quiet and unassuming. Bland is the word that comes to Rory's mind. He doesn't say anything but Rory has no doubt he's taking it all in, listening for inconsistencies and watching for suspicious body language. Rory decides he doesn't like either of them much.

'I understand there was an argument?' Lockyear arches a shapely eyebrow and looks from Sabine to Rory and back again.

'It was nothing really,' Sabine says. 'Leo's been having some issues at school and obviously we want him to do well—'

'Issues?'

'Nothing serious.' Sabine laughs nervously. 'He'd missed a day and was getting behind on an assignment, but you know what teenagers are like. We just talked to him about the importance of school.'

'But it ended in an argument?'

'There were a few heated words, that's all,' Rory adds. He doesn't want them fixating on the row and coming to the wrong conclusion.

'And you've tried all his friends? Anyone he might have gone to stay with?'

'Everyone I can think of. No one's seen him since he left school yesterday afternoon,' Sabine says.

'How does he usually get home?'

'He walks,' Rory says. 'It's not far.'

Lockyear strokes her neck with slender fingers. She's not wearing a wedding ring, Rory notes. 'Tell me about his relationship with Olivia Hunter,' she says.

'They're friends, that's all.' Sabine waves a dismissive hand in the air.

'Sometimes they walk to school together,' Rory adds, wincing at his wife's defensive tone.

'I see.' Lockyear takes a deep breath in through her nose. She narrows her eyes as she observes them both. 'And has Leo ever gone missing before?'

'Never,' they reply in unison.

'Any of his clothes missing?'

'No.' Sabine folds her arms across her chest.

'And you've tried his phone, obviously?'

'It's switched off, but you could trace it, couldn't you? Don't you do that sort of thing?' Sabine asks.

Caulfield speaks for the first time, his bushy, black eyebrows almost taking on a life of their own, bobbing and wriggling as he talks. 'It is sometimes possible, but it can only place someone in an area. You can't pinpoint them like in the movies.'

'It's a start though, right?' Rory says.

'If he has his phone with him.' Caulfield makes a note as Rory gives him the number of Leo's iPhone.

'It must have been tough for the family after Heather Malone's death,' Lockyear says casually.

Shit. So they know about that. Although it was only a matter of time. All they needed to do was put Leo's name in their computer system and they'd have found it. Rory glances at Sabine, but she resolutely refuses to catch his eye.

'Yes, it was,' Sabine says. 'We had to move because of the backlash from the community, even though Leo did nothing wrong.'

Lockyear's chin jolts upwards and her eyes open wide. 'He supplied Ms Malone with the drugs that led to her losing her life.'

'It wasn't his fault she fell from that bridge.'

'That's a moot point.'

Sabine stiffens and her lips turn pale as she presses them together. If Lockyear's trying to get under Sabine's skin, it appears to be working.

'It's funny, isn't it, how trouble seems to follow your son around?' Lockyear steps towards the window overlooking Jerome and Faith's house, leans across the sink and peers out.

'I don't think that's fair,' Sabine retorts coolly.

'Not one, but two missing girls. And now he's vanished himself. It's all very odd, don't you think?' Lockyear turns suddenly, her gaze fixed on Sabine.

'Technically, Heather Malone was never missing,' Rory says. Are they here to help find Leo or not? 'Leo raised the alarm as soon as he saw Heather fall. You can't compare the two things.'

'Can't I? You might not find it suspicious, but I'm afraid I do. Mrs Sugar, do you still stand by the statement you provided earlier in the week that Leo was with you on Monday afternoon?'

Sabine blinks rapidly. She clears her throat, apparently struggling to find the right words. Rory wills her not to lie again. 'Well, I - I...' she stammers.

'A simple yes or no will suffice,' Lockyear says with the innocence of a child. She's toying with them like they're puppets on strings.

'I suppose, now I think about it, I might have been mistaken.'

'Mistaken?' Lockyear's eyebrows shoot up.

'I might have been a little confused about the timings before. But now I've had time to think about it, it's possible I was wrong.'

'Are you saying you want to change your story?'

'Well, yes, I suppose I am, really.'

'Because previously you were adamant that Leo wasn't with Olivia in Clover Wood on Monday afternoon, even though they'd been seen together by an independent witness,' Lockyear says.

Sabine swallows, her eyes fixed on her fingers, which she's twisting nervously. 'I know. I'm sorry,' she whispers.

'So you gave your son a false alibi when you knew full well he *had* been with Olivia Hunter in the hours before she disappeared.'

'It's not like that. You're twisting what I said. He came to help me later, but not when I originally thought.'

'You know it's a serious offence to provide an alibi you know not to be true?'

'I didn't do it deliberately.'

Lockyear taps her foot on the floor. 'And that perverting the course of justice carries a maximum seven-year jail sentence?'

'I'm sorry. Please, I didn't mean any harm.'

'She was worried, that's all,' Rory says, jumping to the defence of his wife. He can't leave her floundering. It's the least he can do. The first step on a long road to redemption. 'There was nothing malicious about it, but she knew you'd eventually find out about Heather Malone and Leo's connection to her death and she was worried it would colour your investigation. She thought you'd jump to conclusions when Leo had absolutely nothing to do with Olivia going missing.'

Rory feels the weight of Leo's burner phone in his back pocket, where he casually slipped it when he heard the police at the door. A physical reminder of another lie. Leo *was* involved in Olivia's disappearance, but not in the way they think. He was helping her. Not harming her.

Should he tell them? Hand them the phone and let them know Olivia's safe so she can be reunited with her parents? He promised on his life that he wouldn't say anything, but if they're going to threaten Sabine with arrest, he will. His own family has to come first, even if it means betraying Olivia.

'You have to understand the hell we've been through these last few months,' Rory continues. 'Sabine wasn't thinking straight.'

'I'm sure Heather's parents would be incredibly sympathetic.'

Rory hangs his head. He didn't mean it like that. Of course it's been awful for them. They've lost a daughter, but it doesn't mean his family hasn't suffered too.

'We'd like to take a look around Leo's room, if that's okay?' Caulfield says.

'Why?' Sabine asks.

'It's just routine. Sometimes people leave clues when they go missing. It could be something innocuous you wouldn't even notice, or something like a diary or a letter or an email.'

'Sure,' Rory says. 'Help yourself. It's the second door on the left at the top of the stairs.'

They wait in the kitchen while Caulfield disappears from the room, the floorboards above their heads creaking as he moves about. Rory doesn't like the thought of someone, even if it is a police officer, poking about in their house, but he can hardly protest. And the most important thing is finding Leo.

Lockyear pulls a notebook from a bag she has slung over her shoulder.

'While we wait, perhaps I can take some details of your movements over the last twenty-four hours?' she says with what she probably thinks is a disarming smile but which gives Rory a chill down his spine.

'Movements?' Sabine asks, cocking her head.

'Yes, if you could, it would be helpful.'
'Why?'

Lockyear lowers her notebook. 'It's routine in these types of cases.'

'You can't seriously think we had anything to do with our own son going missing?'

A cold sweat breaks out over Rory's body, his heart thudding like a rock breaker in his chest. What the hell's he going to say? He can't admit he was with Toni last night. Not in front of Sabine.

'I didn't say you did,' Lockyear says, 'but it would help us eliminate you from our inquiries.'

'I've been in the house most of the time,' Sabine says, 'apart from picking up the dogs and taking them for their walks.'

'The dogs?'

'I look after several of the neighbours' dogs during the day.'

'Oh, yes, of course. Including Mr and Mrs Hunter's dog. Hank, isn't it?' She scribbles a note in her book. 'And what about you, Mr Sugar?' she asks, looking up from her notes and peering at him expectantly. 'Where were you yesterday?'

'I - I was at work all day,' he mumbles.

'And where's that?'

'In London.' He gives her details of the charity and the address of the office.

'And what time did you get home?'

'Actually, I didn't make it home last night,' he says sheepishly. 'I went out for a few drinks after work with colleagues and stayed in a hotel.' He's certain there's a noticeable catch in his voice. A telltale strain that screams he's lying.

'Okay,' Lockyear says. 'Which hotel?'

'The Premier Inn by Waterloo station.' There it is. A big, fat lie and she's writing it down in black and white in her book. But what's he supposed to say? He can hardly tell her the truth.

He forces a smile and tries to make it reach his eyes, but suspects it looks more like he's grimacing.

'And when did you get home?'

'This morning, when Sabine called me to say Leo was missing. I jumped straight on a train.'

'I see. She didn't call you last night?'

'I didn't pick up her messages until this morning.'

Caulfield eventually returns to the kitchen empty-handed. Rory's dying to ask if he's found anything, but keeps his mouth closed.

'Do you have a recent photo of Leo?' Lockyear asks, putting her notebook back in her bag.

'Of course.' Sabine grabs her phone and finds an image of Leo she took in the spring, long before Heather Malone's name was even known to them. He's actually smiling at it. He looks happy and unencumbered. 'Shall I email it to you?'

'Please, then we can circulate it. In the meantime, anything else I should know about?'

Sabine turns to Rory, eyes widening as if she's trying to silently communicate with him. He knows what she's thinking. She wants him to tell them about the phone he's found under Leo's bed. She wants him to tell them he's spoken to Olivia, and that she's safe and well.

'No, that's everything, I think,' Rory says. 'Let me show you to the door.'

Chapter 41

'What the hell was all that about?' I clutch the kitchen counter after the two detectives have left, feeling physically and emotionally spent.

'I don't know,' Rory says, scratching his head.

I watch from the kitchen window as Lockyear and Caulfield climb into a car parked on the road outside. They don't immediately drive off, but sit there, chatting. I guess they're talking about us.

Do they really think Rory and I know more than we're letting on about Leo's disappearance? It certainly felt that way, talking to us like we were suspects. But is it any wonder? I shouldn't have lied to them when they first came here asking about Leo and Olivia in Clover Wood. I should have known they'd have done some digging and found out about Heather Malone's death eventually, and that Leo would naturally come under suspicion.

'Do they really think we're capable of harming our own son?'

'No, that's not what they think.' Rory sucks on his bottom lip, his body tense, like he has all the weight of the world on his shoulders. 'Do you see? They think we're lying about him going missing. They think we've helped him to disappear.'

'What?'

'They think we've made up a story about him going missing so they can't arrest him over Olivia's disappearance. They know Leo was seen arguing with Olivia on the afternoon she vanished, and now they know you gave him a false alibi. What other conclusion would you draw?'

'But it's not true,' I gasp.

'They don't know that.'

'You should have told them about the phone.'

Rory takes a huge breath in, his chest expanding and his shoulders rising, then rubs his beard vigorously. 'I couldn't.'

'Why not? It proves Leo's not done Olivia any harm and that he was only trying to help her.'

Rory shakes his head. His eyes are still puffy and bloodshot, the remnants of his hangover evident all over his face.

'I promised Olivia I wouldn't say anything.'

'But that's crazy. Why are you so keen to protect her over your own son?'

'You didn't hear her, Sabine. She was frantic. I don't know what she's been through at home, but she was adamant she doesn't want to go home,' he says.

'But they think Leo's to blame. All because of what happened with Heather. But he's innocent.'

'Hang on, he's not, is he? He helped Olivia to run away, for whatever reason. But she's only seventeen and even if he thought he was doing the right thing, the police might not see it that way.'

'You should have told them the truth,' I cry. 'You should have told them you'd spoken to her. That she's alive and safe.'

Rory's gone pale, all the colour in his face drained away. A combination of the stress and his hangover, I should think.

'You can talk,' he fires back. 'You gave Leo a false alibi. That's far worse.'

'But I've put that right. I've told them the truth now. You should do the same,' I urge him.

'No,' he snaps. 'I can't. I need time to think.'

'And in the meantime, your son is out there somewhere and we have no idea where he is or what's happened to him.'

'You think I don't know that? I'm just as worried as you, but arguing about it isn't going to help, is it?'

I throw my arms up in despair at the exact moment there's another knock on the door. A crisp, firm tap-tap-tap. We've never been so popular. It's probably one of the neighbours - my guess is Hanna - who've seen the detectives at the house and have come looking for gossip.

'I'll get rid of them,' I announce as I storm out of the kitchen.

But when I open the door, it's not Hanna or any of the other neighbours. It's Lockyear and Caulfield back again. They're looking even more stony-faced than before. Lockyear has her arms crossed over her chest and her lips pressed tightly together like she's swallowed a wasp.

'Oh,' I say, unable to hide my surprise. 'Was there something else?'

DC Caulfield has his notebook open and a puzzled expression on his face, his fuzzy eyebrows knitted together.

'Just something we need to clarify.' Lockyear attempts a weak smile, which looks more like irritation. 'May we come in?'

She pushes past me into the house and marches into the kitchen where Rory's still standing behind the breakfast bar, his face clouded with confusion.

'Mr Sugar, can I clarify something you told us just now? You said you spent last night at the Premier Inn in Waterloo?' Caulfield says.

Rory swallows and wets his lips.

'The hotel has no record of your stay. We've just spoken to them.'

I stare at Rory, wondering what games they're trying to play now. Are they deliberately trying to catch us out?

He glances at me, fidgeting nervously on the spot.

A hollowness spreads from the pit of my stomach.

'Were you at the Premier Inn in Waterloo last night or not?' Lockyear asks, her hands on her hips.

I can almost feel the panic washing off Rory in waves as a sheen of sweat breaks out on his forehead. What's he hiding?

'You see, the thing is...' He's looking at me now, over the shoulders of the two detectives, blinking rapidly. A rabbit in the headlights.

'Rory, where were you last night?' I ask slowly and deliberately as my pulse races.

He hangs his head. 'I'm sorry,' he mutters under his breath.

'Well, let's assume you weren't at the hotel as you told us earlier then,' Lockyear says impatiently. 'Where were you?'

'I stayed with a friend.'

'We'll need a name, an address and a contact number.' Lockyear stares at him.

'I don't know her address.'

'Her?' I yell. 'You were with a woman last night? Who?'

'Mrs Sugar, please.' Lockyear turns and holds up a hand to silence me.

'Her name's Toni. She's a colleague.'

Rory can't bring himself to look any of us in the eye. He lied to me, and to the police. He wasn't in a hotel at all. He was shacked up with some fancy woman from his office. I can't believe it. My chest tightens and I struggle to breathe. Nausea swells in my stomach and my head feels like it's going to float off my shoulders. I grab the doorframe to steady myself, my mind a maelstrom of confusion and humiliation.

'What the hell, Rory?'

'I'm sorry,' he says. 'Nothing happened.'

'And you expect me to believe that?'

'Her full name and a contact number please, Mr Sugar,' Lockyear repeats.

I watch his lips move as he reaches for his phone, scrolls through it, and holds it up for Lockyear and Caulfield to see, but I don't hear anything above the rushing of blood in my ears.

The world slows down and I have a feeling I'm not really present.

So while I was at home worrying myself silly about Leo, my husband was playing away with some tart from the office.

'Who is she?' My voice sounds dull and muted, like I'm wearing a pair of headphones.

Rory glances at me with a blank expression. 'No one,' he says. 'Just someone from work.'

'Who?'

'I told you, her name's Toni. But nothing happened.'

'I don't believe you,' I say, raising my voice.

'I had too much to drink and realised I'd missed my train. Toni offered me her sofa for the night. That's all.'

'I don't believe you,' I repeat.

'Please, Sabine. It wasn't like that.'

'So why did you lie and say you'd stayed in a hotel?'

'Because I knew this is how you'd react. That you'd jump to the wrong conclusion.'

'You're pathetic, you know that?'

I'm suddenly aware the two detectives are still in the room. Lockyear's watching us argue with a smug grin on her face, enjoying the entertainment.

'So now we know you've both lied to us,' she says, shoving her hands in the pockets of her trouser suit. 'Anything else you want to tell us while we're here?'

'We didn't have anything to do with Leo's disappearance, if that's what you're getting at,' I shout, conscious of my voice echoing around the room. 'I know you think we did, but instead of coming around here, trying to trip us up, you should be out there looking for him. And Olivia Hunter. You're wasting your time.'

'Don't you worry, we'll find them,' Lockyear says. 'And we will get to the truth.' Her hard stare penetrates through me.

'I hope you do, and quickly. Now, was there anything else?' I meet her stare with my own. I'm not going to be intimidated in my own house, even if she's just witnessed my total and utter humiliation.

'No, that's all,' she says, turning to leave. But as they reach the front door, she stops and turns back. 'That is assuming your husband's story checks out this time. We'll be in touch, Mrs Sugar.'

And then they're gone. I slam the door shut behind them and slump to the floor, devastated.

Chapter 42

'How could you?' I demand, my jaw so taut it aches.

Rory's staring out of the dining room window with his shoulders slumped. He turns slowly, his face crumpled in anguish. Or is it guilt?

'I'm so sorry,' he says. 'I've been such an idiot.'

I don't recognise him anymore. This man who I loved, who fathered my children, is a stranger in our house. We've been through so much together these last few months and this is how he treats me? With utter contempt? What did I do to deserve it?

'How long has it been going on?' It sounds like a cliché, the kind of thing every betrayed woman who's caught their husband in a lie would , but it's the question I have to know the answer to. How long has he been making a fool of me?

I thought our marriage was stronger than this. We've been through so much, dealt with so much hatred and anger, hostility and resentment, and yet we pulled through it and, I thought, were rebuilding our lives. The one thing that kept me going through the long, dark nights when everything was collapsing around us was that at least Rory and I were united. A team. Indestructible and indefatigable.

And yet it wasn't true. I didn't even know Rory was feeling like this, like I wasn't good enough for him. That he needed more.

'Tell me about her,' I say, with a sudden calm that descends like a heavy velvet shawl.

'Let's not do this,' he says.

'No, Rory, we *are* going to do this. Tell me,' I say through gritted teeth.

He sighs. 'Fine. Her name's Toni and she works with me on the design team, okay?'

I shake my head, trying to recall the name, whether he's ever mentioned her before today. Maybe. It sounds vaguely familiar, but he doesn't really talk to me about work. Not that I'm particularly interested in people I don't know and have never met.

'Is she pretty?'

'Sabine, please. Don't.'

'Is she?' I repeat, raising my voice.

'I don't know. I suppose so.'

'Is she married?'

'No.'

'How old is she?'

He shrugs. 'I don't know. Early thirties, I guess.'

It's another arrow in my chest. This just gets better and better. It's worse than a trashy TV soap opera. 'Almost young enough to be your daughter, in other words.'

'Stop it.'

'So what is it? Am I too old for you? Too boring? Too busy washing your clothes and bringing up your kids to pay you the attention you deserve? Poor Rory.' I pout in mock sympathy.

Rory's chin falls to his chest. 'I'm not doing this, okay? I made a mistake. I should have told you where I was last night, but like I said, nothing happened.'

'And I don't believe you.'

'Believe what you like, Sabine. I don't care anymore.'

'So that's it? Our son is missing, in case you haven't noticed. We should be out looking for him, not having to deal with the fallout from your mid-life crisis, and discussing why you started shagging your secretary.'

'She's not my secretary,' Rory growls.

'You lied to the police.'

'That makes two of us.'

I throw my hands into the air and scream. I can't do this right now. If Rory wants to throw away twenty years of marriage for a thirty-year-old tart from work, I'm not going to stop him. I have more important things on my mind, like finding my son.

I reach out my hand. 'Give me that phone.'

Rory's eyes narrow with suspicion. 'Why?'

'I want to speak to Olivia.'

'I don't think that's a good idea.'

'I'll decide what's a good idea or not,' I snap. I'm done with him telling me what I can and can't do. 'Give it to me.'

Reluctantly, he dips his hand into his back pocket and, with a scowl of disapproval, hands me the phone.

'What's the passcode?'

'Leo's birthday. Zero seven, zero four.'

I punch in the numbers and navigate to the contacts list, which, as Rory told me, shows only one number, listed under the name 'O'. I dial it and put the phone to my ear. If Olivia has any idea where Leo might be, I need to know.

But after one ring, the call goes to voicemail.

'What exactly did Olivia tell you about why she ran away?' I ask, hanging up.

Rory shrugs like a sulky teenager. 'She wouldn't say much, only that Leo was helping her escape from her father.'

'That's a weird thing to say. So what? He's been abusing her?' I ask. It's hard to believe Jerome would raise a hand to his own daughter, but then I know first-hand how melodramatic teenagers can be. 'Why didn't she tell someone?'

Rory shrugs.

I study the phone carefully. Presumably Olivia has one almost exactly the same that she's been using to keep in touch with Leo, and now we have her number, the police should be able to trace her.

'What are you thinking?' Rory asks, watching me suspiciously.

'I'm going to hand it in. I think the police need to know about it.'

'No, Sabine, you can't,' Rory protests, horrified. 'I promised Olivia I wouldn't.'

'We don't have any choice. We can't keep lying. If Olivia has any information that can help us find Leo, we need to know.'

'But -'

'No, Rory. My son is more important.'

He sighs in defeat, knowing better than to carry on arguing with me, especially given the mood I'm in.

'I'm going to run it down to the police station. I'll take the dogs with me and give them a run around while I'm out. I need some time alone to think and decide what I'm going to do.'

Rory stares at me like an abandoned puppy dog. 'Are you going to throw me out?'

'I don't know.' I clear my throat, fighting back the emotion. 'I haven't decided yet.'

Chapter 43

A uniformed sergeant appears from behind the reception counter and drops the phone in a clear plastic evidence bag. I'd hoped to hand it over to Lockyear and Caulfield, but they were unavailable. At least it means I don't have to explain to Lockyear's face why we didn't mention we'd found a phone in Leo's bedroom when they were at the house earlier.

In less than ten minutes, I'm done. The sergeant takes my details and promises to pass everything to the detectives, who'll be in touch if they need any further information. I guess now all I can do is wait. It shouldn't take long for them to locate Olivia now they have her number, should it? And hopefully she'll be able to shed some light on what's happened to Leo. I know he's not a child anymore, but it doesn't stop me worrying about him. Anything could have happened.

When I return to the van, the dogs are unusually noisy and excitable. I've disrupted their routine by bringing them out for a walk at lunchtime, and I guess they're unsettled. Or maybe they picked up on the tension between me and Rory in the house earlier. Animals can be so perceptive, and Rory's revelations have hit me harder than I'd like to admit. Apart from anything else, I feel so stupid because I never saw his betrayal coming.

It's cut like a knife. I never in a million years imagined he'd be the kind of sleazeball who'd be chasing after young women in the office. It's no wonder he's been spending longer and longer at work. And who is this Toni woman, anyway? He says nothing's happened between them, but does he really expect me to believe that? I might feel stupid, but I'm not an idiot. I can read him like a book. The guilt was written all over his face, and I've always been able to tell when he's lying to me.

This couldn't have come at a worse time, when I really need to be focusing my energies on finding Leo. I don't understand how he can just vanish. I know he was at school yesterday. The office confirmed as much. But after that, it's a complete mystery. No one saw him. No one's heard from him. And he's not taken any clothes. I could understand that he was angry with me and Rory after the argument we had, and that maybe he'd taken himself off to calm down, but I would have expected him to keep his commitment to meet with Olivia. After all, he was supposed to be looking after her, wherever she's hiding. He wouldn't abandon her unless there was something seriously wrong. But what?

Has he been in an accident? Has he had some kind of unexplained medical incident? What else could it be? And yet I've called all the hospitals and clinics. So where the hell is he?

I jump in the van and start driving, not really thinking about where I'm going, until I pull into the car park back at Clover Wood. It's been crawling with police looking for Olivia in recent days, but they've gone now, a strip of blue and white plastic police tape fluttering from a tree the only sign they were ever here.

The dogs tumble out of the back of the van with their tails wagging, whining with excitement at an unexpected trip to the woods. They love it here almost as much as I do. It's so tranquil and calming. A place where I can walk and think.

After five minutes, when I'm satisfied we have the run of the woods to ourselves, and the car park is far behind us, I finally let them loose.

Of course, they all dart off in different directions the moment they're free. Hank disappears into the thick undergrowth, snuffling around after the scent of a fox or a badger, while Rosie and Biscuit prefer checking out the smells along the length of the footpath, and never stray that far from my heels. Tyson is nervy, constantly stopping with his ears pricked, listening for the sounds of danger, while Bertie dawdles behind us all and I have to keep chivying him along.

As I'm in no rush to get back to the house and see Rory, I decide to take a longer route than normal, one that follows a t path that loops around the far side of the woods where we rarely venture. The fresh air and exercise will do me good, especially as I didn't sleep much last night, worrying about Leo.

We're at the furthest point from the car park when Biscuit begins to act strangely. She'd been sniffing around happily, trotting along with Rosie, but suddenly stops and stands frozen with her ears pricked, her tail erect like the mast of a yacht, and a front paw raised off the ground.

'Hey, girl, what is it?'

She stares straight ahead, her whole body taut, ignoring me.

Her first bark is a tentative woof, like she's heard something, but is uncertain whether it's something she should be worried about. She paws at the ground, then lifts her head and barks three more times, agitated. I stare into the scrub, following her gaze through the tree trunks, bushes and brambles, but I can't see anything.

'Come on, silly. It's probably just a squirrel,' I tell her, walking on.

But she shoots off, barking loudly as she disappears under low-hanging branches and through clumps of fallen amber and gold leaves. The other dogs, confused, stop to watch as she scurries into the distance. Tyson looks up at me with big, sad eyes and a worried expression and Rosie whines. Something's not right.

'Biscuit? Where are you going?' I call after her. This is becoming a bad habit of hers. If she continues to run off like this, I'll have to keep her on her lead in future.

Her barking fades into the distance.

Even Hank pokes his snout out from a patch of nettles he was investigating to see what all the fuss is about.

'Biscuit! Biscuit!' I yell, but she's gone. I'll have to go after her. 'Stupid dog,' I mutter under my breath.

I step off the path and through the trees, picking my way carefully over and around trailing vines and creeping brambles that threaten to trip me up, through mossy patches and muddy puddles, with the other dogs following behind me, bemused.

At least Biscuit's barking acts like a beacon, guiding me towards her, and when I eventually catch up with her, I'm out of breath and have dead leaves and bits of stick caught in my hair.

She's standing in a small clearing under a broad oak tree that's shed most of its leaves, still barking incessantly, her paws clawing at the ground and her eyes fixed on an unnatural-looking pile of fallen branches, twigs and leaves. It looks as though someone has deliberately piled them up. Probably kids who've been building dens.

As I pant my way towards Biscuit, my senses are on full alert. There's something odd here. Something that doesn't look quite right. A strange feeling I can't put my finger on. And what's Biscuit seen that's upset her so much? A nest of adders? A diseased and injured rabbit? I shudder at the thought.

The other dogs gather around me, unusually subdued. Tyson and Rosie sit and watch Biscuit, while Hank, the bravest of them all, cautiously approaches the strange-looking heap under the oak tree.

Finally, Biscuit stops barking, her tail drops between her legs and she casts a glance at me.

'What is it, Biscuit? What have you found?'

She whimpers, barks once more and turns her gaze back again. There's no mistaking what she's trying to say. There's something under that pile of branches and leaves, and she wants me to take a look.

Chapter 44

Leo's not sure how much more he can take. He's tired, cold and his body aches all over. He's at his lowest ebb and he's about ready to give up all hope. No one's going to find him. He's going to die here, alone and afraid.

Jerome brought him some water and some stale croissants earlier, but his stomach's rumbling and hollow again, and Leo has no idea when or if he's coming back. If he's been left here to rot.

Will anyone even find his body when he's gone? The crate's been well hidden, so unless someone thinks to look in this part of the woods, probably not. It's going to be a horrible way to go. He just prays it won't be painful, that he slips peacefully into a deep sleep and never wakes up.

He tried to do the right thing by Olivia, but he never thought for one moment it would end like this. Jerome knows what he's done. Maybe not everything, but enough. Maybe it's time to come clean. To put an end to his suffering. He doesn't want to, but he doesn't want to die either. Not like this anyway, caged like an animal, hungry, thirsty and in pain. He can't spend another night in this crate.

And so he makes up his mind. When Jerome comes back, he'll tell him everything. He'll confess that he and Olivia planned it together and he'll tell him where he can find his daughter.

It's a difficult decision. One of the hardest of his life, especially as it means letting Olivia down. Breaking his promise to her and condemning her to return home with that monster. But he feels better for it. A little lighter. Like there is hope, light at the end of a long tunnel. Maybe Olivia will find the strength to tell the police the truth, to finally stand up to her father, and maybe Leo's suffering won't be in vain after all.

The sound of a dog barking snaps him out of a light sleep he'd fallen into as the temperature inside the crate rose a few degrees through the morning. It's certainly nowhere near as cold as it was last night, although he's still frozen through and hasn't yet recovered the feeling in his toes and lower legs.

He's heard dogs before, but only in the distance and they've never come close enough to be able to grab their attention. This is different. The barking is getting louder, coming closer, until he's certain the animal is right outside.

His heart soars. Has it found him? Did it come to investigate?

He snatches a breath, hardly daring to believe his luck. If there's a dog, it must have an owner and they can't be too far away. He listens intently, trying to make out the sound of footsteps or the brush of clothing through the undergrowth.

The barking reminds him of Biscuit, the silly cockapoo his mother bought for him and Casper. She's cute, especially when those corkscrew curls of fur fall over her eyes, or she rolls over demanding belly rubs, but Leo would have preferred a proper dog. A big German shepherd or a golden retriever they could have taken on adventures, instead of a ditzy ball of fur like Biscuit. It's not even a proper dog's name.

Leo's chest tightens as he hears scratching and scuffling close by. He closes his eyes and tries to imagine the scene outside the crate. Is there more than one dog? It sounds like there might be, but he doesn't want to risk scaring them off by making a noise. He needs to wait, be patient, until he's sure there's someone close enough to hear his cries for help.

Another dog barks. It's a deeper sound and is accompanied by a guttural growl. Surely the owner has to be near.

And then he hears it. The thud of boots on the ground. The scratch of brambles on clothing. The brush of leaves against legs. Someone's coming!

'What is it, Biscuit? What have you found?'

Leo's heart misses a beat. He'd recognise that voice anywhere. It's his mother. She's found him. Against all the odds, she's stumbled across the crate. Tears of relief and joy trickle down his cheeks.

He bangs a fist against the side of the crate, oblivious to the pain that shoots through his hand.

'Mum!' he croaks. 'Help me! It's Leo. I'm in here.'

Chapter 45

Jerome's been driving around in his van all morning, looking for Olivia, more in hope than expectation. He has to do something. He can't just sit around waiting for Leo to decide he's ready to talk. But it's taking far longer than he expected. It might be time to accelerate matters. He has plenty of tools in the back of his van he could use. He's no monster, but if Olivia's in danger, he has to find her, and time is not on his side.

It's obvious Leo knows where she is, and although it's frustrating beyond belief, Jerome's grudgingly impressed at the boy's fortitude. Most of those snowflake kids his age would have cried for their mothers and spilled their secrets at the first prospect of being sealed up inside that crate.

But not Leo. He's refused to say anything even after almost twenty-four hours stuck out in near-freezing conditions with nothing but the clothes he was wearing and an old fleece blanket.

How long's it going to take? Another day? Another night? Jerome doesn't have that long. His daughter hasn't been home in four nights now.

He has to find her. He can't rely on the police. They've been useless so far. They say they're looking, but they're no nearer to finding Olivia than when he first reported her missing. The only way she's going to be found is if Jerome can get answers out of Leo.

He was going to leave it for a few more hours. Let Leo sweat for a little longer, at least until the early evening when the sun had set and the cold of night was creeping in again. But impatience gets the better of him. It's only lunchtime, but he's going to go back and try again. Give Leo one more chance before he takes more drastic measures to get him to talk.

He's stopped at a petrol station on his way and bought a bottle of Coke and a chicken sandwich for the boy. Playing bad cop's not worked so far, but maybe if he shows some kindness and takes Leo something to eat, it might be enough to finally break his will. Otherwise, he'll have to resort to the hammer and pliers. Not something he relishes, but he'll do what it takes when it comes to saving his daughter.

Jerome rumbles along the rough track to the quiet end of the woods, bumping over potholes and loose gravel, and pulls into the muddy layby where it's unlikely anyone will see him. He grabs the food and trudges into the woods, following a line of trees that marks the spot where he's hidden the crate.

When he hears a dog barking, he slows down to listen. It's not unusual to hear dogs in the woods, but they don't often stray this far from the car park. This one sounds close. Too close. The last thing he needs is to bump into someone who can later place him in the vicinity, especially if things don't go to plan and he has to abandon Leo here to die.

He picks his way carefully through the trees, conscious of the noise he's making as he lumbers through the thick scrub. The big oak tree he's heading for is just up ahead, but as he steps around the trunk of a spiralling ash, he spots a figure.

Is that Leo's mother, Sabine? He recognises her olive-green jacket and loose blonde hair. She's with the dogs and is peering curiously at the pile of branches and leaves he's piled up over the crate where Leo is entombed.

His stomach flips.

How the hell has she found him? And, more importantly, what's he going to do now?

Chapter 46

A dull thud comes from the heap of branches that Biscuit has discovered. It sounds almost like someone hammering with their fist on a kitchen counter and I think I must have imagined it, until it briefly stops and a voice, muted and strained, calls out for help.

'Leo?' I gasp.

Oh my god.

Biscuit goes berserk, barking and wagging her tail, scratching at the ground like a bull about to charge at a matador.

'Mum? Get me out of here!'

Out of where? All I can see is a pile of debris. It doesn't make sense, until I start pulling the branches away and digging through the leaves with my hands, and my fingers strike something hard and immovable. Manically, I dig quicker until I've revealed what looks like a large box made of soft, pale pine that's been meticulously hidden.

What the hell?

'Leo, is that you?' I ask incredulously. Why is my son inside a box buried in the woods? Is it some kind of prank his friends have played on him? A silly game that's gone wrong?

'Please, just open it. Get me out.' His pleas are pitiful.

I drop to my knees and sweep away the rest of the dead leaves and decaying branches, working like a woman possessed, until I've fully exposed what I can now see is a packing crate that looks frighteningly like a coffin, marked with indecipherable symbols stamped across it in blurry black ink.

'Hang on, I'll get you out. Don't worry,' I pant, my hands working around the lid, looking for a way to prise it open.

But it won't budge. I can't open it. The lid of the crate has been nailed down and sealed closed, with my son inside.

What kind of sick monster has done this?

'Mum!' Leo screams. 'Get me out!'

He sounds hysterical, and I'm not surprised, but the more worked up he becomes, the more I panic and the less clearly I can think.

'I'm trying,' I shout.

'Mum!'

But there's no way I can open the lid with my fingers alone, especially as they're now bloody and sore from trying.

'I can't,' I yell. 'I need to get help.'

'Don't leave me,' he screams.

It rips at my heart, but I can't do this alone. I need something to jemmy it open, but I don't have anything like that on me.

'Try to stay calm. I'm going to get you out, I promise, but I need to make a call, okay?'

I pull myself to my feet, pressing my hand onto the top of the lid as if it might miraculously melt away and I can reach in and touch my son.

'Please, Mum.'

'I'll be right back.'

I pull out my phone, but I already know there's no chance of any signal this deep into the woods. I raise it high above my head, praying for a miracle, that some kind of environmental anomaly will mean the signal is strong enough to penetrate the trees and allow me to make just one call.

I stare at the screen and the tiny bars in the top right corner, willing them to light up. For a fleeting second, one bar appears, but it's gone almost as quickly as it appeared. It's hopeless. There's no way I can make a call from here. I have no choice. I'm going to have to leave Leo. I need to head back towards the car park where there's better coverage and, who knows, maybe I'll meet someone on my way who can help, or who I can at least dispatch to raise the alarm.

'Darling, listen to me,' I say, lowering my head to the side of the crate. 'I'm going to have to find help, okay?'

'No, Mum, don't leave. Please!'

'I'll be back as soon as I can. It's going to be fine. I won't be long.'

Chapter 47

Jerome watches silently from behind a tree.

His first instinct is to turn and run. To race back to his van and get as far away from Clover Wood as possible. But he can't run from the police and how long's it going to take for them to come knocking at his door when they find out he's abducted Leo? Meanwhile, he's still no closer to finding Olivia.

He needs to think. No need to panic. After all, it's impossible for Sabine to open the crate unless she happens to have a crowbar hidden under her coat. And there's no mobile signal out here, so she'll have to find help. That should give Jerome a small window to move Leo. But then another thought occurs to him. Maybe he can turn this to his advantage.

He can hear Sabine talking to Leo now, reassuring him, the panic evident in her tone. She stands, pulls out her phone and holds it above her head. He waits. Watches her lower it again in frustration and return to the crate. She's no doubt telling Leo she's going for help and that she won't be long.

She corrals the dogs, puts them on their leads, and turns in a slow circle, trying to find her bearings. He has no idea how she found the crate, but she's clearly lost and is wondering which is the quickest way back to the car park.

For a second, Hank stiffens and stares in Jerome's direction, holding up his snout and sniffing. Jerome snatches a breath. It would be just his luck for that stupid mutt to give him away. He's never liked him much. He never even wanted a dog, but it was Faith's idea. She was insistent when they moved into the new house.

But when Sabine pulls them away in the opposite direction, Hank loses interest in Jerome, and happily trots after her.

As she hurries, stumbling through the trees, Jerome makes a beeline for the nearest path, stalking quietly through the undergrowth, watching where he places each foot, still clutching the plastic bag containing Leo's sandwich and soft drink against his chest.

When he finds the path, he hastens his pace, heading in the direction where he expects Sabine to appear at any moment. He'll make it look as if he's stumbled on her by chance. A fortuitous slice of luck.

A few minutes later, he spots her emerging from the trees ahead, the dogs whining and straining at their leads. At first, she doesn't notice him, stepping onto the trail and marching purposefully away.

It's only when Hank stops, turns around and barks at Jerome that she glances over her shoulder. The relief on her face when she finally spots him is laughable. It's as if she thinks all her prayers have been answered.

'Sabine?' he says, acting surprised.

Hank jumps up, tail wagging, trying to lick his face, but Jerome pushes him away.

'Jerome, thank god.' She's a little out of breath. 'I wasn't sure I'd see anyone.'

He holds up the plastic bag from the petrol station. 'I've been coming out here with my lunch to think,' he says. 'Is everything okay? You look a little flustered.'

'I need your help.' The relief in her voice is palpable. 'I don't suppose your van's nearby, is it? I need a wrench or a crowbar or something.' The words tumble from her mouth in an avalanche. 'It's Leo. I've found him inside a crate and I can't open it. Please, can you help me?'

He feigns puzzlement, knitting his brow. 'Slow down, Sabine. What are you talking about?'

'I don't have time to explain. I can hear Leo inside, but I can't get him out. I think he's been in there all night.'

Jerome shakes his head, staring at her like she's crazy. 'A crate?'

'Yes. Do you have anything in your van I could use to open it? The lid's been nailed down.'

'With Leo inside?'

'Yes. Please, Jerome. There's no time for this.'

He shrugs. 'Yeah, sure. I have a hammer. Will that do?'

'Can you fetch it?'

'Okay. Wait here with the dogs. I'll be back in a sec.'

'Thank you.' Her shoulders slump with relief. 'Please, hurry.'

He turns back the way he's come, his arm pressed against his side, pinning the handle of the hammer he has hidden under his jacket against his ribs.

Back at the van, he times two full minutes on his watch before pulling the hammer out and heading back along the path towards Sabine.

She's waiting where he left her, pacing anxiously up and down on the spot with the dogs pulling at their leads, bored.

'Will this do?' he asks, holding the hammer aloft.

'I hope so.' Her face is pale with worry. 'It's this way.'

She charges back into the woods, through the trees, crashing noisily through bushes and sticky, muddy puddles.

He keeps close and eventually she pulls up in the clearing close to Leo and the crate. It stands out in stark contrast to the vegetation.

'What the hell?' Jerome gasps, secretly pleased with his acting skills and making it seem like he's genuinely surprised.

'Can you open it?' Sabine begs. 'Leo's in there.'

He casts her a sideways glance, maintaining the pretence of confusion.

'Sure,' he says, approaching the box cautiously, eyeing it up as if he's trying to work out where to start.

He crouches with one knee on the soft ground and slides the claw of his hammer into a narrow gap between the lid and the crate.

Sabine stands close by, clutching her hands to her face.

Jerome grunts as the first nail gives and the lid opens a fraction of an inch. Methodically, he goes around them all, lifting them one by one, until the lid comes free. He slips the hammer back into his jacket pocket, stands and tosses the lid to one side.

Leo blinks up at him, his eyes narrowed against the sudden bright light. He looks pale and pinched, his hair all messed up and his eyes puffy. Jerome steps back as Sabine rushes forwards, virtually pushing him out of the way.

'Oh, Leo, thank god you're safe.'

'Mum?' he croaks.

'It's okay, baby. I've got you now.' She pulls him up until he's sitting awkwardly, wincing and stiff.

She throws her arms around him and pulls him into a smothering hug, crying and wailing, making such a fuss.

'You're okay now,' she soothes. 'Are you hurt? Let me look at you.'

She pulls away and holds his head in her hands, examining his face tenderly. She wipes away a smear of dirt on his cheek with her thumb.

'I'm okay, Mum,' he mumbles. 'Just a bit sore and thirsty.'

Jerome's hand snakes into his trouser pocket, searching for the knife.

'What happened to you?' Sabine asks. 'Who did this?'

Leo coughs, his body wracking, doubling over as he clears his lungs. When he finally catches his breath, he looks up and spots Jerome by the trunk of the shady oak.

Jerome stares at him. Leo holds his gaze defiantly.

Then their stupid dog comes bounding up, nuzzling under Sabine's arm to lick Leo's face. 'Hello, girl,' he says, a smile cracking across his lips. 'I've missed you.'

Sabine pulls off her coat and wraps it around her son.

'Let's get you out of here.' Sabine looks to Jerome. 'Is your van close? We need to get him to the hospital to get checked over.'

Jerome doesn't move a muscle. He just stands glaring at them both, the hammer in one hand, the other wrapped around the knife in his pocket.

'Jerome, please, help me.'

'He's not going to help, Mum. He's the one who put me in here.' Leo's voice is so whiny and weak, it's like fingernails being scratched down a chalkboard.

'What?' Sabine's expression clouds. 'Jerome did this?'

She looks at him as if expecting him to deny it.

'All true, I'm afraid,' he says. He pulls out the knife, extends the blade, and holds it loosely at his side.

Sabine's eyes open wide. 'What? But why? I don't understand.'

He finds her confusion endearing. 'Leo knows where Olivia is, but he's so far refused to tell me,' Jerome explains. 'I just want my little girl back.'

He doesn't take his eyes off Sabine for a second. He doesn't trust her not to make a run for it.

'Jerome, this is madness.' There's a panic in her voice that thrills him.

He wishes Sabine and her arty husband had never moved onto the estate with their awful, unruly kids. That he'd never set eyes on the family, that Olivia had never met Leo. If Jerome had known about Leo's past and what he did to that poor girl who fell from the bridge, there's no way he'd have allowed his daughter anywhere near him. But nobody knew. It's their little secret they brought with them and kept to themselves. They disgust him.

Sabine's gaze roams across his face, as if she's trying to read him. It's about time she appreciated what he's capable of. His daughter's life might depend on it.

'I don't understand what's going on,' she murmurs.

'He wouldn't tell me the truth.' Jerome keeps his tone even.

Sabine glances at the knife at his side. 'Let's discuss it,' she says, like she can talk her way out of it.

'As soon as your son tells me what he's done with my daughter, I'd be happy to.'

'I - I don't think he knows anything,' she stammers.

That's typical. She's going to defend him even now. He lunges at her, snarling. 'Of course he knows,' he bellows in her face, spittle flying from his mouth.

Sabine screams, stumbling backwards and almost tripping over the end of the crate.

'Mum!' Leo yells.

'Shut the fuck up!' Jerome hollers, raising the knife in Leo's face.

Sabine sobs. Big, fat tears of self-pity. *Boo-hoo*. Doesn't she get it? He never wanted any of this. He just wants his daughter back. Why can't they understand?

'Tell me where she is!' he yells at Leo.

Sabine throws herself at him, trying to grab his arm and knock the knife out of his hand. Such a stupid thing to do. He's more than a foot taller than her and is probably twice her weight.

He pushes her away, flicking her off his arm as easily as if he was dispatching a fly.

She stumbles and loses her footing, Leo's expression contorting in terror. As she falls, Jerome snatches her by the elbow and drags her back to her feet. He pulls her close and spins her around, her back pressed against his chest. She's so bony and thin, he has no idea what Rory sees in her.

He puts the blade to her throat and nicks her skin. Just a small prick that produces a bead of blood. She squeals, but he holds her tight, one arm across her body, pinning her so she can't move.

Leo stares at his mother in horror.

'For the last time,' Jerome says as Sabine squirms, 'tell me where I can find Olivia.' He angles the blade of the knife under Sabine's chin, its tip pressing into the soft flesh below her jaw. She stills. 'Or I swear to god, I'll cut your mother's throat.'

Chapter 48

Leo's so weak and stiff he can hardly stand up, let alone help his mother fight Jerome. All he can do is watch her eyes widen with fear as Jerome holds her tightly. He stares at the blood trickling down her throat and seeping into the collar of her jumper and reminds himself this is all his fault. If his mother dies, he'll never forgive himself.

Olivia never asked him for help, so what was he thinking? He should have learnt his lesson, that he can't solve other people's problems by himself. What did he think he was doing when he took it upon himself to help her with her problems? Playing the hero?

'Let her go!' His voice is reedy, his words lacking conviction.

'Of course,' Jerome says. He has a mad look in his eye, like he's deranged. 'As soon as you tell me what you've done to Olivia and where she is.'

'I've not done anything to her!'

'Where is she?'

Leo glances at his mother. He's never seen her look so scared. He's never felt so scared himself. What's he supposed to do? What's he supposed to say? He'd decided he was going to tell Jerome everything, but that was before his mother came and Jerome put a knife to her throat. If he tells Jerome the truth, what then? Will he kill them both?

'Leo, love,' his mother says, between snatched gasps of breath. 'If you know anything about Olivia, you need to tell us. You're not going to be in any trouble, I promise.'

He opens his mouth to speak but can't find the words.

'Listen to your mother,' Jerome growls. 'Just tell us the truth and no one has to get hurt.'

Leo doesn't believe him. He's hardly going to trust the word of the man who forced him into a crate and left him nailed inside overnight. Or who thinks it's acceptable to take a woman hostage with a knife. Jerome's dangerous. A complete psycho. It's no wonder Olivia was so upset and thought there was no other way out.

'How long do you think it will take her to die?' Jerome asks, lifting his mother's chin. The blade of the knife is perilously close to her milky-white skin. 'A minute? Two? Enough time to tell her you love her? That you're sorry?'

'Please,' Leo whimpers. 'Let her go.'

'As soon as you tell me what I need to know.'

A couple of the dogs have picked up on the tension and are watching with interest. Biscuit starts intermittently growling and barking at Jerome. She comes closer, snapping at his heels, with Rosie, her long-eared spaniel friend, at her side.

'Get off me, you stupid dog,' Jerome snaps, kicking out at them.

His foot strikes Biscuit on the side of the head and she howls before retreating to a safe distance with her tail between her legs. She whimpers and lies down with her head on the ground, jammed between her front paws.

'We just want to know the truth,' his mother says. She's up on her tiptoes with her back arched and her face taut with fear. 'If you know anything about what's happened to Olivia, please, say something.'

Leo hangs his head. 'You're right, we had an argument,' he says. 'I can't even remember what it was about. Something trivial. Something that had happened at school, I think. She went off in a huff and I didn't see her after that.'

'Don't lie to me!' Jerome screams, a vein throbbing in his temple.

'I'm not. It's the truth.'

'You don't think I'm serious, do you? That I won't really hurt your mum. But I care about Olivia more than anything in the world and I'm not bothered who gets hurt if it means getting her back.'

'Just tell Jerome what you know,' his mother encourages him.

'I've already told you—'

Jerome throws his mother violently to the ground, shoving her with such force that she falls to her knees with a whelp of surprise and pain. He snatches a handful of her hair and pulls it hard, yanking her head back so forcibly she yells in agony.

Jerome brings the blade of the knife back up to his mother's throat, right in front of Leo's face. He's so close, he can see the clumps of eyeliner that have collected in the creases of her eyes. The fine down of hair on her cheeks. The freckles on the bridge of her nose. He can feel her breath, ragged and warm, and can virtually taste her terror.

Jerome clutches the knife so tightly, his eyes fixed on Leo, that his knuckles are white.

'Stop!' Leo yells. 'Don't hurt her.'

Jerome's hand stills, but Leo can't take his eyes off the blade. With a flick of his wrist, the psycho could kill her.

'Something you want to tell me?' Jerome asks.

Leo lowers his head in defeat. He can't put his mother through this. Can't risk her life. He made a promise to Olivia, but surely she'll understand Jerome left him with no choice? He has to give her up.

'Alright,' he says. 'You win. I'll take you to her. Just don't hurt my mum, okay?'

Chapter 49

Sabine left the house more than two hours ago and should have been back by now. She was only going to drop off the phone he found in Leo's room at the police station and take the dogs for a quick walk. So where is she?

Rory paces up and down the living room, unable to settle. He ought to be working on the set of social media posts he said he'd deliver for the fundraising team by the end of the week, but his mind's not in the right place. First Leo goes missing. And now Sabine has vanished. What the hell is going on? Is she still punishing him? Angry that he spent the night at Toni's flat? Maybe she's left him. Perhaps she's walked out and plans never to come home. But that's not Sabine. If she was planning to leave him, there's no way she'd let him stay in the house. He's certain she'd kick *him* out.

He's tried her phone a few times, but it cuts straight to voicemail. Sabine always keeps her phone on for emergencies, so it's odd he can't get through, although if she's taken the dogs into Clover Wood, reception down there can be patchy.

He's probably worrying about nothing and she's taking some time out to think things through. He doesn't blame her. He's let her down. He's abused her trust, but she can't stay out forever. They need to talk.

He needs to reassure her he's not a cheat. It was one lousy, drunken, mistaken night of crap sex. He can't let her walk out on their marriage and destroy the family for that.

For a brief, horrible moment, he pictures himself living alone in a dingy bedsit with mould on the walls, a lumpy bed and the sound of arguing coming from the neighbours downstairs. He shudders. He doesn't want to be a forty-something divorcee, kicked out of his own home. He wants Sabine. And he wants things to go back to how they were.

He just wants a normal, uncomplicated life.

Surely the police must have traced Olivia's phone by now, although he's kept an eye on Jerome and Faith's house from the kitchen window all day, hoping to see her brought home and reunited with her parents. But it's been desperately quiet at the house opposite. Only the solitary police car on the drive that's been there most of the week.

He still feels bad that he's broken his promise to Olivia. He vowed not to say anything, but as soon as the police find her, they'll have no choice other than to take her home and reunite her with her parents. With Jerome.

Rory was lucky. He always had a good relationship with his parents, but you read about these horrors that happen in apparently respectable homes, don't you?

He perches on the edge of the sofa with his elbows on his knees and his fingers steepled against his lips. Olivia said she didn't know what'd happened to Leo, but was she telling the truth? They've probably cooked up some scheme between them and are holed up together somewhere. If the police find Olivia, what are the chances they'll find Leo with her? But what's taking so long?

If only he could work out where they are. He thinks back to the phone call with Olivia, searching his memory, but it was such a brief conversation and he can't really remember what was said. All he can recall is Olivia pleading with him not to tell her parents or the police and that she sounded so scared.

But there was something. He hadn't given it much thought at the time. He hadn't really even registered it. A noise in the background. A low-level sound that was so familiar, it wasn't even noteworthy. Except it was. And it could be the key to finding Olivia and Leo.

But like a song playing in your mind you can't quite place, he can't put his finger on it. It dances and writhes before his face like a wisp of smoke from an extinguished candle. Impossible to grasp.

What was it?

Rory closes his eyes and focuses on the memory as a dull, rhythmical thud-thud-thud seeps through the walls of the house. It's been such a constant soundtrack to their days since they've moved in that he no longer hears it most of the time, even when he's working from home.

Rory's eyes spring open as it hits him.

It's the same noise he heard in the background when he spoke to Olivia. He's certain of it.

With a sudden clarity, he jumps up and grabs his keys from the side, pretty certain he knows where Olivia Hunter is hiding. Where Leo is probably holed up, too. He's going to find them and he's going to bring them both home.

Chapter 50

Leo walks a few paces ahead, glancing back nervously from time to time as Jerome hollers out directions. Eventually, we stumble out from the trees and onto the footpath. Jerome has a tight grasp of my arm and the knife pressed into my side above my kidney. Every time I trip or stumble, he growls in my ear and pulls me roughly, his breath sour with stale coffee and warm on the back of my neck.

We've had to abandon the dogs. The last I saw of them, Biscuit was watching me with concern from a safe distance, with Rosie at her side. The others had wandered off, taking advantage of their unexpected freedom. I just hope they'll survive on their own, or maybe find their way safely home. There's nothing I can do for them though, not with a knife in my side and Jerome behaving like a madman.

Up ahead, I spot his van parked off a muddy track under the branches of a tree. He unlocks it with a remote key and orders Leo to open a sliding side door.

'There's a box with some electrical wires in there,' he says. 'Fetch it.'

Leo looks terrified. He's pale and his eyes are jet black. He looks to me for reassurance. I nod, encouraging him to do as Jerome asks.

He reaches into the van, finds a cardboard box and puts it on the ground at Jerome's feet. Then Jerome orders us both onto our knees with our hands behind our backs, facing away from him, towards the van.

'Are you okay?' I whisper to Leo as we kneel.

'Shut up! No talking,' Jerome yells before Leo has a chance to answer.

I mumble an apology. I don't want to wind him up any further. We're in big enough trouble as it is.

Jerome wrenches my hands painfully up my back as he binds my wrists with a length of black flex. Then he does the same to Leo and orders us to stand.

He pushes me into the van, forcing me to lie on my side on the gritty, hard floor. Then he shoves a dirty rag in my mouth. Leo is bundled in next to me and we curl up together, our bodies tense. I catch his eye, but I can't smile with a gag in my mouth. Instead, I nod, and he nods back at me. At least we're together and we're alive.

When the door slides shut with a rumble and a thud, we're pitched into semi-darkness. I want to hold Leo tight, give him a mother's reassurance that everything is going to be okay. I want to press his head into my shoulder and inhale the familiar scent of his hair. But we're both as helpless as each other, trussed up and completely at Jerome's mercy.

The van rocks on its axles as Jerome climbs into the front. He glances over his shoulder at us and demands to know where we're going.

Leo mumbles something incoherent through the rag in his mouth.

Jerome reaches over and yanks it out. 'What was that?'

'The new houses,' he gasps. 'She's in there.'

'The new estate?'

'Yes. Drive to the top of Pheasant Lane. There's a loose fence panel,' Leo explains. 'It's how we've been getting in and out without being seen.'

Jerome nods, apparently satisfied, and shoves Leo's gag back into his mouth.

'Pheasant Lane it is, then,' he says cheerfully, as if he's taking us on a day trip to the seaside, rather than holding us as hostages.

The drive is less than five minutes, but it's one of the most uncomfortable journeys I've ever made. The track is rutted and potholed and we're pitched and tossed around in the back, clattering our heads, shoulders and knees against the metal bodywork of the van. I can feel bruises swelling all over my body.

Looking up through the windscreen, I snatch glimpses of the sky and the blur of passing trees and little else, but I can picture the route perfectly. We're not far from home, at the far end of our estate, where the second phase of building work is going on. Another twenty executive homes on big plots of land.

Jerome pulls up and kills the engine. The silence thrums in my ears as my shoulders, arms, and legs scream out in pain. Leo sits bolt upright, his eyes alert. I just hope he doesn't feel the need to play the hero and end up getting himself hurt. He just needs to go along with what Jerome wants. At least for the time being.

'Get out,' Jerome demands as he throws open the side door.

Leo rolls his legs out of the van in one fluid motion, making it look effortless, while I have to shuffle on my bottom and wait for Jerome to hoick me onto my feet by my arm like I'm an invalid.

I stand blinking, taking in the surroundings. We're at the edge of the woodland with a canopy of trees above us. A little further along the lane, I can see the hoardings that have been erected along the edge of the building site, painted in sage green and plastered with evocative photographs of children playing, a little girl with blonde braids, skipping. Beyond the hoardings, I can just make out the first skeletons of the new homes that have risen from the earth.

Jerome reaches into the van and retrieves a long, leather case. He flips it open and pulls out a shotgun, which he swings around and points directly at us. The shotgun he was showing off at the barbecue in the summer.

'Don't make me use this,' he warns with a menacing growl. 'If you try to run, I'll shoot.'

I catch Leo's eye. He swallows hard, his body tense. It didn't come as much of a surprise that Jerome owned a shotgun, although I'd been surprised when he brought it out at the party to show everyone. I bet he'd happily use it too if he came face to face with a burglar in his house.

'Right, where's this fence panel?' he asks.

Leo nods at a point further up the lane and we all set off, Leo and I walking ahead, with Jerome and his gun close behind. Leo stops in front of a panel where the paint is peeling and the bare, ugly chipboard is showing through.

'This it?'

Leo nods.

Jerome stares at the panel blankly. I can't see any opening either, although the light is fading fast and the November afternoon gloom settling heavily around us.

'Show me.'

He spins Leo around and unties the wire binding his wrists.

Leo runs his hand down the length of the board until he finds a small opening just big enough for his fingers to slot into. With a grunt, he yanks it back, opening up a gap barely wide enough to slip through.

'You expect me to get through there?' Jerome asks as he sizes it up.

Leo shrugs.

'Fine. You go first. But don't try anything.' He levels the shotgun at my head.

Leo's eyes open as wide as dinner plates. And then he's gone, scurrying through the gap between the boards.

It's a bit more of a struggle for me, but Leo helps by forcing the panel back from the other side. Finally, Jerome follows, leading with his gun.

We stand together on the other side, taking in the extent of the construction work that's been taking place out of sight over the last few months. There are six partially built houses spread out across the site, all of a similar design to the properties in our street. Handsome, modern buildings with a nod to some Georgian heritage. None of them has windows or even a roof in place yet, but the trusses are all in and you can tell it's not going to be long before they're finished and ready to move into.

Jerome casts his eyes around, looking less than convinced. 'You sure she's here?' he grunts.

Leo nods and Jerome removes his gag.

'We've been coming here to hang out after school,' he says, wiping his mouth with the back of his hand.

'Why the hell would you want to come here?' Jerome asks with disgust.

Leo shrugs. 'There's no one here after four when the builders have gone home. We have the place to ourselves and can have a good nosy around.'

I had no idea. It's utterly irresponsible. Leo knows full well how dangerous building sites can be. At least he should. Why does he think they lock the gates at night and surround it with a ten-foot hoarding?

'Is she in one of these houses?' Jerome asks, looking at the brick shells dotted around.

'Not these. That one.' Leo points towards the main entrance where a set of gates are chained and padlocked closed. Alongside them is a house that's already been finished, complete with a neatly mowed lawn, pockets of shrubs and rows of box hedging.

'That one?' Jerome says suspiciously.

'Yeah,' Leo confirms. 'The show home. That's where Olivia is.'

Chapter 51

Casper saunters up the drive with his rucksack hanging off one shoulder, excited at the prospect of the weekend ahead and two days off school. Two lie-ins. Two days of no classes. Two days of no teachers on his back. Plus, it's Barnaby's party tonight, assuming his parents let him go.

As he approaches the front door, it swings open, and he's surprised to see his father emerge from the house. He's not normally back this early, even on a Friday.

'Dad? What are you doing home?'

'Have you seen Mum?' his father says, frowning. He looks distracted. Like there's something on his mind.

'Probably out with the dogs. Why?'

'She's been gone for ages.'

Casper shrugs. She's often not home when he gets in from school. 'Is there any news about Leo?'

He wasn't in school today and it's not like his brother to stay out overnight. Not that Casper's particularly worried. He heard every word of that big row Leo had with Mum and Dad the other night. He's probably gone off in a huff, although it's weird that he's vanished so soon after Olivia went missing. Probably just a coincidence.

'Dad?' he says when his father doesn't answer.
'No, not yet.'
'Are you going out to look for him?'
'What? No, I need to pop out to... to do something. I'll be back later.'

His father brushes past him and hurries down the drive. Something's going on, but nobody ever tells him anything in this family. He might be the youngest, but he's not a baby. It's about time they started treating him like an adult.

Oh, well, at least he has the house to himself.

He lets himself in, tosses his shoes and bag to one side and heads straight for his father's study.

The computer's switched off, although he assumed his father must have been working from home today. Maybe he took a day off instead. He didn't come home last night and his mother's pissed off with him. He's probably got another hangover and called in sick.

Casper pushes the door closed behind him, and heads for the bookcase pushed up against the wall next to the desk. He locates the thickest book, *The Decline and Fall of the Roman Empire*, reaches into the gap behind it and finds the old tin with the hinged lid. It's where his father has always kept it, supposedly hidden, even in their old house.

With a tremble of anticipation, Casper opens it and peers inside. The last couple of times he's looked, he's been disappointed, but today he's hit the jackpot. Inside is a small, transparent plastic bag containing a white powder.

Casper's heart races, although he's not entirely sure what it is. Cocaine probably. The only other white powder he knows is heroin, and he's pretty sure his father wouldn't touch that stuff.

Carefully, he puts the tin on the desk and helps himself to a sheet of plain white paper from the printer. He folds it into an envelope like he's learnt on YouTube, and then removes the plastic bag from the tin, peels it open and taps out a few grams of powder. He checks the bag, holding it up to the light of the window and decides he can get away with taking a little more. His father's not going to notice, and even if he does, what's he going to do? Nobody's supposed to know about his drugs. Casper only found them by accident last year when he was bored and snooping around.

He folds the envelope closed and slips it into his pocket, before replacing the powder in the tin and putting it back behind the big book of Roman history.

When he's done, he backs out of the study, checking he's left everything as he found it. He pulls the door closed and hurries up to his room with a grin on his face.

It's going to be a wicked party.

Chapter 52

Jerome shoves the shotgun into the small of Leo's back. 'Show me.'

But Leo digs his feet into the ground and refuses to move. 'Not that way,' he hisses. 'We have to go around the back.' He points to several hexagonal metal boxes propped up on tripod legs, like robotic aliens that have landed from outer space. 'We need to avoid the security cameras.'

Jerome stares into the distance for a moment or two and then nods.

Leo skirts around to the right, picking a path that hugs the tall boundary fence.

'Slowly!' Jerome warns.

He pushes me between my shoulder blades, urging me to follow, but my foot snags on a rock and I stumble, unable to break my fall with my arms tied behind my back. My scream of pain is muffled by the gag in my mouth, now soaked with my saliva.

'Stand up,' Jerome orders angrily.

Slowly, I get to my feet and turn to him. I can hardly breathe with the cloth in my mouth.

He must see the panic in my eyes because he puts a finger to his lips and slips the gag out.

'Don't make a sound,' he warns. 'Or I'll put it back in again.'

I nod my understanding. There's no point screaming for help, anyway. No one's going to hear us. Our house might be a stone's throw away, behind a narrow strip of woodland that separates the two estates, but it might as well be a thousand miles away. I'd never be heard.

I've no idea where we're going, whether Leo is leading us on a merry dance or if he's genuinely taking us to Olivia. For days, I've been pushing away the memory of seeing him fighting with her in the woods, of finding that bloody knife, not letting my suspicions have a voice. What if he's hurt her? Has her tied up and held hostage? Or worse, killed her? Maybe not deliberately, but what if she's had an accident, and he's hidden her body on the building site? I suppose it would be an ideal place to conceal a corpse with all the digging and mud and concrete foundations being laid.

I shake my head, clearing the thoughts from my mind. It's crazy. Leo wouldn't have done anything like that. He may have issues, but he's not capable of anything as heinous as murder. I know my son.

Leo waits for us to catch up at the rear of the show home. He's agitated, fiddling with his fingers. Chewing his nails. Jiggling his legs.

'Right, so where now?' Jerome asks.

Leo pulls a bunch of keys from his pocket and selects one before heading around the front of the building. He slots a key into the lock of an integral garage and, to my surprise, the bright red door clicks open.

'Where did you get that key?' I ask.

He grins. 'We found a bunch of them.' He points to a section of muddy tarmac road that runs through the entrance gates and stops a little further past the show home, ready to be completed once the rest of the houses have been built. 'One of the sales reps must have dropped them.'

Leo rolls open the garage door wide enough for us to crawl underneath.

'You first,' Jerome hisses, waving his gun at Leo.

Leo darts inside and I follow him, wincing as I crouch, my body battered and bruised from the punishing, short trip in the back of Jerome's van. I emerge into the darkness of the empty garage with its dusty smell of newly laid concrete and wait as Jerome struggles behind me, grunting and groaning with the effort.

As soon as he's inside, Leo disappears through a door into the house with a cry of, 'In here.'

'Wait!' Jerome growls.

Leo pops his head back out and apologises. 'Sorry, I thought you were right behind me.'

It's a missed chance. He should have run while he could. He could have raised the alarm and saved us both, but he seems caught up in the moment. Excited by the adventure.

As I step into a utility room with an abundance of cupboards and empty worktops, a blinding light comes on. I turn my head away and narrow my eyes.

'What are you doing?' Jerome bowls past me into what I can now see is a well-appointed kitchen, complete with a bowl of fake oranges on the side.

He grabs Leo by the throat and pins him to a wall. Leo's eyes bulge in their sockets in terror.

'Turn the bloody light off, you idiot,' Jerome yells in his face.

'Why? Nobody can see. We always put the lights on.'

Jerome loosens his grip, watching Leo warily, and finally lets him go.

'So, where is she?' he asks.

It's a good question. The house is immaculate, a manufactured fantasy of what life could be like for any prospective buyer. All the fittings and furnishings are modern and desirable, the walls painted in neutral tones, designed to appeal to the widest tastes. The only sign that none of it's real, that it's been set up to show off the house and the lifestyle it promises, are the fake oranges and the desk at the back of the kitchen-diner for the sales team, near the bi-fold doors that open up into what will eventually become the garden.

A chill runs down my spine.

What is Leo playing at? Olivia's not living here. How could she? The show home is open all week, even at weekends, and there must be at least one sales person stationed here full time to deal with enquiries and viewings. It's impossible that Olivia could be staying here unnoticed. Jerome's going to flip when he realises Leo's lying.

'Why don't you put the gun down, Jerome,' I say softly. As far as I can tell, he's left the knife in the van. 'Nobody needs to get hurt and if we work together, I'm sure we'll be able to find your daughter.'

When his head snaps around to face me, his eyes burn with such fury I take an involuntary step backwards.

'Shut up!' he hisses. 'You said she was here. So where is she?'

Above us, a floorboard creaks. We glance up in unison as if we all have X-ray vision and can peer through the ceiling.

'Up here.' Leo dashes into the hall.

'Follow him. Quickly,' Jerome orders me.

I race up the stairs and find Leo already on the landing, reaching into a cupboard. He pulls out a long, thin stick with a hook screwed into one end.

'Put that down.' Jerome points the gun over my shoulder, aiming it with steady hands at Leo.

But Leo ignores him, using the stick to prod open a loft hatch above, and then hook down a set of aluminium steps.

'Olivia,' he shouts, placing the feet of the ladder on the floor. He climbs four steps and pokes his head into the loft while Jerome keeps the gun trained on his back.

'Leo? Oh my god, I thought you were dead.' Olivia's head and shoulders come into view. 'Where have you been?'

Leo climbs back down and steps off the ladder. 'You'd better come down,' he says solemnly, but Olivia's already on her way, hurriedly clambering down.

At the bottom, she spins around, her face full of joy and relief, about to throw her arms around Leo, but her expression clouds when she first notices me and then her father.

'Olivia!' Jerome cries. 'Thank god, you're alive.'

He lowers the gun and shoves me out of the way.

Olivia recoils in horror. 'Dad?' she gasps. 'What are you doing here?' Her eyes widen as she backs away.

'We've been so worried. Are you hurt?' Jerome looks her up and down. Her clothes are a little grubby and her hair could do with a wash, but otherwise she appears in good health.

Olivia shoots an accusatory, narrow-eyed glance at Leo. 'Did you bring him here?' she asks incredulously. 'Why would you do that? You promised.'

'I'm sorry,' he mumbles. 'I had no choice.'

Jerome attempts to put an arm around Olivia and pull her into a hug, but she pushes him away like he's toxic. She shuffles backwards, out of his reach, past the ladder and along the landing. 'Don't touch me,' she shouts.

'Don't be silly, darling. It's me. Your dad. Why are you being like this?'

She looks absolutely terrified as Jerome advances towards her.

I catch a glint of anger in Leo's eyes and in a flash, he darts between them, creating a physical barrier between Olivia and her father.

His instinct to protect Olivia, his loyalty and bravery, is commendable, but as his mother, I wish he hadn't done it. Jerome has a gun and if he's capable of imprisoning Leo in a crate in the woods overnight, he's more than capable of using the gun on him.

'She said she doesn't want you to touch her,' Leo growls in Jerome's face, his shoulders back and his chin jutting out. My little boy growing into a man.

'Get out of my way.' Jerome attempts to push him to one side, but Leo stands his ground, swatting the older man's hand off his shoulder.

'I said, don't touch her. You've seen she's safe and now you can go.'

'I'm not going anywhere. Olivia, darling, whatever's wrong, let's talk about it,' he says, lowering his voice.

'I think you know what's wrong,' Leo says. 'You're a monster. A filthy, depraved monster.'

Jerome swings his fist so fast it's a blur. But I hear it clearly as it connects with the side of Leo's face. A horrible, echoing thud that momentarily stills my heart. Leo stumbles, clutching his nose, blood pouring through his fingers.

'Stop it!' I scream. 'Don't you dare touch him.'

Leo inspects the blood in his hand. Then smirks and stands up tall again, uncowed.

Jerome cocks the shotgun and takes aim at Leo's chest at point blank range. 'Still want to be the hero?'

'Leo,' I cry. 'Let it go. You're going to get yourself killed.'

He shakes his head. 'I can't, Mum. I'm not letting him hurt her again.'

'Please,' I plead.

'Listen to your mother, why don't you? And get your nose out of my family's business.'

Leo crosses his arms across his chest, his nose and mouth smeared crimson. Behind him, Olivia cowers, trying to make herself small, whimpering with fear.

'You should be ashamed of yourself,' Leo says, his voice guttural, as if his nose might actually be broken. 'She's only a kid, but you took that away from her the first time you climbed into her bed, you disgusting animal.'

Suddenly, everything becomes clear. Why Leo's been protecting Olivia. Why he helped her run away.

He never planned to hurt her. He was saving her.

The problem is, Jerome's found his daughter, and although it's three of us against one of him, he's the one holding the gun.

Chapter 53

Rory should have worked it out sooner, but he hadn't connected the dots. Now he's convinced Olivia is somewhere on the building site behind the house where they're constructing the next phase of the estate.

The monotonous thud of pile driving, the rumble of bulldozers and dumper trucks and the tap-tap-tap of nails being hammered have become so familiar in recent months, he hardly hears it anymore. It's no surprise it didn't register when he was on the phone with Olivia.

Now it's all he can hear in his mind when he thinks about the call, like one of those optical illusions where you can't see the hidden object no matter how hard you look, until you can, and then you can't see anything else.

Olivia sounded so scared, but she's only seventeen. The same age as Leo. So it's no surprise. It's not right for a teenage girl to be camping out on a building site. It's not safe. Anything could happen to her. Although he knows Leo was only trying to do the right thing, he wishes he'd come to him and Sabine for help, instead of taking matters into his own hands. They could have sorted something out between them. Resolved the problems Olivia was having with her parents.

He ought to leave it to the police now they have Leo's phone and Olivia's number, but he can't sit back and do nothing, especially as Olivia is so close. The girl's vulnerable, and obviously afraid. Maybe he can help, even if she doesn't want to go home and face her father. At least he can talk to her and make her see sense. Maybe even offer her a bed in their house until they can sort out her disagreements with Jerome. But whatever, he can't let her face another night outside on her own.

At the entrance to the construction site, Rory finds the gates locked, secured by a thick chain and a substantial padlock. The last of the work crews have long gone with the weekend looming. 'Keep Out' and 'Danger' warning notices pepper the perimeter.

He can't just break in, even if Olivia is in there somewhere. There are bound to be security cameras everywhere, and he doesn't want to be caught trespassing.

He slides his fingers through the mesh wire of the gates and peers inside. It's a mess of mud, piles of bricks, heaps of sand and the silhouettes of half-built houses standing isolated and forlorn. In contrast to the chaos, there's a single house that's been completed ahead of all the others. A show home with a manicured lawn, curtains in the windows and an incongruous air of homeliness in what looks more like a battlefield than a housing estate.

There are even lights on in the windows, as if someone's home. Probably intended to make it look appealing for anyone passing or who's come to look out of hours. What a waste of electricity, like the office blocks in the city where they leave the lights on all night, even though there's no one inside working.

A crazy thought strikes him. What if that's where Olivia's camping out? But how would she have gained access? She doesn't have a key, and it's unlikely she'd have been able to sneak in during the day with all the sales people and customers pottering around.

It's hopeless. Rory doesn't know what he's doing here. He really should leave this to the police. What was he thinking? He shakes his head, but as he pushes himself off the gate, about to head back home, a blinding flash lights up one of the upper windows in the show home. A fraction of a second later, it's followed by a loud crack, like a firework going off.

Rory stumbles backwards. What the hell was that? It was almost like a gun being fired. But that's impossible. More likely some kind of electrical fault. Two live wires badly connected, causing a mini explosion? The sort of thing that could easily start a fire in a house.

But what if Olivia *is* inside? It's the only logical place on the site where she'd be hiding. None of the other houses even have roofs. He doesn't think twice. If Olivia is in that house, she could be in danger. He begins to scale the gate, the wire digging into his fingers and his feet slipping as he tries to find purchase. The adrenaline pumping through his veins gives him a strength and a dexterity he never knew he possessed. The gate creaks and sways, but he makes it to the top in a matter of seconds and throws himself over and onto the other side, where he lands with a grunt on his hands and knees.

He picks himself up, dusts himself down and sprints towards the house, not stopping once to think about his own safety. All he can think about is that Olivia might be inside the house and that she could be in danger.

Chapter 54

'Shut your mouth. You don't know what you're saying,' Jerome yells.

He waves the gun and his fists around wildly, becoming increasingly agitated.

He and Leo are about the same height, but at seventeen, Leo is much slighter than Jerome, who has a thick neck and powerful arms and shoulders, but even though he's no physical match for Olivia's father, Leo doesn't back away. He stands there, nose to nose with him, unwavering.

'You should be thanking me,' Leo says. 'When I found Olivia, she was ready to take her life. She couldn't bear it anymore. If it wasn't for me, she'd probably already be dead.'

Olivia was going to kill herself? Is that really true?

I remember the knife I found in the woods. The blood. Was that what I saw? Olivia taking the knife to herself and Leo fighting with her to stop?

'When I found her, she was heading into Clover Wood, determined she was going to do it,' Leo continues. 'How badly do you think she must have been hurting that cutting open a vein on her arm was preferable to going home?'

It must have been the knife I found. How could I ever have doubted my own son?

'You're lying,' Jerome spits. 'I'd never do anything to her.'

'I despise you. And so does your daughter.'

'I'm not the one who killed a girl.' Jerome looms over Leo, his jaw tight with anger. 'You see, I know all about you, too. Why you and your parents had to move here. I know about how you killed Heather Malone. How you supplied her with drugs even though she was only fifteen. You're a drug-dealing, murdering junkie. And I won't have my daughter ruining her life because of you.'

'He didn't kill her!' Olivia stands up straight, appearing from behind Leo, her head bobbing above his shoulder. 'You don't know anything. He didn't even give her the drugs.'

'It's okay,' Leo says. 'Don't.'

I don't blame Leo for lying to Olivia, telling her he wasn't responsible for Heather's death. No teenager wants that kind of reputation, but Leo *was* to blame, at least inadvertently. He confessed everything to the police, how he'd given Heather a single tab of LSD, a small square of blotting paper laced with lysergic acid diethylamide, at a party and let her climb up onto the parapet of a bridge, knowing full well she didn't know what she was doing. It wasn't his fault she fell, but she wouldn't have fallen if she hadn't taken the drugs Leo had supplied.

'I don't want him believing all the lies like everyone else. Leo's a good person. And he's right, if he hadn't found me when he did, I probably would be dead,' Olivia says.

'Don't be ridiculous,' Jerome snarls. 'Now come here and let's go home.'

'No,' Olivia says defiantly. 'I'm not going anywhere with you.'

'You'll do as I say,' he barks. 'I'm your father.'

'I'm never going to let you touch her again.' The blood that was flowing from Leo's nose is finally congealing. He's a mess, but I hope it looks more serious than it is.

Every maternal instinct in my body is screaming at me to do something. I want to take hold of my boy, clean him up and get him out of this house and to safety, but what can I do with my hands tied and Jerome holding a gun?

'This has nothing to do with you.' Jerome attempts to barge past Leo to reach his daughter again, but Leo pivots and twists, with Olivia clinging onto him, using him as a shield from her father.

'It has everything to do with me. I'm looking after her now,' Leo says.

His words sound so grown up, but he's still only young. He's not even shaving properly yet. He can't look after Olivia. He can barely take care of himself.

Jerome laughs cruelly. 'You? Don't make me laugh. Now get out of my way.'

'No.'

'Don't make me do something I'll regret, lad.'

'Yeah, like what? What are you going to do? Olivia doesn't want you in her life. You deserve to be locked up and never let out.'

Jerome takes a step back and raises the gun. His hands are shaking with anger as he lifts the barrel and aims it at Leo's face. If he shoots, he'll kill him. There's no way he can survive being shot at point-blank range.

Jerome's finger coils around the trigger and my heart rattles in my rib cage. I've been wrestling with the wire around my wrists while Jerome has been distracted, but I've not loosened it at all, and now my fingers are sore and my shoulders aching. I'm helpless.

'You don't have the balls to shoot me,' Leo says, reaching behind his back, snaking one arm protectively around Olivia.

'You don't think so?'

'No, I don't. You're a coward who makes himself feel like a man by abusing his own daughter.'

Why's he winding Jerome up? He should be trying to reason with him, to get him to put the gun down. Not challenging him to use it.

Jerome's body stiffens and I'm certain he's about to fire. He's not going to let Leo talk to him like that. His pride won't stand for it.

It's now or never. I do the only thing I can. I tense all the muscles in my upper body and, with a scream, charge at Jerome.

When I drive my shoulder into his back, it's like hitting a brick wall, but the surprise knocks him off balance and causes him to stumble.

I'm vaguely aware of Leo flinching and ducking as the gun goes off with a deafening bang that leaves my ears ringing. The whole hallway momentarily lights up in an explosive flash.

'You stupid cow —' Jerome yells, turning on me with a face like fury.

But I'm not listening. My focus is entirely on Olivia, who's still standing close to Leo, but staring down in horror at the crimson stain of blood that's creeping across her chest and stomach. When she finally looks up, she's pale, her eyes wide with shock. Her face crumples.

And then she drops to the floor and her eyes flutter closed.

Chapter 55

Rory rattles the front door, but it's locked and all the windows are shut. He's about to try around the back when he notices the garage door is open a fraction. Dim light from inside spills out, fanning out across the drive's blockwork paving.

He yanks the door up and hurries inside, through a door into the house and into a large kitchen. The layout mirrors their own home, but there's notably less clutter everywhere, and it smells clean and new. He darts for the stairs, taking them two at a time with his pulse pounding and his thighs burning.

He freezes when he reaches the landing, staring past the aluminium ladder propped up in the open loft hatch. He never expected to find Jerome Hunter here, on his knees next to his daughter. He's cradling her head in his lap, sobbing. Rory snatches a breath as he catches sight of her bloodstained clothes. Her oversized hoodie soaked through.

'What happened?' he gasps, spotting a shotgun lying on the floor.

Leo is here too, standing over Jerome and Olivia with a look of utter shock and horror etched on his face, while Sabine is propped up against a wall, her mouth hanging open and her hands apparently tied behind her back.

It's such a surreal scene, full of people he didn't expect to find, that Rory struggles to make sense of it. It's like something from a horror film. He expected to find Olivia here. And possibly Leo too. But Jerome and Sabine? What the hell is going on?

'He shot her,' Leo croaks. 'Jerome shot Olivia. Oh my god, is she dead?'

Time seems to slow down while Rory's brain races to catch up with what he's seeing.

Why would Jerome shoot his own daughter?

'It's all my fault,' Sabine whimpers.

Rory shakes uncontrollably, his mouth dry. What does he do now?

Call the police?

Try to save Olivia?

Untie his wife's hands?

Grab the gun?

It's all too much to process. Too overwhelming.

'I pushed him,' Sabine sobs. 'I thought he was going to shoot Leo.'

Rory shakes his head, trying to bring his thoughts into focus. 'What?'

'He was going to shoot Leo, so I pushed him, but the gun went off and now... and now...' Sabine's body convulses with emotion.

'Okay,' Rory says. He attempts to take a deep breath, but his lungs are too tight. He can barely breathe. 'Okay,' he repeats, blinking.

'For god's sake, untie me,' Sabine wails.

'Right. Yes.'

Her hands are pale and turning blue. As he struggles to untie a length of electrical cable that has been bound tightly around her wrists, Leo suddenly throws himself at Jerome, pushing him away from Olivia's motionless body.

'Get off her! Just leave her alone!' he yells. 'You did this! You killed her, you monster.' His hands fly to Jerome's thick neck, his face twisted into a grotesque mask of anger and hatred.

Jerome, momentarily caught off guard, falls sideways with Leo on top of him, but quickly regains the initiative and for a second or two, there's a blur of flying hands, legs, feet and elbows as the two of them wrestle.

In a flash, Jerome's turned the tables on Leo and now Leo's on the floor with Jerome pinning him down with his knees on his biceps and his hands around Leo's throat.

'You killed her,' Leo croaks, his words strangulated by Jerome's tight grip.

Rory finally loosens the wire around Sabine's wrists and sets her free. But he's unsure how to separate Leo and Jerome. If he doesn't do something, Jerome's going to kill him.

'That's enough,' Rory yells, but Jerome doesn't react. His entire focus is on throttling the life out of Leo.

Rory flies across the landing and grabs the back of Jerome's jacket, tries to pull him off, but Jerome's too strong. Too determined. And he's not letting go of Leo.

In a panic, Rory looks around the landing and spots the discarded shotgun.

Rory's never held a gun in his life, let alone fired one, but he reaches for it without hesitation, stands and cocks it against his hip. He aims the barrel at Jerome's back. He's seen enough guns in films and on TV to get the general idea. It's a double-barrelled shotgun which means it holds two cartridges. He's only heard one shot, so he's banking on the gun being loaded with a second cartridge.

'Let my son go,' he shouts as the fight drains out of Leo, his face turning a worrying puce.

'I said, let him go or I'll blow your brains out!' Rory screams at the top of his lungs, surprising even himself with the aggression of his tone.

Startled, Jerome finally releases his grip. Leo rolls over, groans and coughs.

'Stand up! Slowly,' Rory orders. 'I don't know what's gone on here, but I need to get my head straight. Is she still alive?' He nods at Olivia's prone body. There's so much blood. It's everywhere, even beginning to pool on the floor under her body.

Leo hauls himself to his knees and drags himself across the floor. He brushes Olivia's hair out of her eyes and runs the palm of his hand tenderly along the curve of her cheek.

'I don't know, Dad,' he wails, tears springing from his eyes. 'You have to get help.'

Jerome has his hands up, palms out, standing directly in front of Rory now. He's panting and has a wild, untamed look in his eye.

'Tie him up until the police get here,' Rory tells Sabine, who's taken cover behind him. He nods towards the coil of wire that had been used to tie Sabine's hands. 'And then maybe one of you can start explaining what the hell happened here.'

'It's Jerome,' Sabine says. 'He's an abuser. Leo helped Olivia to run away, and she's been hiding here ever since.'

Jerome edges closer, a despicable sneer on his face.

'Stand still,' Rory orders. He digs into his pocket for his phone but struggles to dial one-handed while keeping the gun level and an eye on Jerome. 'What do you mean, an abuser?'

'Don't you get it, Dad?' Leo cries. 'He's been doing it for years. Sneaking into her bedroom when her mother was asleep and doing horrible, awful things to her.'

Rory's stomach tightens and flips. 'Is that true?'

'Of course it's not true,' Jerome says, shuffling another couple of inches closer. 'You know what teenagers' imaginations are like. They'll say anything for attention.'

Rory gives up with the phone and tosses it to his wife. 'Call the police and get an ambulance. Hurry.'

'You want me to tie him up first?'

Rory shakes his head. 'We need to get Olivia to hospital.'

He's assuming she's still alive, because he can't face the alternative. There's no way that poor, sweet girl from across the road can be dead, shot and killed by her own father. It would be too awful for words.

Sabine moves to the top of the stairs to make the call while Rory keeps his eyes locked on Jerome. He doesn't want to shoot him, but he'll do it if his family is in danger, and he'll worry about the consequences later.

'Hello? Yes, police and an ambulance. It's urgent,' Sabine says. 'A girl's been shot.'

At almost the same time, the sound of sirens reaches them. They're a short way off, but getting closer. Too quick to be as a result of Sabine's call, as she's not even given them the address yet.

Jerome glances over his shoulder.

Maybe the police have traced Olivia's phone after all and now they're coming to find her. Although it's a bit late, Rory thinks ruefully, glancing at Olivia's body. It'll be a miracle if she survives.

The sirens get closer and closer. Louder and louder.

'Is she telling the truth?' Rory asks. 'Were you abusing her?'

'Of course I wasn't.'

'So why did she run away?'

'Because your son dripped poison into her head. Why do you think?'

Rory shakes his head. You hear about these things happening in the news sometimes, but usually in broken homes and deprived neighbourhoods. You never expect it to be going on in the same street. That your own neighbour is a monster in disguise.

He has the urge to punch Jerome. To cause him acute, physical pain. It's not a new urge. Rory's never liked him, not since his behaviour at their party in the summer, all over the women, Sabine included, with his tongue practically hanging out with lust.

Rory's never hit anyone, at least not since school. It's not in his nature, but he could make an exception with Jerome, and who could blame him?

'Why don't you put the gun down?' Jerome says. 'Let's talk about this. We don't want anyone else getting hurt, do we?'

There's a nervousness about his manner that wasn't there a few moments ago. Is it the thought of the police arriving? Is he finally afraid justice is going to catch up with him?

A loud crash outside suggests the gates at the entrance of the site have just been demolished. The sirens are ear-piercing now. Rory hears cars pulling up outside. Doors being opened and slammed. Blue lights wash across the landing.

Leo stands and peers out of a window.

'It's the police,' he says. 'There are loads of them.'

Thank god. It's nearly over.

Jerome lunges at Rory while his attention is briefly distracted, but he's not quick enough. Rory steps to one side and jabs the barrels of the gun into Jerome's stomach. 'Back off! I'm warning you,' he cries, clutching the gun so tightly, the muscles in his hands ache.

A thundering bang echoes through the house as the front door is smashed open. Feet thunder into the building and up the stairs, while Rory keeps the sights of the gun trained on Jerome's head.

'Armed police! Put your weapon down!' voices scream, filling the house with noise.

Instinctively, Rory wheels around towards the source of the commotion racing up the stairs, the gun still cocked and loaded.

Two loud cracks ring out.
Rory pitches backwards, his legs giving way under the weight of his body.
And then he crashes to the floor.

Chapter 56

What happens next is a complete blur. The house is overrun with people in uniforms, police and paramedics, shouting and screaming, creating utter chaos. We're all ordered onto the floor and told to put our hands on the backs of our heads, not to move, ugly-looking weapons pointed at us. Meanwhile, a flurry of activity takes place around Olivia and Rory, a desperate battle to save their lives.

I watched in disbelief as my husband fell to the ground, his eyes opening wide with surprise as he was shot. Not once, but twice. They didn't have to shoot him. He wasn't a threat. He wasn't the one who shot Olivia. Although he was an idiot not to have dropped the gun when he heard the police breaking in.

'Is he going to be okay?' I mumble, my face pressed into the carpet as I'm roughly handcuffed from behind.

But nobody answers. They treat me like I'm a suspect. That I was the one running around with the gun.

With my cheek pressed into the floor and my head angled sideways, I can just about make out two paramedics kneeling at Rory's side, talking to him, ripping open his clothing, running lines of fluid into his body.

Someone hauls me to my feet and I'm taken downstairs where there are a staggering number of police officers, most of them carrying guns and wearing helmets and protective vests.

I'm escorted into the kitchen-diner where the detectives, Lockyear and Caulfield, are waiting. I'm surprised to see them, but I guess it's their case and they wanted to be here when Olivia was found. Of course, they want to know everything, exactly as it happened, and it all comes tumbling out of my mouth in an avalanche. How Biscuit helped me find Leo in the crate in the woods and how we were both abducted by Jerome Hunter at knifepoint. They must have seen and heard some incredible stories during their careers, but even they look astonished.

As soon as it's clear I had nothing to do with shooting Olivia, they remove my handcuffs and reunite me with Leo. I throw my arms around his neck and hug him more tightly than I've ever hugged him before. I don't ever want to let him go.

'How's Dad?' he asks.

I lower my head. 'I don't know.'

'They're still working on him upstairs,' Lockyear says with a note of sympathy.

'You didn't have to shoot him.'

'I'm sorry. They had no choice. He had a gun, and he turned it on an officer. They couldn't take any chances.' Lockyear shoves her hands in her trouser pockets and stands with her legs wide apart, her long raincoat hanging open.

'What about Olivia?' Leo asks quietly, as if he already suspects he knows the answer.

'I don't know. I'm sorry.'

'She can't die,' he says. 'Not after everything.'

'So this is where you were hiding her?' Lockyear asks.

'Yes, but—'

'He didn't mean her any harm,' I say, jumping in. I know how the police will twist things if I'm not careful. I don't want them thinking Leo abducted Olivia. 'Her father had been abusing her, so Leo helped her run away. They came here to hide. He thought he was doing the right thing.' He should be commended for his intentions, if not his actions.

Lockyear and Caulfield exchange glances.

'Abuse?' Lockyear asks, arching an eyebrow.

A heavy weight hangs around my heart as I reflect on what that poor girl must have been through, suffering in silence, thinking there was no one she could turn to for help. 'She told Leo he'd been sexually abusing her for years.'

Lockyear strokes her chin. 'She said that?'

Leo nods.

'I see. I think we'd better continue this conversation at the station. I'll need statements from you both.'

'Are you arresting us?' I ask.

'Not at the moment. You'll be helping us with our inquiries unless something new that you've not told us comes to light. As Leo's only seventeen, you'll be able to accompany him during the interview.'

'What about Jerome? What's happening to him?' I ask.

'He's been arrested.' Lockyear doesn't elaborate.

They put us into the back of a waiting patrol car, accompanied by two uniformed officers, while Lockyear and Caulfield follow on in a car behind.

Leo stares out of the window, a silent, brooding presence. I reach for his hand, intending to give it a reassuring squeeze, but he pulls it away and buries it in his lap.

'Do you think Dad's dead?' he asks with tears in his eyes.

'I don't know.' I can't think about it. I don't want to lose myself in the fear that he might not survive. That he'll bleed to death, the trauma of being shot too severe, and that he'll make me a widow and leave the boys fatherless. It's too much to bear. I just have to pray he's going to survive.

'It's all my fault, isn't it?'

I let out a long, slow sigh. 'No, but I wish you'd come to us when you found out about Olivia. We could have helped.'

'You wouldn't have listened to me.'

I'm stung by the vehemence of his tone, but what hurts more is that he thinks we wouldn't have been there for him. That he couldn't come to us.

'That's not fair. You know you can always talk to us about any problems you have. We've always been clear about that.'

'Yeah, right,' he huffs.

'Leo.' I swivel to face him. 'We've always been there for you and your brother.'

'Until you thought I'd supplied drugs to a fifteen-year-old.'

'Let's not go over that again.' I glance at the officer driving, catching his eye in the rear-view mirror, conscious he's listening to every word. 'It was a mistake, and you learnt your lesson.'

'You do know it wasn't me, don't you?'

'Yes, we've been through this. It's not your fault Heather fell,' I say.

'That's not what I mean. I didn't give her those drugs. She didn't get them from me.' He turns his head to stare out of the window again.

'But you confessed to the police.' I frown, not sure where this is all coming from.

'Yes, but it doesn't mean it's true.'

I snort. It's a bit late to start lying about his involvement now. 'Okay, so who did? Who is this mystery person who supplied LSD to Heather Malone?'

He bites at a tag of skin around his thumbnail and shrugs.

'No, come on, Leo. If you didn't give Heather those drugs, who did?' I say, raising my voice.

'I can't tell you.'

'Why not?'

'Because you wouldn't believe me,' he snaps.

'So you took the blame for something someone else was responsible for? Something that ended up with a girl dying?'

'Yes.'

'But you won't tell me who? In which case, you're a fool. No friend is worth that. You could have gone to jail.'

'You don't think I know that?'

'So why lie for someone else? It doesn't make any sense.'

'I knew you wouldn't understand. That's why I didn't say anything before. But you never believe anything I say, do you?'

'That's not true,' I protest.

'Come on, admit it, you think I'm a waste of space. A failure. You always have. You even thought I'd killed Olivia, didn't you?'

'No, of course not.'

He glowers at me. 'Really? Because that's not what you were saying a few days ago. You thought I'd killed her and hidden her body.'

'No! Don't say that. I didn't!'

'And that's exactly why I didn't come to you in the first place.'

At the station, I'm escorted into an interview room with Lockyear and Caulfield while Leo's taken off to a different part of the building to wait. We sit at a table in a bare room and I go through everything again, starting with how I thought I'd spotted Leo and Olivia in Clover Wood on Monday afternoon, but couldn't be certain. And why I lied to them and gave Leo a false alibi. I might as well be honest. I don't have anything else to lose.

'I knew he didn't have anything to do with Olivia's disappearance—'

'But he did,' Lockyear corrects me.

'I mean, I knew he wouldn't have hurt her. He's not like that. He's a good boy at heart. But I was worried that if you suspected him, and you started digging around, you'd find he had a recent police caution and you'd jump to the wrong conclusion.'

Lockyear studies a sheet of paper lying flat on the table between us. 'Ah, yes, Heather Malone. Leo admitted supplying her with a small quantity of Class A drugs.'

I hang my head. 'Yes, LSD. I never even knew he was taking drugs.'

'And she was later found dead?'

'She'd fallen from a bridge. But it wasn't Leo's fault. He didn't make her climb it.'

'He'd met Heather at a party?'

'She pestered him for drugs. She was practically begging him. It's not like he forced them on her.'

'She was only fifteen,' Lockyear reminds me.

'I know. It was wrong. Trust me, I couldn't believe it myself. And he's regretted it every day since.'

Lockyear sits back and draws in a long breath through her nose, folds her arms and instructs me to continue.

With as much detail as I can remember, I explain how, after Leo went missing, Biscuit must have picked up Leo's scent and I stumbled across the crate in the woods.

Oh god, I've completely forgotten about the dogs I had to abandon when he abducted us. They could be anywhere by now. Scared, alone. 'Someone needs to look for the dogs,' I say, frantic. 'There were five of them I was looking after. They'll be in the woods somewhere, but they're not dangerous.'

Lockyear looks to Caulfield and nods. He pushes back his chair and leaves the room without a word.

'Okay, we'll look into it,' Lockyear says. 'Carry on.'

I tell her about Jerome's van, the shotgun he produced, and how Leo led us to the construction site and the show home where Olivia was hiding.

'How did you get into the house?' she asks.

'Leo found a key for the garage.'

'And Olivia was camping in the loft space?'

'That's right.'

Lockyear's eyebrow shoots up. 'Any idea why Mr Hunter shot his own daughter?'

I swallow, my mouth suddenly dry. No more lies. Only the truth. 'Because I shoved him from behind when I thought he was going to shoot Leo.'

'So it was an accident?'

'I suppose, although it wouldn't have happened if he hadn't brought a gun.'

'No need to get defensive, Mrs Sugar. We're only trying to establish the facts.'

They keep making me go back over the same ground, asking the same questions, until I query my sanity. But after nearly an hour, Lockyear finally wraps up the interview and tells me to take a ten-minute break. After that, they want to take Leo's statement and I'll need to be with him as his parent.

I leave the interview room exhausted, my head spinning. There's so much to process and after the prolonged rush of adrenaline that's been keeping me going, every limb is heavy and I feel like I could sleep for a week.

I still don't know what's happening with Rory. Biscuit and the other dogs are all missing. And, as I slump in a seat in a small waiting room with Leo, I realise there's a phone call I need to make.

Chapter 57

'Mum? Where are you? I thought you'd be home ages ago,' Casper says, answering his phone on the first ring.

In all the excitement, I completely forgot Casper was home alone. He's probably frantic with worry.

'They've found Olivia and Leo.' I choose my words carefully.

'Great.'

'Leo had been helping Olivia hide out on the building site behind us.'

'Okay,' Casper says uncertainly, clearly picking up on the stress in my voice.

'But Olivia's been shot.'

'What? Shot? By who? Is she okay?'

'I don't know. Dad's also in hospital. He was injured when the police arrived.' I deliberately don't tell him the whole truth, not until we have some concrete information. He'll only worry unnecessarily. 'We're waiting for news.'

'Where are you?'

'With Leo at the police station. They're taking statements from us both.'

The line goes quiet in my ear. I should be home with Casper, not delivering news like this over the phone. It's too much to expect a fifteen-year-old to cope with.

'I'm not sure when we'll be back,' I say. 'It's going to be awhile yet. Can you find something in the freezer for dinner? Or order in pizza?'

'Okay.'

'I'll let you know as soon as I have any more information about Dad.'

'Mum?'

'Yes?'

'There's a party tonight at Barnaby's house. I've kind of said I'll go. Is that alright?'

'A party?'

How can he be thinking about going to a party at a time like this? Hasn't he heard a word I've just said? Casper's supposed to be the sensible one, and anyway, we've told him before, he's too young to be going to parties, especially after what happened with Heather. There's bound to be alcohol there, and maybe even drugs. It's bad enough having one wayward son. I can't cope with another one going off the rails.

'I won't be back late,' he says, completely missing the point.

'No, Casper. You'll have to tell him you can't go. I've got too much on my plate to worry about you sneaking off to a party.'

'Oh, Mum, please?'

'Casper, no. And that's my final word. Don't be difficult.'

'That's so unfair.'

'Casper—'

But he hangs up before I can utter another word. I scream in frustration, drawing a concerned look from a passing female officer as she heads for a vending machine at the back of the room.

'What's up?' Leo asks, leaning his elbows on his knees and wringing his hands with anxiety.

'Nothing. It's fine.'

DC Caulfield appears with two cups of coffee. 'We're ready for you now,' he says.

I jump up and smooth down my hair, as if anyone is paying any attention to how I look. I'm still in my dog walking clothes, my muddy boots and the treat pouch around my waist. I'm not even wearing any make-up, which I only realised when I nipped to the toilet and caught my reflection in the mirror. My eyes look sunken in their sockets and my skin pallid.

'We've sent a patrol out to Clover Wood to see if they can find the dogs,' Caulfield says as he elbows open the door to another interview room. 'I'm sure they'll find them.'

'I hope so. Most of them aren't mine.' I hate to think of them all out there alone overnight. Poor Biscuit will be beside herself with worry. She's always been an anxious dog. Although with Rory in hospital, shot by armed officers who should have been protecting us, it should be the least of my worries.

'Now, Leo, why don't you tell us everything you know, leading up to the events at the building site earlier this evening,' Lockyear says with a faux-friendly smile as we take seats around a small rectangular table.

She looks as hard as nails. I'd hate to get on the wrong side of her.

Leo begins by telling them about how he'd spotted Olivia heading for Clover Wood on Monday afternoon.

'I could see she was upset,' he says. 'It looked like she'd been crying, but when I called for her to stop, she ignored me. That's not like her.'

'You're good friends, are you?' Lockyear asks.

Leo's cheeks flush. 'Yeah,' he says, looking down at his hands.

'But nothing more?'

'She's not interested in me like that.' There's a note of regret in his voice. 'When I finally caught up with her, I saw she had a knife.'

'What kind of knife?'

'I don't know. Like a knife you'd use in the kitchen. I think she'd taken it from home. She was saying all this crazy stuff about how she wanted to kill herself and that she couldn't go on.'

'Did she say why?'

'Her father was... doing stuff to her.'

'What kind of stuff?'

'Like sexual stuff, you know?' Leo's cheeks flush with embarrassment. 'I mean, I don't know exactly, but she said he used to go into her bedroom when her mother was asleep and... It was horrible.' Leo clenches his hands into tight fists.

'And how did that make you feel?'

'Like I wanted to kill him.'

Caulfield scribbles a note in a notebook on his knee. I wish he hadn't said that, but it's out there now, and hopefully they'll understand. It's a natural reaction. 'Then what happened?'

'Olivia pulled up her sleeves and started hacking at her arms,' Leo continues, staring at the back wall blankly as if he's reliving the horror of it in his mind's eye. 'It was like she was trying to find a vein or something. She said she wanted to die.'

'So you tried to stop her?'

'Yeah. I grabbed the knife from her and she screamed. That's when my mum saw us.'

'Go on. What happened next?'

'We ran off and I told her I'd help her run away. I didn't want her going back to... to him.'

'So you went to the building site?'

'It's where we used to hang out sometimes after school. I reckoned she'd be safe there, at least until we could come up with a long-term plan.'

'And the knife? What happened to it, Leo?'

I hold my breath.

'I don't know. I think she dropped it.'

Should I confess it's in our cupboard at home? That I put it through the dishwasher to clean it because at the back of my mind I was terrified Leo had used it on Olivia? That I suspected my own son was capable of such brutality? I decide to keep my mouth closed. It's not as if it's a murder weapon.

Leo tells the detectives how he bought two burner phones so they could keep in touch with each other and that he'd destroyed Olivia's smartphone and removed the SIM card so she couldn't be traced by the police. How he'd been sneaking food and water out of the house for her. Taken her some warm clothing and a sleeping bag. And that eventually they'd discovered a way of getting into the show home and set up a camp for Olivia in the loft.

'So that's where you were when you should have been at school?' I say, everything slowly slotting into place.

He shrugs. 'I didn't like leaving her alone, and she didn't have anyone else.'

'But her father, Jerome, suspected you were involved in his daughter's disappearance?' Lockyear says.

'I don't know how. I suppose someone must have seen us.' Leo continues to explain how Jerome picked him up as he walked home from school, took him to Clover Wood in his van and forced him into a wooden crate, a cruel torture to persuade Leo to confess what he knew.

It's awful to listen to. He must have been so scared. So cold. I shouldn't have delayed calling the police when he went missing. I should have listened to my gut instinct, instead of listening to Rory, who was convinced Leo had taken himself off somewhere to calm down after our row. I've let him down dreadfully.

The interview lasts for almost two hours, but eventually we're allowed to go home. A patrol car drops us back at the house, although I wonder whether I should have asked them to take me to the hospital. They told me Rory was taken straight to surgery, and that although he's in the best hands, it's still touch and go whether he'll survive.

He was shot in the upper chest and one bullet narrowly missed his lungs. All I can do is hope and pray for a miracle. After the efforts I've made to keep this family together, I can't have my husband die on me.

The house is in semi-darkness. The light in the hall is the only one that's been left on.

'Casper?' I call out as I let myself in. 'We're back.'

Silence. Not even the sound of a video game thumping in the background.

Leo takes himself straight to his room. He needs to sleep. It's been a tough twenty-four hours for him.

I can't find Casper anywhere. He's not downstairs watching TV, and he's not in his room. The only sign he's been here at all is a couple of leftover slices of pizza in a box on the kitchen counter.

Please tell me he hasn't disobeyed me and gone to that party after all.

I call his phone, but there's no answer. A mixture of anger and worry stirs up my blood. I'm not sure I can cope with dealing with this on top of everything else that's happened tonight.

Chapter 58

Although I'm overwhelmed with exhaustion and my bed is calling, I know I won't be able to sleep. My mind's too active. The adrenaline still pumping furiously through my veins. I'm worried about Rory and whether he's going to pull through. Whether I should be at the hospital by his side. He betrayed my trust when he spent a night with a colleague, and although he's denied sleeping with her, it's going to take me time to forgive him, if I ever do. But I don't wish him dead. Of course I don't. And now I feel bad that our last words were cross ones. That I was considering throwing him out. I'd hate it if that was the last conversation we ever had.

On top of that, I can't stop thinking about Olivia, lying motionless with her clothes soaked in blood. I'm worried about Biscuit, afraid and alone in the woods all night. And I'm worried about Casper, imagining him collapsed in a bush, drunk... or worse. He's still not answering his phone and part of me is beginning to wonder whether I ought to head over to this party and drag him home. I'm sure he said it was at Barnaby's, although I have no idea who he is or where he lives.

I try watching TV to take my mind off everything, but I can't concentrate and mindlessly flick between channels until I give up and switch it off.

I guess at some point I must have dozed off because I'm jolted rudely awake by my phone ringing on the arm of the chair. It's well past midnight. The number is unfamiliar, so I snatch it up, fully expecting it to be the hospital with an update on Rory's condition. Please god, don't let him be dead.

'Hello?' I gasp, my voice thick with tiredness and anxiety.

'Is that Casper's mother?'

'Yes.' My heart sinks.

'It's Barnaby's mum. Penny Forsythe.'

I sit up straight, clearing my throat. 'Oh, hi. Is everything okay?'

'No, I'm afraid it isn't.' Her tone is icy.

What the hell has happened now? Surely, the day from hell can't get any worse.

'We've caught your son with... a substance,' she says sternly. 'At our house. We told Barnaby we didn't mind them having a couple of cans of beer as it's a Friday night, but I take a dim view of drugs, Mrs Sugar.'

The blood drains from my veins and the walls of the room feel as though they're suddenly closing in.

'I - I'm sorry,' I stammer. 'I had no idea—'

'My husband was all for calling the police.'

'No! Please don't do that.' I've had enough of the inside of police stations for one day.

'But I said it was better to let his parents deal with it.'

'I'd offer to come and pick him up, but I'm afraid I'm without my van tonight,' I say. It's still in the car park in Clover Wood. I was going to pick it up in the morning.

'My husband can drop him home.'

'That would be... Thank you—'

But she's already hung up, behaving like it's my fault. I didn't even want him to go to the bloody party.

I drop the phone and hang my head in my hands. Where did we go wrong? I thought we were good parents who'd brought up decent, respectable, sensible boys who knew the difference between right and wrong, who understood the dangers of drugs. They've had a good home life. It's not as if they've ever wanted for anything. So what is it with the drugs?

I blame Leo. He started this, dabbling with acid of all things, behind our backs. And now Casper's obviously copying him. Leo should be setting a good example to his younger brother, not leading him astray. And if I find out that Leo's been supplying Casper, I swear I'll kill him. I'm not going to stand for it, not while they're both living under my roof.

For the next twenty minutes, I pace up and down the kitchen, waiting for Casper's return, rehearsing in my head what I'm going to say. Finally, the headlights of a car glisten through the window and Casper is delivered home by a cross-looking bald man in mustard-coloured corduroy trousers and a holey green jumper.

'Thank you for bringing him back,' I say, rushing out to the drive and forcing a grateful smile.

The man gives me a withering look before jumping back in his car and driving off.

'Sorry, Mum,' Casper says, unable to look me in the eye. At least he has the decency to look sheepish.

'Get inside,' I hiss through gritted teeth. I don't want to wake the neighbours with what I have to say to him.

He tramps into the house with his head down like a man walking to his execution.

'What the hell do you think you're playing at?' I yell the second I've closed the door. 'I thought you knew better than that.'

He looks up at me through his long lashes, his face a picture of innocence and naivety.

'I told you I didn't want you going to the party, especially not tonight, and you've not only wilfully disobeyed me, but I've had the embarrassment of having you sent home in disgrace. What do you have to say for yourself?'

He shrugs. 'I'm really sorry.'

'Drugs, Casper? Seriously?'

'It wasn't much.'

'That's not the point! What was it anyway?' I'm hoping it's just a joint. A little cannabis he was sharing with friends. Not that I approve, but it's better than finding out he was taking something harder.

'Just some powder.'

Oh my god.

'What powder?' I yell.

'Some coke. It's no big deal.'

I feel like my head is going to explode. Cocaine? Casper's fifteen years old. What the hell is he doing with cocaine? 'No big deal? After everything we've been through this year? How much did you take?'

He shakes his head. 'I didn't take any. Barnaby's mum caught us before we had the chance. She flushed it down the toilet.'

'Just you wait until your father hears about this.'

Casper's eyes open wide. 'Well, he can hardly say anything, can he?'

The landing light flicks on and Leo emerges in a T-shirt and shorts, looking bleary-eyed. 'What's going on?' he asks, padding down the stairs bare-footed.

'Nothing. Go back to bed.'

Casper casts a glance over his shoulder and shares a look with his brother.

'What do you mean about your father?'

'Where do you think I got the drugs in the first place?' Casper says.

'Casper, don't!' Leo hisses a warning from above.

'What's that supposed to mean?'

'I took them from Dad's stash, alright?' Casper says. 'If anyone's to blame, it's him.'

'Don't you dare try to blame this on your father. You know he's in hospital after being shot?' I ask incredulously.

Casper's head jolts backwards. 'Shot?'

'He's going to be fine,' I lie.

'Who shot him?'

'It doesn't matter and don't change the subject. What do you mean, Dad's stash?'

'I'll show you.'

Casper marches down the hall and stops outside Rory's study, glancing back at me. He reaches into the room and flicks on a light before disappearing inside.

When I catch up with him, my mind a fog of confusion, he's standing by the bookcase next to Rory's desk. He reaches behind one of the books and pulls out a small tin.

'Here, see for yourself.' Casper shoves the tin under my face.

'What's this?'

'It's Dad's. Look.'

I take the tin and gingerly lift the lid. Inside, there's a transparent plastic bag containing a small amount of white powder.

'What is it?' I ask, my hands trembling. This can't be what it looks like.

'Dad's cocaine, like I said.'

I shake my head. There has to be a mistake. Rory doesn't take drugs. At least, he hasn't for a long time. Not since he was a student, but everyone was experimenting back then.

'You're lying.'

'He isn't,' Leo says. I hadn't noticed he was standing in the doorway, watching.

So now they're ganging up on me?

'I found the tin last year. He keeps all sorts in there. Powders. Pills. Tabs,' Casper says. 'I don't think he knows I found it.'

Tabs?

I turn to Leo, who has his arms crossed and his jaw clamped shut.

It's like finding an elusive last piece of a puzzle. 'The LSD you gave to Heather. It was your father's?'

'I took it,' Casper says. 'It wasn't Leo. I gave it to Heather.'

I spin around, blind-sided. 'You?' I gasp.

'Leo had nothing to do with it.'

'I - I don't understand.'

Leo sighs. 'I didn't want you to find out. I'm sorry, Mum.'

'Casper gave her the drugs?'

Leo nods. 'He was trying to impress her, so he came up with a plan to invite her to our party, even though it was only supposed to be for the sixth-formers. They sneaked in through the back garden. I had no idea he was planning on coming.'

'I didn't know she was going to go off her head,' Casper says.

'Woah, slow down.' I can't keep up. All this time, I believed Leo was responsible for Heather's death, but it was a lie. It was Casper.

'I told her I could get her into the party and that I had some drugs,' Casper says, chewing his lip. 'I don't think she would have wanted to hang out with me otherwise.'

'Hang on, have I got this straight? You're telling me *you* stole the LSD from your father?' I shake my head, my mind flipping somersaults. 'And you gave it to Heather?'

'I didn't know she was going to go crazy. She thought she could fly. That's why she was on the bridge. I tried to stop her, Mum, but she wouldn't listen to me. She wouldn't come down.' Casper's shoulders slump.

'You were with her when she fell?'

'Yes.' The word catches in Casper's throat and barely comes out as a whisper.

I frown. That doesn't make sense. 'But it was Leo who called for an ambulance. They traced his number.'

'When she fell, I panicked,' Casper says. 'I didn't know what to do, so I ran back to the party and found Leo and told him everything. I didn't know whether she was dead or alive. I just ran. Leo said he'd take care of it and sent me home.'

I cast my mind back to that evening. Casper didn't come home. He was supposed to be staying with a friend at a sleepover.

'She wasn't breathing when I found her,' Leo says, 'so I called for an ambulance, but didn't leave my name. I didn't think they'd be able to find me. I thought we could get away with it.'

His naivety is astounding. Did they really think the police wouldn't investigate, especially when they found traces of an illegal drug in her blood? Of course, they'd want to know who'd supplied it and whether she'd been on her own when she fell. I can't believe they could both be so stupid.

'But why would you take the blame?' I ask.

Leo runs his hands through his hair and lets it flop back down with a sigh. 'Casper was so scared. He was in pieces, worrying about the police finding out. He thought he would go to jail, so I decided I'd admit it was me if they found us. I wanted to do the right thing.'

'You confessed to the police to protect your brother?' I ask, astounded. They've never been close, less so since their teens, so it's hard to believe Leo could have acted so selflessly.

And all this time, I've been so angry with him for what happened. Angry with him for taking drugs. For supplying them to a teenage girl. For letting her do something as dangerous as climbing a bridge while she was off her head, tripping. Yet, he's not guilty of any of these things. It was Casper, and Leo was trying to protect him.

I don't know whether to laugh or cry.

The enormity of it all hits me like a sledgehammer and my legs turn to jelly. All the lies. All the deceit. All the stress and anxiety. All the rows. The upheaval of moving. Changing the boys' school. Dealing with the trolls. And the haters. And all this time, it had nothing whatsoever to do with Leo.

Is there anything about this family that's not built on lies and deceit? Even Rory's been lying to me about the drugs, and the affair. I know about Toni now, but how many others have there been? And how long has he been taking drugs behind my back?

Don't they know how hard I've tried to keep this family glued together? To hold off the onslaught of the outside world which seems determined to destroy us?

Or is it? Have we brought this all on ourselves? Perhaps it's nothing to do with the outside world. We've been wrecking our family from the inside. It's just I didn't realise it.

'I - I don't know what to say,' I mumble.

'Mum—' Leo steps forwards, his hand out towards me.

'Just - just go to bed,' I sob. 'Both of you.' Tears bubble in my eyes, the emotion constricting my chest.

The boys exchange a look and shrug.

'We'll talk about this in the morning,' I yell after them as they shuffle out of the room with their shoulders hunched.

When they've gone, my legs finally give way and I fall to the floor, bury my head in my hands and weep.

Chapter 59

THREE MONTHS LATER

I watch through the window from the shadows of the kitchen as a young couple with a small child arrive at Jerome and Faith's house opposite and greet an estate agent with handshakes and broad smiles. Are they going to fall in love with the house and make an offer on the spot? Are they going to be our new neighbours? I guess it depends on whether they have any idea about the history of the house.

They look like decent people, well dressed and respectable, but I've learnt there's truth in the old saying, don't trust a book by its cover. When I first met Jerome, I thought he was a bit of a creep, maybe, but harmless enough. Even when I caught him staring down my dress at his barbecue last summer, I didn't think much of it. Boys will be boys, after all. But I had no idea what was going on behind closed doors. The police have since charged him with multiple counts of rape and child sexual assault. All I hope is that they find him guilty on all charges and he goes to prison for a long, long time. The horrors he put his own daughter through are beyond thinking about.

Thankfully, Olivia has made a remarkable recovery from her physical injuries after being shot. She'll always bear the scars, physically and emotionally, but at least she still has her life. A future to look forward to. I've heard they've offered her a place at Oxford, if she gets the grades, although I imagine she might have to defer for a year while she continues her recovery.

Not that I've seen her, or her mother, Faith, recently. In fact, not since the shooting. All my information has come second or third-hand. They've moved to somewhere secret. Somewhere where no one knows their story. They're attempting to rebuild their lives and start afresh, exactly as we did after Heather Malone's death, and I know just how tough that's going to be for them.

Of course, Olivia will have to come back to give evidence at her father's trial, assuming he continues to deny all the charges, but after that, she'll be free of this town and the gossips.

With any luck, it'll be a long time before Jerome's free and he'll spend an unpleasant lifetime behind bars trying to avoid kettles of boiling sugar being thrown in his face by inmates who take particular exception to child molesters, especially those who target their own child.

I never got to the bottom of why Olivia's cardigan was in Hanna and Fergal's house, but I'm sure there's an entirely innocent explanation. I was only suspicious because of the rumours at the time that Olivia had been seeing an older man, a rumour that turned out to be, like so many rumours, entirely spurious. Olivia wasn't seeing anyone, either her own age or older. And I fear that because of what she's gone through, what Jerome did to her, it's going to be awhile before she's ready to take that tentative step, anyway.

The couple at the Hunters' house disappear inside, no doubt sizing up the rooms, the layout and whether it's a house that will work for their needs. I wasn't sure about our house when we first moved to the estate, taking on a modern new-build after our old Victorian semi with all its charm and character, but I've come to love it. It's a quiet neighbourhood, now at least, and we have some really lovely neighbours who've been so supportive since they found out about our past and we finally came clean about why we had to move.

I've even expanded the business and taken on four more clients and their dogs. They're all neighbours who've heard about me from my existing customers. More dogs means more chaos in the house, but I love having them here. Although at the rate I'm going, we're going to need a bigger property and I'm going to need another pair of helping hands.

I'm conscious of a tug at the leg of my jeans. When I look down, Biscuit's sitting on the tiled floor, tail wagging, and staring at me expectantly. She barks, her bottom shifting briefly off the floor. Then Rosie wanders into the room to find out what all the fuss is about, yawns and shows off a long, lolling tongue and a set of sharp teeth.

The police found Biscuit and Rosie huddled up together close to the crate where Jerome imprisoned Leo, waiting patiently for us to return, which, of course, we never did. Bertie wasn't far away, and they eventually located Tyson shivering nervously under a tree. If there was ever a misnamed dog, it's Tyson. Not in the least bit as fearsome as his boxing namesake.

Hank was missing for twenty-four hours. I've no idea where he went after we abandoned him in the woods, but knowing him, he was off exploring, oblivious to the fact I was missing. Hunger must have eventually won him over as Hanna found him sniffing around Jerome and Faith's front door, begging to be let in.

He lives with us now and is settling in well, although Biscuit's made it clear she's the boss. She might be smaller than him, but with a low growl, she puts him in his place whenever he steps out of line. There was no way Faith and Olivia could have kept him with everything else going on in their lives, and offering him a home while they sort themselves out was the least I could do. Whether he stays with us forever, or they ask for him back when some sort of normality returns for them, we'll have to wait and see. I don't mind either way. For now, I'm happy he's living with us.

The low rumble of a car pulling into the drive snatches my attention back to the window.

'Leo! Casper! Are you ready?' I yell.

A few moments later, they thud down the stairs, Leo leading the way. He spills into the kitchen, yanking on his coat.

'Bye, Mum. Love you,' he says, pecking me on the cheek.

'Hey,' I say, affronted. 'What about my hug?'

He mock-rolls his eyes, puts his arms around me and holds me for precisely one second, but it's better than nothing. I miss the days when the boys were toddlers and actively sought cuddles with me. It's the price of them growing up, I guess.

Leo heads off to find his shoes, making way for Casper. I wet my thumb and wipe a smudge of jam from his cheek before straightening his coat and pulling him into a hug.

'Mum!' he complains, swatting away my hand. Sometimes I forget he's not still five years old.

'What? You're not too old yet.' I grin at him.

'Love you.'

After everything that's happened these last few months, Heather's death, Olivia's disappearance, the drugs and the lies, we're actually closer than ever as a family. What could have torn us apart has made us stronger.

Leo's behaviour at school has improved no end since the truth came out about Heather. His grades are up, I've had no more threats from the school office about expulsion, and he's even talking now about retaking the year and applying for a place at Oxford himself.

It's taken a little longer to forgive Casper. I know as a parent you're not supposed to have favourites, but as the youngest, I'd always had a soft spot for him, especially as I thought he was the easier of the two boys. He was the son who never strayed from the straight and narrow. So to discover he'd not only been taking drugs, but supplying them to other kids had been a massive shock. We have an appointment fixed next week to see a drug counsellor and Casper's promised me faithfully that he's never touching them again. I believe him, but it may take some time for him to win back my trust.

It was noble of Leo to take the rap to protect his brother, although I wish he hadn't. Having a police caution to his name might well haunt him for the next few years, at an important time in his life when he's looking to go to university and build a career.

I was all for marching them both down to the police station to clear Leo's name, but he was adamant he didn't want to. He said he'd had enough of speaking to the police and that it would only rake up old mud. So we left it, against my better judgement.

I've always done my best for my family, but maybe if I'd been a better parent, we wouldn't have ended up where we are. If I'd been closer to them, maybe Leo and Casper would have felt able to come to me after Heather's death and we could have worked it out together. And when Leo found out about the abuse Olivia was suffering, he would have talked to me about it instead of taking matters into his own hands.

A knock at the door sends Leo scurrying into the hall.

'Hey, Dad,' he says, throwing open the door.

'You ready? Where's Casper?'

Rory appears at the entrance to the kitchen dressed in about ten layers under his coat.

'Are you sure you're going to be warm enough?' I can't suppress my smile.

'What?' he says. 'I feel the cold. You know that.'

'You're only going to a football match. You're not hiking across Antarctica.'

I let Rory move back into the family home while he was recuperating from his surgery, but I made him stay in the guest room. I wasn't ready to welcome him back into the marital bed. It gave me time to think about things, to consider what I wanted from life. It would have been easy to pretend nothing was wrong, to go back to how we were to keep the family intact. After all, that's all I've ever wanted. But I couldn't get over the way he'd abused my trust. It wasn't just that he'd spent the night with another woman. I could put that down to a mid-life crisis. A drunken mistake. It was the secrets and the lies, the way he'd disengaged from the family when we needed him most.

He admitted he'd been using drugs on and off for the last five or six years as an escape from the drudgery of his life, in his words. A desperate attempt to feel young again and capture the elusive rush of doing something illicit. He said he knew I'd disapprove, which is why he kept it from me. But it was like discovering I'd married a stranger. Someone I didn't know anywhere near as well as I thought. And so, when he was well enough, I asked him to leave.

'We'll grab something to eat after the match and I'll drop them back after that,' Rory says. 'If that's okay?'

'Yeah, sure. I'll enjoy the peace while the boys are out.' I force a smile. I hate it when the house is quiet and I'm here on my own, but it's not fair to deprive Rory of spending time with the boys. He is their father, after all.

He's making a real effort with them, taking them out to places to do things, like watching the football and going to the cinema. Next week, he says they're all going bowling. Part of me is a little jealous. It would be nice if the four of us could do something like that together.

Maybe in time we will. Maybe I'll learn to forgive Rory, and when my wounds have healed, I'll invite him back to the house and we can start over. It's still too fresh at the moment. Too raw. The problem is, time is ticking. The boys aren't getting any younger. Before we know it, they'll both be off to live lives of their own. And then it will just be the two of us.

'Right, well, I'll see you later then,' Rory says.

It's the most natural thing in the world when he comes over and plants a kiss on my cheek.

'Love you.' The words slip out of his mouth before he realises what he's said. He flushes with embarrassment. 'I'm sorry,' he stammers. 'I shouldn't have... I didn't mean—'

'It's okay,' I assure him with a smile. 'I love you too.'

And in a way, I mean it.

I just need to learn how to feel it again. And that's going to take time.

Also By AJ Wills

The Phantom Child
Karina's worst nightmare comes true when her four-year-old son vanishes while on holiday in Turkey. But is he really missing? Or did he never really exist?

The House Guest
When Marcella is invited to stay with Carmel and Rufus, she thinks it's a chance to steal their perfect lives. But the couple have other ideas and Marcella soon realises they may not be who they're claiming to be.

The Lottery Winners
When Callum and Jade win the lottery, they think all their dreams have come true – until they're approached by a stranger begging for help and they discover the cost of their winnings may be more than they're willing to pay.

The Warning
When Megan discovers a text message on a phone hidden in the loft of her new house with

a chilling warning about her husband, she's forced to confront some dark truths about their relationship...

The Secrets We Keep
When a young girl vanishes on her way home from school, a suspicious media suspects her parents know more than they're letting on.

Nothing Left To Lose
A letter arrives in a plain white envelope. Inside is a single sheet of paper with a chilling message. Someone knows the secret Abi, and her husband, Henry, are hiding. And now they want them dead.

His Wife's Sister
Mara was only eleven when she went missing from a tent in her parents' garden nineteen years ago. Now she's been found wandering alone and confused in woodland.

She Knows
After Sky finds a lost diary on the beach, she becomes caught up in something far bigger than she could ever have imagined - and accused of a murder she has no memory of committing...

The Intruder
Jez thought he'd finally found happiness when he met Alice. But when Alice goes missing with her young daughter and the police accuse him of their murders, his life is shattered.

Let's stay in touch

If you'd like to keep up to date with all my writing news, please consider joining my weekly newsletter. I'll even send you a free e-book! You can find more details at bit.ly/hislostwife or scan the QR code below.

Or follow me on Facebook - @AuthorAJWills, find me on my website ajwillsauthor.com join me on Instagram at @ajwills_author or find me on Goodreads @ A.J.Wills

I look forward to seeing you there.

Adrian

Printed in Great Britain
by Amazon